"It is a very touching story and I wish you the best with it. I hope you can sense how much I enjoyed the book. Thanks for sharing it with me."

Dr. Kraig Adler, Professor
Department of Neurobiology and Behavior
Cornell University
Ithaca, New York

The Lullaby Lost

A novel

by

Paul William Barada

and

J. Michael McLaughlin

I missed hearing the music
of my parents' lives.
But this is what happened
when I followed the lyrics
they left behind...

authorHOUSE®

AuthorHouse™
1663 Liberty Drive, Suite 200
Bloomington, IN 47403
www.authorhouse.com
Phone: 1-800-839-8640

First published by AuthorHouse 1/3/2008

ISBN: 978-1-4343-4611-7 (sc)

Printed in the United States of America
Bloomington, Indiana

This book is printed on acid-free paper.

For Connie and our sons, Paul Jr., Will, and Jon. Especially for Connie who was gracious enough and patient enough to endure the creative struggles of a would-be first-time novelist. And to our sons who, perhaps, weren't sure it could be done at all, but were kind enough not to say so...

Acknowledgements

Writing this novel has been a very personal and, at times, a very emotional experience for me. Most of the story is based on actual happenings in my life. Some of it obviously is fiction, although there were times when I sincerely wished it ALL could have happened. There were also times, to be honest, when this novel seemed to write itself, truly magical moments when it seemed as though I was only an observer, watching the words appear before me.

There are, nevertheless, a few people who deserve to have their contributions honored.

The first is Dr. Joan Farrell who is a kind, compassionate, and sympathetic friend and guide who helped me finally understand that I needed to write this story, not just for myself, but for others who might relate to its message and be comforted by it.

Next is my second son, Will, who showed me a new way to think about the story that was touching, insightful, and intriguing. His sensitivity and understanding of how important telling this story was for me has been extremely gratifying. I love him all the more for it.

Then there is Karmen Gulde who read and re-read the manuscript for errors in grammar, punctuation, and content. She was kind, tactfully blunt, and unafraid to voice her valued opinions. If the finished product sparkles with any precision it is because of her.

Dear friends Dan and Betty Green helped conceptualize and create the design for the cover of this book. They instantly saw what Mike and I were trying to evoke and managed to capture it on film.

Finally, I'd like to acknowledge my co-author, fraternity pledge brother, and life-long pal, Mike McLaughlin. Mike also understood why this story needed to be told. It is essentially my story, but Mike gave life and breath to it. This novel would never have seen the light of day but for his skill, talent, experience, and unique ability to "turn a phrase." But most importantly, Mike's willingness to help make this novel come alive was done out of nothing more than his desire to help me, with no thought of personal gain for himself -- because he is my friend. This is "our" novel.

To the extent that there were many magical moments during the creation of this novel, my fond hope is that readers, too, will experience some of that magic as they travel with me through these pages.

Paul William Barada
Rushville, Indiana

October, 2007

Author's Note

The principal characters in this story were real. Their lives and love, however, were cut tragically short. Who can say what joys they might have shared, where the paths of life might have taken them? And most importantly for me, what might have turned out very differently had I been there to alter their destiny in some small way?

For so many years I have thought about the music they could have written, the happiness we all might have shared. I've wondered about the dreams they left unrealized, the plans they held in store for me. But these were only imaginings borne of an unfulfilled longing. I wanted truth.

This is a story of my journey to find that truth - to fill a haunting emptiness in my soul. This is the story of my quest to make peace with history. And the surprises I found along the way.

Prologue

November 10, 1945: Elsie Bradshaw stared out the window at the desolate snow-covered prairie stretching off into the distance. Sitting at the dining room table, she peered through the sheers at the bleak, windswept South Dakota countryside she had endured through a lifetime of winters, more or less like this one. The snow was drifting behind the back of the barn like it always did when the wind blew out of the northwest. Only this time it looked so much colder outside than before. The old place seemed more colorless than she had ever seen it. The emptiness wasn't in the landscape surrounding the weathered clapboard Bradshaw farmhouse at the edge of the little town called Elm Springs nestled at the foot of the Dakota Badlands. It wasn't the monotonous horizon that caused her lack of focus. The emptiness, the sadness she felt was inside her. This was about loss. Life was not supposed to be like this; mothers weren't supposed to bury their sons in unfamiliar graveyards clear across the country or to ride alone on half-empty trains back to homes filled only with memories. The child who always seemed to understand her loneliness, the child who was so sensitive, so talented...was dead!

But a lifetime on the prairie – much of it as a widow – had taught Elsie Bradshaw to be a realist. This had happened. And now the thing to do was cope with this new reality and bear up under this tragic loss as bravely and with as much dignity as God would see fit to grant her. She felt the familiar tightness in her chest returning. It was not a new sensation, but in the past the feeling had quickly passed. Instinctively, she knew these twinges of pain were warnings – that the time was coming when the cold and the wind and the loneliness would no longer matter.

At the funeral back in Indiana, people had been kind. It wasn't a bad place, really. She told herself; Paul had been truly happy there. He had found a place where his musical gifts were valued – working with boys. His musical talent had always made her proud.

She glanced across the dining room at the old upright piano in the dim hallway; the same one Paul practiced on as a child. She could almost see him there.

"Paul, you've been practicing for over two hours. Don't you think that's enough for now?"

"Not yet, Mama, just a few more minutes. I know how I want this to sound; I can hear it in my head, I just can't make my fingers do it yet!" The music seemed to flow effortlessly from his slender hands. He was only twelve years old, but he was big for his age, his gangly legs easily reached the brass peddles on the bottom of the piano. The light from the kerosene lamp on top of the piano filled the hallway with a warm yellow glow, as he played.

"It's going to be dark soon," she chided.

"I know, Mama, I know! Just a couple more minutes."

"Your father could use some help splitting that cord of wood. You know he hasn't felt well..." Paul's natural talents, coupled with his willingness to practice for hours at a time were a rare combination, seldom found in boys his age. She wanted him to be a regular boy, but he was clearly more than that and, well, to keep him from his music would have been to deny his natural gifts. The music continued to flow from the old piano, like water rushing down the mountain streams of the Badlands in spring.

"Paul! Go help your father this minute!"

"All right, Mama, I'll help Papa," Paul answered with disgust. He hopped up from the piano bench, grabbed his hat, and was out the door in an instant. The rickety screen door slammed. The noise startled Elsie. She turned quickly toward the door, but it was only the wind. She looked back at the piano. He was not there. The hallway was dark. Her little boy had been there, but only in her imagination.

His musical ability had led him away to college after high school, the first in his family to go that far. After graduation, he had found a job teaching music at a small military school in Indiana. He wrote often, but Elsie missed him terribly.

She looked again at the piano in the darkening hallway. Years had passed since he sat there practicing, improving his skill. Elsie let out a long sigh. "Oh, Paul, I miss you so," she said aloud.

He had found a wonderful girl to marry – a girl who loved him deeply. That was her picture on the mantle in the living room. A pretty girl; quick to smile, fun-loving – "good for him," everybody said when they got married. And now there was the new little grandbaby – less than two months old.

The teakettle in the kitchen began to wheeze and Elsie had struggled to her feet by the time it made a whistle. She'd almost forgotten she had started to make a cup of tea before going through the papers she had brought back from Indiana.

There was a large yellow envelope with clippings and letters and a few other things someone at the funeral home said she should have. The envelope seemed to be filled with things of Paul's...things "You might want to save," the man in the military uniform had said. She hadn't opened the packet on the train. She couldn't. There didn't seem to be any hurry about opening her heart to more sorrow.

Now, with a cup of steaming tea beside her, Elsie bent back the clasp on the envelope and slowly slid out the pile of papers and a small black leather coin purse. There at the dining room table, she sadly beheld the collection of memories from her son's all-too-brief life.

There were other memories, too, stored in the bottom drawer of the corner cupboard in the far corner of the dining room: letters she had been saving for a very long time, letters from her son when he was in college imploring her to get better, to see a doctor about the pain in her chest. They were sweet, thoughtful letters that had given her strength when she most needed it and helped forge an even stronger bond between mother and son. There were also photographs and yearbooks, and more. Keepsakes. "Is this all I have left of him?" she asked aloud. Quietly she began to cry.

It was nearly dark when she was done looking through the letters, awards, citations, clippings, concert programs, student grade books, and a few casually scrawled musical manuscripts, Elsie rose again and walked slowly over to her late husband's favorite reading chair. Beside it was the sewing kit she used when she mended things. That was where the light was best, and she could see well enough to do the needlepoint she had eventually learned to enjoy after her husband had passed away. Out of the sewing kit, she took a roll of bright blue ribbon. "This will do," she said to herself. "I will tie all this up for safe-keeping. This won't end here and now. Not if I can help it. A blue ribbon for safe-keeping." Very carefully, she sorted the pile of papers and all the letters into little bundles, wrapped them in tissue paper, and tied each one securely with a small blue bow. A mantle clock across the living room chimed six times, and the house fell back into lonely silence.

Out in the hallway, near the treadle sewing machine that had belonged to her mother was a new cardboard box. Carefully, she placed the papers and the musical manuscripts on the bottom of the box. Next came the books and photographs – she looked at each picture one final time, memories of happier times swept over her. Again she thought of him practicing at the piano and smiled, how sweet and precious he was as a child. Gently, she kissed the picture of her little boy and placed it inside the box. Next, she neatly placed the carefully tied bundles of letters on top. Last of all, she tucked the little coin purse deep in the corner of the box. Finally, she closed the lid.

Steadying herself against the sewing machine, she slowly lifted the box from the floor. At the end of the hall was the doorway to the attic. A steamer trunk waited for her at the top of the dark narrow staircase. "One step at a time, Elsie," she said to herself, "One step at a time." It seemed like an eternity before she reached the attic door. The wind outside was blowing even harder than before; the whole house shuddered against its unrelenting force. She opened the attic door and stared at the endless flight of steps that led upward. Carefully she placed the box on the second step while she lit the old kerosene lamp she kept on a little wooden stand by the door – the one that used to sit on the piano. There was no electricity in the attic. "One step at a time," she told herself again. Painfully, she lifted the box once more and, holding the lamp in her left hand, began the ascent to the attic.

Gasping for breath, she finally sat on the dusty attic floor. Before her was the wooden, copper-trimmed steamer trunk. She released the latch and lifted the heavy lid. Everything that mattered to Elsie Bradshaw was in that trunk: her wedding dress, tiny linen gowns her children had worn as babies, the family bible; memories of a lifetime were in it – now she was adding more. She placed the box in the one remaining empty corner of the trunk. She knew her daughters would find it. She closed the lid and then the latch.

Gradually the light from the kerosene lamp began to fade, but she did not notice. She did not notice the chill that crept over the house as the snow continued to swirl violently outside.

Chapter One

September 12, 1997: It had been a hectic week at the office. I was ready for some peace and quiet. My back hurt from sitting in front of a computer screen most of the day. "I'm getting too old for this," I said to myself as I arched forward to relieve the pain. I was ready to be done with the impersonal clicking of computer keys, blended conversations of employees at their jobs, the endless chiming of telephones, and all the usual cacophony of disconnected sounds that are part of a busy office. Tomorrow would be Saturday, the office would be closed, and there would be peace. In just a few more minutes, I'd be out the door and on my way home.

I stared vacantly out the window, lost in idle thought; the sounds of the office gradually faded away. It was a beautiful late summer afternoon, but the signs of autumn were already apparent: the brisk chill in the early morning air, the brilliant tinges of red and orange just beginning to accent the dark summer green around the edges of the swaying maple trees on the courthouse lawn across the street, and the brilliant afternoon sun beginning to drop below the flat Hoosier horizon a little earlier each day.

The changing seasons reminded me of the circle of life itself – of birth, of life, of love, and of death. I knew I was no longer a young man, and the circle of my own life seemed to be moving, had already moved, well into middle age. I could see my reflection, a shadowy transparent portrait, looking back at me from the office window. The thinning hair I now had to "arrange" instead of actually comb, the gray at the temples, the age lines that crossed my forehead, all were unmistakable signs that time was passing – just as the seasons passed, inexorably, from one to the next. I looked at my hands. Long, slender fingers were beginning to show the first signs of age, signs that I had recognized before – when I was a boy.

"How old are you Aunt Nell?"

I never got a straight answer from her, no matter how many times I asked.

"Just sweet sixteen and I've never been kissed," she would always say with a gentle, loving smile.

I knew she was old, nevertheless, at least older than my friends' parents. I caught myself. That kind of thinking about the past was nothing short of a flashback to my childhood and the kind of Victorian philosophy I had "inherited" from my two great aunts, my grandfather's sisters, who had raised me.

My brief nostalgic reverie was suddenly shattered by the shrill familiar voice of one of my senior associates, Mary Stevens.

"Paul, I don't know what to do about this report. I just can't finish it this afternoon. I'm tired. It's been a long week. Can't I just put it off until Monday?"

I could feel the heat rising in neck and face as I tried to contain my anger. I looked at the report; it was from one of our best clients in Chicago! I glared at her through narrowed eyes.

"Look, damn it," I shouted. "I don't care how tired you are or how late you have to stay, this report has to be done and mailed before you leave! This business isn't being run for your personal convenience!"

Mary tried to speak, "But, I only thought..."

"There's nothing to think about. Do the damn report and I mean right now!"

Mary was dumbstruck by my outburst. "Yes, sir," she said quietly as she backed quickly out of the room.

Regaining my composure, I wondered what made me explode at Mary that way. I had always had a hair-trigger temper, even as a child, but I sensed I was becoming less and less patient with people as I grew older. I wondered why such a deep sense of frustration always seemed to lurk just beneath the surface, waiting to burst forth at the least provocation. And yet, I knew there was also a vulnerable, more emotional side to my personality as well – one that I worked very hard to hide from others. Sometimes it seemed as though an angry, frightened, and very lonely child was hiding somewhere deep within me, callously mocking every attempt I made to be more even-tempered. Now I was embarrassed, knowing that others in the office had heard my verbal outburst and I felt ashamed.

I sensed someone else entering the room. I spun around in the chair, it was my bookkeeper, Judy Rhodes, one of those attention-to-detail people without whom I doubted I could get through the day, but at that moment I would have liked to try! She obviously had heard my outburst and approached me cautiously. She had seen these explosions of temper before. Judy was a short, delicately constructed woman with carefully curled honey-blond hair. Prone to allergies, she always carried a tissue securely tucked between the buttons of her blouse, reading glasses perched on the end of her nose. In summer she always wore loose open-toed sandals, but she also never went without nylons, even on the hottest summer days. Her sole mission in life, it seemed to me, was to please others – almost at any cost.

"Mr. Bradshaw, ah, please don't forget to take that box home," she said gently. What box was she talking about? I didn't remember any sort of package arriving for me at the office that day.

"What box?" I snapped at her, annoyed by another interruption. There was no answer. Judy flip-flopped hurriedly out of the room. I took a deep breath. I knew there was no reason to be that abrupt, but sometimes it almost seemed as though I could not help myself.

In she walked again carrying a nondescript brown cardboard box that apparently had been delivered earlier in the day. I looked at the large mailing label; it was clearly addressed to me. About two feet square, I had no idea what it might contain. I couldn't recall ordering anything recently that might have come to the office like this – unwrapped, just an old brown cardboard box held together with twine and clear heavy masking tape. It was so unremarkable, in fact that I didn't particularly want to deal with it at that moment. But there Judy stood her eyes just visible over the top of it. She was eying me cautiously as if using the box for protection against another possible fit of temper. The box was obviously heavy.

"Where shall I put it, sir?" she mumbled meekly, the side of the box pressing against her mouth.

"I don't care. Over there, I guess," pointing casually to a nearby chair. It went down with a thud. "It might be important," she said in a more forthright tone I seldom ignored.

I walked over and looked at the box more closely. The return address was clearly marked; it was from someone in South Dakota, someone named Jean Myers.

"Who the hell is Jean Myers," I said to no one in particular.

"I don't know, sir."

"Well, don't worry about it." Now I felt a stinging twinge of remorse for having snapped at her. I looked up at her, smiled, "Thanks for reminding me about it, Judy."

"You're welcome, sir. If it's all right, I'll be going now."

"Of course. Have a nice weekend."

At least it wasn't a misdirected birthday gift or something my wife, Connie, had ordered without telling me. No, this was something from someone named Jean Myers. Then, with a flash of unexpected recognition I remembered! Jean Myers was a distant cousin! That's who Jean Myers was! I wondered if I was getting absent-minded, along with all the other things that let me know that time – my time – was passing.

"You've got the box, don't you?" Judy called out from the top of the stairs as I headed toward the door that Friday afternoon.

"Yes, I've got it," I answered back, half annoyed by her persistence.

As I walked to the car, I wondered why I was taking this heavy box home at all. I hefted it into the back seat of the car and headed out of the parking lot.

It was a short drive, five minutes, tops. The car's air conditioner had barely started lowering the temperature as I pulled into the driveway.

Connie, my wife and partner for over 25 years, mother of our three sons, was working in the flowerbed in front of the house. I waved as I drove up to the garage. She had been planting mums all afternoon and was dripping wet with perspiration. Her hands were covered in brown, soft dirt. She was wearing skimpy navy blue shorts and a white sleeveless top which was moist with perspiration. Her figure was still appealing. Narrow, soft shoulders, a slender neck, the sensual outline of her breasts accentuated by the damp clingy top. Long, smooth, shapely legs... The frustrations of the day seemed to melt away as I watched the graceful movement of her body. Connie radiated an unintended sexuality that had always attracted me. A pleasant, unexpected surge of desire filled my thoughts.

Nearby, red and white geraniums that had been blooming all summer, were still blooming in fact, were sticking pathetically out of a dark green trash bag. I was particularly fond of geraniums.

"Why are you getting rid of the geraniums, already? I love geraniums," I asked impatiently. The ceremonial uprooting of the geraniums was another unwelcome sign that another summer was coming to an end.

Connie stood up, wiping her forehead with the back of her hand. "Because it's time to plant the mums. *Now* is when you *plant mums.*"

"Oh, well, then," I said sarcastically. "That makes sense. Rip out perfectly good geraniums because it's time to plant mums." I climbed wearily out of the car, leaving the door ajar.

"You must have had a bad day. You don't seem to be in a very good mood."

No, I wasn't in a good mood. I couldn't really remember the last time I had been in a good mood. I stood there and lamely tried to offer an explanation. "It's hot. I've spent another Friday leaving messages for people on their impersonal answering machines. Apparently everybody starts their damn weekends on Thursdays. Everybody but me. Sometimes it's really frustrating."

"What's in the back seat?" Connie asked. Oh, yes. The box.

Connie came over, looked at the label. "Who's Jean Myers?"

"A cousin of mine from someplace out in South Dakota. I think I may have mentioned her to you before."

"No you haven't. I had no idea you had a cousin in South Dakota. Who is she?"

"I think she's my father's sister's daughter."

"Wait, say that again."

"She's the daughter of my father's sister."

"Oh, well, you've never mentioned her to me before. What's in the box?"

"No clue." I gathered up the box, my suit jacket and what remained of the morning's Indianapolis Star – the sports section – and walked into the entryway of our house. The deliciously cool air-conditioning swirled around me as I walked toward the kitchen.

"Don't forget the box." Connie scolded – getting back to the wholesale destruction of perfectly good geraniums. What was it with women and this goddamn box? Anyway, was it the cocktail hour yet?

Surely, somewhere in the world – it was legitimately *cocktail hour*. The box got as far as the kitchen counter.

In due course, Connie followed me into the kitchen. "You're not going to leave that *there*, are you? The cleaning lady came today. I'd like to keep the house straightened for maybe just one whole day before it starts getting cluttered again." Along with that comment, I got 'The Look.' 'The Look' was unmistakable. The box went immediately to the library, where Connie had a slightly less strict tidiness code – at least where making messes was concerned. The library was a special room we both wanted when we built the house in 1988. All four walls were floor to ceiling dark cherry bookshelves. The one major break was a bay window along the north wall. Neither Connie nor I could bear to part with a book. We both had started saving books during college, and we had been acquiring more books over the last quarter-century, so when the house was built we finally had a place to put them. All the shelves were full. The library also contained a large cherry desk with an inlaid burgundy leather top and matching leather button-back swivel chair behind it. It was my favorite room in the house – a cozy repository for a vast amount of information.

After a drink I retreated there, planning to go through some of the week's mail. I looked over at the box. "OK, let's see what we've got," I said to no one in particular. "This shouldn't take long."

A letter opener slid easily along the edges of the box and then sliced down the middle through the masking tape. Inside was a top layer of coarse packing material included, no doubt, to protect its contents from any damage in shipment. So far – nothing unusual. I saw several stacks of old snapshots, carefully wrapped in tissue paper – probably to keep them dry and separated from the other contents. Next, I saw stacks of letters and greeting cards – all neatly tied up in faded blue ribbons. The little bows had been carefully tied but were mashed flat from what appeared to be years of storage.

My mind involuntarily flashed to the hands that had tied those ribbons – apparently a very long time ago. Whose hands were they? What, if anything, did they have to do with me?

Next, I spied some old school yearbooks. I recognized one of them as being a copy of "The Holcad," the traditional name given the annual published each year by the graduating class of Rushville High School. The date on the cover immediately caught my eye: 1928, the year my mother graduated.

Under the yearbooks I saw a few dusty old photographs in cardboard folders of various sizes, the kind professional photographers used to give out as frames with graduation portraits or wedding photos. There were other things deeper in the box – also carefully wrapped in discolored tissue paper. I looked again at the return address on the mailing label – incredulous to believe this package of family history had unexpectedly arrived for me on that particular Friday afternoon. It was surreal. Uninvited. Almost uncomfortable, as I began to think about it.

A strange tightness stirred somewhere deep in the pit of my stomach as I tried to retrace the sequence of events that had brought me to this confrontation with a far distant past about which I seldom thought – or even allowed myself to think.

I thought again about the connection. My father's niece, Jean, had sent this box. We had never really met. In fact, over all the intervening years, from childhood on, I seldom had contact with anyone from my father's family. They lived out West where my father had been raised, but I had been born in Indiana. My father's sister, Aunt Grace, had sent Christmas cards with brief endearing messages when I was a small child, but after she died, I lost track of her children, my cousins. Only now had I remembered there was a daughter, Jean – married name Myers. She had somehow ended up with this strange collection of family memorabilia and, for some unknown reason, had sent it all to me.

I looked again at the stacks of letters and snapshots piled on the larger photographs and old yearbooks. I suddenly felt a strange, disconnected sensation I did not understand, and for some unexplainable reason I didn't want to know what was in those letters. I didn't want to see those photographs or to know what else might be in that box – and yet I did! As I stared at all of it, I experienced a strange, unexpected rush of anxiety. I almost felt magnetically drawn to that old brown cardboard box! It was like being pulled in two emotionally opposite directions at the same time!

It didn't make sense! The contents of the box represented a very dark and very lonely place to which I did not – had never wanted to go. But, without warning, another disturbing wave of anxiety seemed to command me to discover the long-hidden answers to all the disquieting questions about my past!

"No! Stop it! Don't think about this! This is about things from a faded, long distant past you've managed to suppress for fifty years," I told myself. What would be the point of going back to that sad and dimly remembered past now?

It was becoming clear that this could be a disturbing emotional journey, the question was whether or not I was willing to make it... I was born on October 5, 1945, just over a month after the official end of World War II, when the whole world was still reeling with the overwhelming joy of newfound peace. My father, Elsie Bradshaw's little boy, had died tragically of a sudden and massive heart attack on October 13, 1945, a little over a week later, while coaching an intramural football game at Culver Military Academy, a small private school in northern Indiana. I was just nine days old. He was only 41.

My mother, I had always been told, never got over the shock of her husband's death and died quietly on a peaceful

Sunday morning, March 9, 1947, of what had gently been described to me as "a broken heart." I was barely 17 months old.

What little I knew about my mother, I had heard from my great-aunts when I very was small. To have heard them tell it, my mother had been the most wonderful little girl who had ever lived, but there was never any reality about her for me. No connection. Just this wonderful little girl I didn't know and couldn't remember.

"Your blessed mother would come for long weekend visits with my sister and me – when she was not much older than you are now – especially in the summertime! We would play dress-up and have tea parties, and we would take snapshots of her in the backyard sunlight," Aunt Nell would say. "We had such fun. She was like the daughter we never had. Your poor grandfather! He would scold us for spoiling her. 'Girls,' he would say, 'it's going to take us until a week from Friday to get her behaving again!'"

During all my growing-up years, I had seen only a few snapshots of her, taken with an old Brownie box camera when she was a very little girl. They were always kept in a small cardboard box in the far back corner of the top drawer of the large bureau in the spare bedroom upstairs. To me, as a child, that's where she lived. That's where I could always go to find her – if I wanted. And that was that.

The four of us, me, my two great-aunts, and my grandfather lived in a large Victorian home on Perkins Street in Rushville, Indiana. My grandfather, however, had not been around much when I was a small boy: he never played with me...never taught me how to throw a football or play baseball or how to do any of those other things small boys need to learn. Upon more mature reflection, I suspected that I reminded him too much of the girl who died on that long-ago Sunday morning in March. He gave me all the love and affection that was left in him to give, but during all those growing-up years he never talked about his daughter, my mother...not even once. I was twelve years old when I was sent to Culver for the first time, for the 1958 summer session, to the very same school where my father had taught and where my parents had lived – and died – in the 1940s. My grandfather never came to visit. I wished terribly that he had, but the memories of what was lost at Culver must have been too much for him to bear. William Winship, my grandfather, died in 1962. I was in high school.

As a boy, people had often said to me how awful it must have been to have lost my parents when I was so young. My stock answer was that it hadn't bothered me at all because I didn't remember either of them. "It's hard to miss people you can't remember," I would say.

As I sat there, looking at that old cardboard box and thinking about the past, the words rolled over and over in my head, "People I can't remember." People? My mother and father... were never really "people" to me, just impersonal images in a formal black and white photograph, the only one I had ever seen of the two of them together in all my life. There was nothing inside me that had ever connected with the images in that picture.

Now, here before me was this box from the past. I knew I would feel no emotional connection to the memories the box contained; yet, I felt compelled to go there, to experience that past! Another unexplainable surge of anxiety engulfed me like an angry, roiling ocean wave... My throat tightened. I felt cold perspiration forming on my forehead. My hands began to tremble involuntarily. A gut-wrenching queasiness began tearing at me somewhere deep inside!

At that precise moment I made a decision! I would *not* go back there. I did *not* want to go back there. I did *not* want to know more. I had gotten along just fine without my mother and father, not knowing them, not knowing who they were, not knowing about their lives, or wondering what *our* lives might have been if only... I caught myself. Sighed a long, slow sigh. I looked out the bay window and reflected. What difference did any of it make now? It had all been so long ago, and there was nothing I could change now, even if I wanted to... That one formal photograph of the two of them had been enough! That one photograph had been enough to take pride in and to be able to prove that I, too, had once had parents, just like my friends. Before I consciously realized what I was doing it, I had slammed the cover back on the box, and found myself pushing it into a far corner of the hall closet. Like those old box camera photos of my mother as a little girl, I would always know where to find these things – if I ever really wanted to go there – someday, perhaps. This was a journey I was not prepared to make, not now. I went back to the library, physically drained and emotionally exhausted.

Connie and I went to bed early that Friday night. I scrunched the pillows and settled into the soft embrace of the down comforter. Sometime around 3:00 A.M. I was unexpectedly awakened by an odd, unfamiliar sound. Half asleep, I turned my head slightly to listen, but couldn't identify it. I blinked, opening my eyes to the darkness of the bedroom. There was nothing unusual to be seen; just the indistinct shapes and shadows that always filled the room during the stillness of the night. At first I thought it might have been just my imagination, but I could still hear...something.

The sound wasn't like the usual noises that can occasionally disturb the darkness, not the creaks, or rattles, or moans, or bumps that houses sometimes make, nor was it like any of the sounds that drift in from the countryside on sultry late-summer nights. It was not like the early-rising clamor of restless songbirds or the repetitious chirping of unseen insects; it was more like a distant hum, faintly melodic, but nothing like I had ever consciously recalled hearing before. This strange, slightly disconcerting sound did not seem to be coming from the bedroom or from anywhere in the house. It seemed to be coming from somewhere far away, out in the pale blue-gray darkness beyond the bedroom window. As the cobwebs started to clear my mind, I thought perhaps it was the low moan of an animal caught in a trap, or the approach of a very early train announcing its arrival with a long, deep-throated whistle. No. I knew those sounds, and this was not like either of them!

I sat up slowly, listening, confused, and a little apprehensive. What was that *sound*? It had been a hot day, but now the night air was cool. Rain was coming; the smell of moisture was in the air. Almost absentmindedly, I decided I'd better make sure the window was closed against the coming rain and listen more closely to this faint, unfamiliar hum that had awakened me.

Carefully pushing back the comforter, I slid slowly out of bed to avoid waking Connie. I walked gingerly over to the bedroom window. In the dim light, I could see that it had been raised a few inches. I listened again. Now, just slightly more audible, the sound was like someone faintly humming some sort of tune very far away. I knew from experience that sounds can sometimes travel long distances, carried along on the wind. Perhaps that was what I was hearing, but by whom and from where? Somehow I felt compelled to listen. All that came to my drowsy mind was the absurd recollection of the Siren's song from the tales of Odysseus.

Carefully I opened the window to the top. Connie sighed and stirred slightly. I didn't want to wake her. I knew how much trouble she had falling asleep once awakened. I had not been careful enough...

"Paul, what are you doing?" Connie's voice sounded sleepy, but she was still annoyed.

"Just closing the window. Feels like it might rain." I could hear the covers rustling as she rolled over. Without thinking, the words came.

"Do you hear that?" I asked.

"Hear what?" I could hear the impatience in her tone. "I don't hear anything but you banging around!"

"I'm not sure; it almost sounds like somebody humming far away."

"Did you forget and leave the television on again?"

"No, it's not coming from inside the house, I don't think. It seems to be coming from outside someplace..."

"I'll bet it's the air conditioner you hear. I've been telling you that thing is about to go, but you won't listen. I guess it'll just have to quit altogether before you do anything about it. It's a good thing this is September and not May..." Connie's voice trailed off and, much sooner than I expected, she was asleep again.

She was wrong about one thing, though, I was listening. I was listening to some distant "melody," for lack of a better word to describe it. I strained to hear it more clearly. It wasn't particularly an unpleasant or even discordant sound, but who or what could be causing it in the middle of the night? Sometimes wild coyotes would howl in our nearby woods, but their mournful call was almost like a woman's scream. This sound was entirely different, almost soothing. Minutes passed. I stood at the window listening. It was softer and more distant than the other night sounds and beneath the murmur of the freshening wind that promised a coming rain. Finally, still unable to understand what it might be, I carefully closed the window again.

This was, as subsequent events would show, only the first in a series of road signs that would point the way to the beginning of that very long journey I was destined to make. As I got back into bed, it started to rain.

Chapter Two

Connie was already up when I awoke again. It was another Saturday morning, just after 8:00 A.M. The morning sunlight flooded into the bedroom wiping away the last traces of pre-dawn gloom. Now there was clear definition and clarity to what had been only the indistinct shapes and forms allowed by the darkness a scant few hours before. I let my eyes adjust to this new daylight reality. There was the dark oak dresser with its brass drawer pulls that had belonged to Connie's grandmother. Across the room was the tall matching wardrobe that contained too many sweaters –sweaters I had saved that were either too small or desperately out of style – cleaning out that wardrobe was another chore, along with mum planting, Connie wanted done. Our four-poster bed completed the set. The bed had always fascinated me. It was a solid, tastefully ornate piece of furniture, handmade by some long-forgotten craftsman who had clearly taken pride in carving the spiral swirls and delicate finials that crowned the top of each post. I wondered about its uses – sleep, love, birth, and death. How many times had it been a marriage bed? How many times a place to die?

Tossing back the covers, I eased myself to the floor and walked slowly over to the window again and put it up; the morning air rushed in fresh, fragrant, and cool. The green shade trees near the house shimmered with wetness in the sunlight, still dripping from last night's rain. I leaned against the window frame, inhaling the sweet, clear air. Everything around me looked just as it should – just as always. More importantly, everything *sounded* just as it should, there was no sound of a faint, distant, unintelligible hum lingering on the wind this morning. I wondered if last night's experience had been just a dream. It had been so vivid I shuddered involuntarily at its recollection. It had to have been a dream! ...It wasn't.

When I got downstairs Connie, still in her floor-length red and white striped flannel gown, was in our kitchen having a cup of steaming coffee, and reading the morning paper. She looked up as I walked in wearing my old faded pajamas and equally faded, but very comfortable, ratty bedroom slippers. Her eyes were wide and alert, beautiful brown eyes, framed by the graceful lines of her face.

"What was that all about last night?" she asked as those lovely eyes locked tightly on me. At that very moment I felt the same surge of passion for Connie I had first experienced over a quarter century before when I saw her for the first time.

"What was what about?" I knew perfectly well what she meant, but didn't want to acknowledge it, avoiding what I knew could quickly turn to a penetrating glare.

"You remember! Hearing voices outside the window in the middle of the night!"

"I wasn't hearing 'voices,'" I said with mild indignation and no small measure of embarrassment. "It was probably nothing but the wind. You know how the wind sometimes sings and whistles through the trees just before a storm. It just sounded odd, that's all. I was wondering what it was and thought you might have heard it, too. Besides, the window was up and it was going to rain."

"Well, it was probably just the air conditioner under the deck you heard. You need to look at that thing and see if it needs to be replaced. It makes all sorts of peculiar noises. It wheezes and whines all the time – that's probably what you were hearing." Connie had been more awake last night than I realized!

"OK, I don't have much on my agenda today anyway. I'll look at it." I knew next to nothing about fixing air conditioners, but if it would please Connie, I would "look" at it.

"And don't forget you promised you'd help me finish planting the mums today." Oh, yes, the ever-popular pre-autumnal mum planting! It had almost slipped my mind... "I think I'm going to plant the rest of the rust, white, and yellow mums behind the screened porch. That combination will look nice there, but I need you to help me unload the extra bags of potting soil from the back of the Jeep. You'll need to put them in the wheelbarrow, and bring them around to the back yard so I can finish my planting. Those bags are just too heavy for me to lift."

"Sure, I'll be glad to do that." The truth of the matter was sitting *on* the porch was really what I had in mind, not hauling heavy bags of dirt and planting mums in the flower bed *behind* it. Happily, I had the presence of mind not to express that thought. I was at least awake enough for that!

It was clear Connie was about to launch into one of her Saturday missions. Just then the phone rang. Connie glanced at me hoping I would answer it. It rang a second time, more insistently. I feigned deafness.

"I'll get it," Connie said disgustedly, as I shuffled over to the refrigerator to pour a glass of orange juice, my old slippers rhythmically slapping the tile floor with each step. Connie picked up the phone.

"Hello? Yes? Oh, just fine, thanks, and how are you?" she said airily. Connie had the annoying habit of never saying the _name_ of the person who was calling! "How nice! They're all fine. No, not yet."

As she listened, I whispered, "Who is it?" thinking it might be one of our boys or someone from the office... She waved off my question with an impatient frown and dismissive sweep of her hand.

"I'm sure that would be fine. Yes, he's right here. I'll be happy to put him on." Connie handed the phone to me.

I put my hand over the phone. "Who is it?" I whispered again.

"Janet Mosley!" Connie whispered back.

Janet Mosley! I hadn't talked with her for months. What could she be calling about so early on Saturday morning?

"Hi, Janet!" How good to hear from you!"

I had known Janet all my life. She had always been very kind to me when I was a boy and had always been interested in how our own boys were doing. Well into her 70s, Janet had never married; she had lived a life of quiet, proper elegance, her life's one true passion playing the grand old pipe organ every Sunday morning at historic Main Street Christian Church – for nearly fifty years. She was a mainstay in our community, one of those people who had earned deferential treatment and respect over the years. When Janet spoke, people listened. When she entered a room, heads would turn toward her instinctively and voices would be lowered until she had finished surveying the scene before her. Janet was the quintessence of proper Victorian decorum.

"Paul, it's very nice to hear your voice. Connie says you and the boys are all fine." She paused for an instant.

"Yes, everyone's fine,"

"Paul, it's been ages since I've paid you and Connie a visit, and I'm in the process of resurrecting my Saturday afternoon visits. When I was a girl, you know, everyone went visiting on Saturday and Sunday afternoons. I think it's a delightful custom, and I'm taking the initiative to bring it back! I've even had calling cards printed!" Janet said with enthusiastic determination. "Are you busy this afternoon?"

I looked over at Connie, "Ah, no, not really..."

"Good, let me put on my glasses while I check my appointment book. I'd like to stop by at 2:00 P.M., if it's not an imposition."

"Let me, ah, check with Connie – just to make sure there's nothing on the calendar. Can you hold for just a second?"

"Of course."

"Connie, she wants to come over this afternoon. Are we doing anything?" I whispered.

"What on earth for?"

"She said she wants to stop by for a visit," I shrugged.

"Tell her it's fine, I guess. We can finish the planting this morning." Connie whispered back.

"We'd love to see you, Janet. Two will be fine."

"Wonderful! I'll see you then. Good-bye."

Before I could reply she had hung up. I looked at Connie, "Sometimes I think Janet's a little...peculiar. I thought 'visiting' went out of fashion with high button shoes and parasols, but she says she wants to revive the custom."

Connie took another sip of coffee. "How odd. Well, I'll throw on some clothes so we can get those mums planted."

We spent the balance of the morning planting. Three or four trips were necessary to deliver all the exotic potting soil from Connie's car to the backyard. Hauling sanctified dirt was not the only job to which I became heir. Water was also required – to insure that the precious mums got a healthy start! By noon we were hot, sweaty, and tired, but the mums were all dutifully planted, watered, and ready to burst forth, or whatever mums are supposed to do, to brighten our surroundings.

After a quick lunch, showers, and a change of clothing we were ready. I glanced out the window precisely at 2:00 P.M. Up Janet drove in her spotless, chrome-accented, midnight blue 1970 Cadillac Coupe de Ville. The car looked showroom new.

I opened the front door as she came up the walk. "Janet, it's so nice to see you!" I stepped aside as she came in.

She turned and looked at me, nodded rather formally. "Yes, it's nice to see you, too." Her hair was a shimmering silver-white, but her blue eyes still sparkled with the lingering exuberance of youth, as bright as a cloudless autumn afternoon sky. She had high, prominent cheekbones, accented by a sweep of rouge. Carefully applied lipstick and makeup gave her skin the look of fine porcelain. The aroma of lilacs surrounded her like a delicate lace train. She was wearing a fine floral-print silk scarf carefully secured at the neck with a single overhand knot, a pleated beige skirt with matching jacket. She carried a small handbag held by a slender gold chain on her arm, and was clutching a carefully wrapped package with the other. Her garden party appearance stood out in stark juxtaposition to my casual golf shirt and khaki shorts. She was also wearing white gloves!

"Won't you come into the living room?"

"Yes, thank you very much." She formally handed me one of her new "calling cards," her name embossed in Old English script.

Connie was already there. "Janet, how nice of you to come by! Would you care for some iced-tea or lemonade?"

"No, thank you, but a glass of pinot-noir would be very nice."

I glanced at Connie, shrugged. She caught my eye and smiled. "Fine. I'll be right back." Janet Mosley was not one to mince words and obviously preferred an afternoon drink with a little more "character" than iced-tea or lemonade. I liked that about her.

Janet gracefully took a seat on the sofa as Connie returned with a small glass of red wine carefully placed on a small filigreed silver tray and offered it to Janet. It would have been unthinkable to simply hand her a glass of wine...

"Thank you very much," she said with a smile. Janet took a tiny sip from the glass, put it down carefully on the end table, and said, "Gracious living just isn't what it used to be when I was a girl. I was very fortunate to have grown up in a family that appreciated proper amenities. Life has become so much more..." Janet paused as if searching for just the right word to come to mind. "Coarse... Don't you agree?"

"Well, yes, I suppose so...I, ah..."

"Paul, the most unusual thing happened the other day." Janet interrupted. "I was cleaning out the hall closet and came across some things my sister Judith asked me to keep for her. It's my opinion, you know, that closets should be cleaned out at least once every year." Connie nodded in definitive approval. "Well, the first little stack I took out of the closet included this…" Janet handed me the package she had been holding on her lap. It was wrapped in brown paper and carefully tied with twine.

"Would you like me to open it?"

"Well, of course! It's one of the reasons I wanted to stop by this afternoon," Janet said emphatically.

I carefully untied the twine and gently folded back the paper. Inside was a beautiful dark mahogany frame with a velvet-covered maroon easel back. I glanced up at Connie, who was sitting on a straight ladder-back chair across from the sofa with her hands politely folded. I shifted my gaze to Janet who was smiling expectantly. Slowly I turned the frame over. I was holding a black and white photograph of my mother as a young girl, perhaps around twelve or thirteen years old! I was stunned at the coincidence! It was obviously a posed portrait, probably taken during the early 1920s. She was wearing ribbons in her hair and a freshly starched and pressed white dress with neat creases along the sleeves and a wide pointed collar. There was something almost magical about the expression on her face. Youthful innocence, soft beautiful eyes, and an amazingly sweet smile. Suddenly I had the strangest sensation that the girl in the photograph had been waiting patiently all these years to finally see me, just as I was finally seeing her, even though I knew this was just an ordinary photograph. It was a hypnotic moment. I could hardly look away.

"Isn't she lovely?" Janet said wistfully. "You may know that Shippy, your mother, and my sister Judith were the best of friends." I forced myself to look up. "They grew up together. This picture of her was on the table next to the settee in our living room for as long as I can remember. But I never knew what became of it after Mama and Papa passed away. Anyway – and this is so strange – when I started cleaning out the hall closet, there it was – right on top. As soon as I saw it, I thought of you...I want you to have it." Janet looked at Connie, smiled, as she took another sip of wine.

I handed the photograph to Connie. "This is a lovely photograph, the frame is gorgeous, and I know just the spot for it! Paul, let's put it on the table next to the little slipper chair in the library! Janet, we have this lovely little slipper chair that used to be in the house where Paul grew up. I think the table next to it would be the perfect place!" Our quaint little slipper chair was a small, high-backed upholstered chair that got its name not from its shape, but from its intended use. It had a fairly low seat and was supposed to be placed in bedrooms for proper ladies to use when dressing and putting on shoes.

"I remember that chair from the house on Perkins Street! It's the only one I've ever seen like it. It was always in your grandmother's upstairs sitting room. That does sound like the perfect place, where people can see it," Janet said. Quickly she finished her wine, stood up and checked her small appointment book "Well, I've completed my first visit of the afternoon. Now, I should be off. Civility, like time and tide, waits for no man!"

I walked Janet to her car. "I can't thank you enough for the picture, Janet. I've never seen many photos of my mother, so this is a very special gift."

"Something told me you should have it," Janet said with a smile, as she slipped back into her car.

"Thank you so much for coming out. It was a delightful visit!"

"I knew you would enjoy the photograph."

Janet drove her car back down the driveway and was gone. I walked back into the house.

"See what you think of this," Connie called out from the library. She had placed the picture of my mother on the little side table next to the slipper chair. She turned it so it was facing toward the door.

"Perfect spot," I said, but little did I know nor could I have guessed where this long-forgotten photograph was about to lead me.

Chapter Three

The next day, Sunday, was my traditional bill-paying day. Outside, it was another brilliantly sunny late summer afternoon. Not only did I hate paying bills, but I hated spending part of the dwindling supply of perfect days inside, particularly when they were slipping by so quickly. I would have almost preferred planting mums – almost. After lunch, I headed again to the library.

"Connie, I'm off to pay bills." Reluctantly, I flopped down in the chair behind the desk, checkbook in hand. If bills had to be paid, this was the room in which to do it, cozy, quiet, and comfortable.

"Fine. I'll be there in a minute to 'report' on the checks I've written this week."

My method was sadly antiquated; I knew that, but it worked for me. I kept track of deposits and checks written in a simple blue ledger book. Our oldest son, Paul Jr., constantly chided me about getting with the times, paying bills online, and using a computer program to track deposits and withdrawals. "Dad you won't even need a checkbook, just pay the bills online! It's all right there!" It was sometimes tedious work, but at least I could keep track of cash on-hand in our joint checking account in an actual book that didn't need a power cord to tell me what I needed to know! Connie didn't particularly like my method, either – having to account for checks she'd written each week.

In she walked with her list of checks. "I thought you liked it where I put it."

"Put what?" I said without looking up.

"The picture of your mother!"

"I do like it."

"Then why did you move it?"

"I haven't touched it; what're you talking about."

"Look!"

I looked up. The framed photo on the table wasn't facing the door, but turned toward the desk, toward me.

"I didn't move it. Frankly, I really hadn't looked at it."

"Well, I haven't moved it," Connie said as she turned the photo back toward the door.

"Maybe the wind moved it," I said as I turned to a fresh page in the ledger book.

"Right, and the windows haven't been up in here for days. Wind can do that," Connie said sarcastically.

"Honestly, I didn't move it! I like it where you have it!"

"Maybe it moved all by itself. Well, anyway, here's my list of checks." With that, Connie spun quickly on her heel and was out the library door in a gust of silent indignation. I was left to finish my weekly accounting job. I walked over and sat in the low slipper chair, looked again at the picture of my mother. She really had been a beautiful little girl. Whoever had taken that photograph all those years ago had tripped the shutter at precisely the right moment. The expression on her face had a warm, soft quality about it. I could almost feel the warmth.

I looked at her for another long, lingering moment. But, still, I felt no emotional connection to the innocent face in the mahogany frame. The balance of the afternoon was quietly spent on our screened porch, reading the Sunday paper, followed by a quiet evening of uneventful TV watching.

It happened again late that same night. Not much after 3:00 A.M. I was awakened by the same odd sound I had heard two nights before. The only difference was that on this night the voice sounded much nearer, neither as faint nor as indistinct. More clearly than before, the voice now seemed to be definitely female, humming some sweet, still unrecognizable melody. It was another cool evening, the window was up, but this time the humming didn't sound at all like a distant voice being carried along on the wind. There was no wind! I sat up in bed quickly, listened. At least I was awake, I was sure of that. The voice was very much closer.

"Connie! Do you hear that voice?" I blurted out.

"Oh, no! Not again," Connie muttered sullenly, half awake. "What is it this time?"

"Don't you hear that voice? It sounds like a woman humming a tune. Don't you hear it?"

Connie turned over, listened. "Paul, there's nothing to hear out there. What's the matter with you? I don't hear anything but crickets."

"You're kidding! You don't HEAR that voice?"

"No! And you're either not awake or you're imagining things. Go back to sleep."

I was NOT imagining this! I could hear a woman's voice, nearer now. Then farther away. A beautiful voice humming a soft, lyrical, enchanting melody. It sounded very close, swept along and flowing all around the house! After a few more minutes the voice began to fade and gradually was gone. I lay back down on the soft linen-covered pillows, wide awake, staring at the shadows cast by the dim light that drifted silently into the room. Why couldn't Connie hear the voice? Was I imagining it? Was this just part of a waking-dream?

The next morning, as I dressed for work, I thought about the strange serenade of the previous night. Perhaps it had been a dream after all. Connie hadn't heard anything, but it had seemed so real... I gathered up the bills I'd paid the day before from the top of the dresser and headed down the stairs, through the dining room with its long table surrounded by high-backed chairs, and into the kitchen. Again, Connie was already there when I arrived. There was no warmth coming from her large brown eyes this morning! Her face was set and drawn.

"And how are you this morning?" Connie asked in a feigned tone of casual pleasantness that barely masked her anger.

"Fine, great night for sleeping."

"I wouldn't know," Connie said with disdain dripping from every word.

"Oh, didn't you sleep well?"

"Well, I might have if you hadn't wakened me again – for nothing! Paul, we can't have another night of your imaginary nocturnal musical interludes. I don't care if you're hearing a full choir, would you mind not waking me again, particularly when there's nothing to hear?"

"I'm sorry. It won't happen again. It was just so real..."

"I don't care if the Robert Shaw Chorale is camped in the backyard, if that's what you think you hear! Just don't wake me to hear it with you!!

"OK, I get the point," I replied meekly, as much embarrassed as annoyed by, what seemed to me, her lack of understanding and, apparently, her loss of hearing! How could she not have heard that voice last night? This, however, was not the time to debate the point. I quickly gulped down a glass of orange juice and hurried out the door...

Monday was another ordinary day at the office, until just shortly before lunch. I was about to head down the stairs when the phone on my desk rang impatiently. I walked back over and hit the speaker button,

"Yes?"

"There's a Betty Brown on the line for you." It was the receptionist from downstairs. "Do you want to take the call?" Betty Brown and her husband, Dan, had been friends for years. They ran a very successful photography studio just two blocks down the street from my office.

"Sure, I'll take the call." The phone rang again. I picked up the receiver.

"Hi, Betty! What's up?"

"Hi, Paul!" Betty said brightly, "I'm on a little quest for the local historical society and thought maybe you could help."

"Sure. What have you got in mind?"

"We're planning to do an exhibit of memorabilia from all the local high schools that used to be in the county before the days of school consolidation. My part is to see if we can put together a display of all the yearbooks, at least from the schools large enough to have had a yearbook," Betty laughed. In years gone by, every little crossroads town in our county had its own high school. Sometimes the graduating classes would contain only a few dozen students. All of those tiny high schools had been closed in the late 1960s when consolidation was the rage, but school loyalties were still strong, even though there had been no schools, save one, in our county for over thirty years.

"OK. I'm with you so far!"

"Well, we've got almost all the old 'Holcads' from Rushville High School, all the way back to 1914, but one. The only yearbook we're missing...is from the late twenties, 1928 to be exact, and I was wondering if you might have that one and if we might borrow it for the display; or if you don't have it, perhaps you might know someone who does."

My God! I knew I had one and I knew *exactly* where it was. It was in that brown cardboard box in the hall closet, but the words would not come, somehow they stuck in my throat when I tried to answer!

"Paul? You OK?" I took a deep breath and let it out slowly.

"Sure... Wow, I, ah, don't think so. What made you think I'd have that particular one, Betty?"

"Funny you should ask. We were at the museum – the people on my committee – just looking through some of the old yearbooks for fun and somebody, I think it was Janet Mosley – you know Janet – was looking at the one for the previous year, 1927, and she asked us if we recognized the picture of some girl in the junior class. Well, none of us did – 1927 was a long time ago – and Janet said, 'That's Margaret Winship. She's Paul Bradshaw's mother.' I don't think any of us knew that! Well, anyway, Janet thought you might have a copy of the 1928 Holcad since your mom would have been a senior that year."

"Gosh, Betty, I don't think I do." I knew that was a lie! "Ah, but Janet's sister, Judith Mosley, was also in that class. Maybe she has a copy."

"Janet thought so, too. Said she'd have to go through some things of Judith's at home and see if she could find it." So that was how Janet had found the mahogany-framed picture of my mother! She was looking for a copy of that 1928 yearbook! Her unexpected visit now made more sense.

"I'll be happy to look, but I don't remember ever seeing a copy of it." I was still lying, but I didn't really know why.

"That's fine," Betty said, "If you do find it, we'd love to borrow it for our display."

"No problem! Say 'Hi' to Dan for me!"

"I will. Bye."

Why had I lied about having a copy of that yearbook? I felt guilty about not telling her the truth: but, for some irrational reason, I still didn't want to revisit the contents of the box, or loan out the yearbook I *knew* was there – and I didn't really understand why – yet.

Chapter Four

I'd been home from the office about an hour that Monday afternoon when Connie walked into the living room, apparently on another mission.

"If you don't like that stupid picture where I put it, why don't you just tell me?"

I let out a long, slow sigh. "What stupid picture?"

"You know the one, don't try to pretend you don't!"

"No, really, I don't know the one."

"THE PICTURE OF YOUR MOTHER IN THE LIBRARY! Why did you move it again?"

"Connie, I haven't touched it!" I got up and walked into the library with Connie hot on my heels. There was the picture on the little table next to the little slipper chair pointing toward the desk again!

"Check it for fingerprints if you want to. You won't find mine there!" I was becoming annoyed by these false accusations. Once more Connie turned it back toward the door and put it down with an audible thud, as if attempting to glue it in place.

"Well, pictures don't move themselves!" Connie snapped as she left the library, still obviously perturbed with my alleged picture readjustment. I looked once more at the lovely face in the photograph. Her smile was as sweet as before, but I could almost sense a strange new sadness in her eyes I had not noticed before. It was an unusual, disquieting sensation... sadness for her and...for me.

The rest of the week was normal. There were no more nighttime concerts to disturb the tranquil silence of the cool, humid nights. Then, exactly one week later the voice, or whatever it was, came again. But this time it *was* a dream. It had to be a dream! I seemed suspended above the back of a large, dusty, dimly lit rehearsal hall, an unseen observer looking down on a small handful of people gathered around a plain upright piano, the top of which was covered with sheet music. A woman was standing alone behind some sort of boxy microphone in the center of the cavernous stage far beneath me. Her back was to me, I could not see her face. Not far away, a single light bulb, on a tall stand, was the only stage illumination. Then, the woman at the microphone started softly humming. The people around the piano turned slowly toward her. In my dream, somehow I knew this was the same voice I'd heard the week before. But this time the voice seemed to be coming from within me! Then it was all around me, and, for the first time, I could hear the words and the melody echoing softly amplified throughout the empty hall!

"Long ago and far away,
I dreamed a dream one day,"

Then, suddenly, in a heartbeat I was awake! I was in our bedroom, everything familiar, dimly illuminated by the soft gray moonlight shining through the window. The rehearsal hall was gone, no one was there, and the bedroom was empty, except for Connie sleeping quietly next to me. Tonight I would not wake her...but I could still hear singing. I glanced at the digital clock on the nightstand next to the bed. The soft red glow said it was just after 3:00 A.M. I lay there listening. It was the same voice, beautiful, everywhere, and nowhere...

> *"And now that dream is here beside me;*
> *Long the skies were overcast,*
> *But now the clouds have passed;*
> *You're here at last!"*

Was I really awake or was this still a dream? I wasn't sure. The voice seemed very near, close to me. It was comforting and yet somehow deeply disturbing, both at the same time!

> *"The dream I dreamed was not denied me.*
> *Just one look and then I knew*
> *That all I longed for long ago was you."*

A woman's voice...lovely, haunting...very real.

> *"Chills run up and down my spine,*
> *Aladdin's lamp is mine;*
> *The dream I dreamed was not denied me."*
> *Just one look and then I knew*
> *That all I needed long ago was you."*

I had the strangest feeling this melody; this particular *song* was meant for me... The voice began to fade. I was suddenly overwhelmed by a profound sense of loneliness and grief I could not explain. I did not want the song to end or to never hear that voice again! Then the voice was gone. In the shadowy darkness of our bedroom I felt completely and totally alone, disoriented, abandoned! Fear came. I could feel the cold wetness of perspiration on my face and forehead, on my hands, and a gripping, wrenching tightness in the pit of my stomach! An uncontrollable panic rose up trapping me in its terrible frigid grip!

"Don't go! Please don't go! Don't leave me!" I sobbed out loud. The words just came, poured out of me. I don't know why. I would not help it.

"Paul! What's the matter with you?" It was Connie's voice now.

"I don't know," I gasped. I could feel myself trembling, tears streaming down my face. "Something's wrong! I don't know what it is," I cried out. I couldn't get my breath! I gasped for air!

"What's the matter with you? Why are you acting like this?"

"I don't know! I don't know! Trembling, sobbing, I reached for Connie and held her close.

Neither of us said another word for what seemed to be a very long time. When I awoke, Connie was not there. Another Saturday morning had arrived. But the memory of the previous night was still vivid and profoundly disturbing. The first thing I did was hurry downstairs to the computer in the living room to see if there was a real song that contained the lyrics I had heard the night before, so touching, so poignant. I carefully typed in the only line of the song I could remember: "long ago and far away." Instantly, there appeared on the screen the same lyrics, word for word! "Words and music by Ira Gershwin and Jerome Kern, 1944." What I had heard in the darkness was a real piece of music which, according to the information on the screen, had been recorded by several vocalists, bands, and orchestras over the last fifty years!

Then, in a sudden flash of wide-awake insight, I wondered if there could be some sort of meaningful coincidence between what I had heard and the arrival of the long-lost photograph

I had been given. No! That was an absurd notion! "If you aren't careful," I told myself, "You'll let your sleep-shrouded imagination turn all this into some sort of phantasmagorical ghost story." This wasn't a meaningful coincidence; this had to be just a chance occurrence of ordinary events. Connie was right, pictures don't move by themselves and perhaps I had just imagined that a song was being sung for me. After all, people sometimes hear all sorts of things in the disorienting darkness of night that can seem very real – at the time. But this was a real song! And my unexpected emotional reaction to it was equally real. Perhaps, just perhaps, more of this story remained to be heard...if I listened for it.

"Paul, is that you?" It was Connie's voice. In she walked, red and white-stripped flannel gown billowing along behind her. Her face was drawn and stern.

"What happened to you last night?" she said with a serious, concerned tone clearly in her voice. "That's the third time you've awakened me because you were hearing things! And then...last night...sobbing like a child? A man doesn't act like that over some kind of silly bad dream. You've got to do something about these ridiculous nightmares, or whatever they are! You're frightening me!"

Connie was both annoyed and genuinely worried at the same time, I could tell that. I'd never seen her like this. It frightened me, too. I also felt ashamed by the depth of my reaction.

"A little compassion would be nice," I countered, wishing I could minimize the humiliating events of the previous night.

"Compassion!? You need more than compassion! Did you dream you were hearing voices again? That's the third time in the past week! Paul, you've got to get past whatever it is that's troubling you. It's not normal, crying like that. You're not a frightened child. If you need help, for God's sake – get it! Don't talk to me about compassion." With that, she stalked out of the room.

Maybe she was right. These weren't just ordinary nightmares. They seemed too real, which was worrisome in itself, to say the least. Last night had been a full-fledged panic attack, much worse than the feelings evoked earlier by the contents of the box...and I'd better face it. Both events had been disturbing, but there was more going on than the physiological reaction to these unexplainable events. Perhaps they were hallucinations! It seemed clear that there was more to this than I could understand on my own. It was clear, I *did* need help, and for more reasons than I could have realized at the time.

Chapter Five

Facing the realization that I needed psychological help wasn't easy. I felt a deep sense of shame and, in some ways, guilt that my unconscious thoughts were somehow in control of me. So I put off trying to find a psychologist for several days.

"Have you made an appointment with anybody yet to talk about your nightmares?" Connie asked one morning as I was about to leave for the office.

"No, not really. But I can handle it. They're just bad dreams."

"Have you even thought about it?" There was a definite edge in Connie's voice. I looked away, avoiding her eyes. "Look, Paul, you've obviously got a problem. I don't like the idea of being married to a man who's having silly, childish nightmares. A man should have more control over his emotions! Sometimes I think you actually enjoy it, wallowing around in whatever's bothering you, feeling sorry for yourself, thinking about it." Connie was glaring at me – and doing more than a little mind-reading!

"I don't want to think about any of it, and I certainly don't want to 'wallow around' in it! I've been trying to leave the past *in* the past for a long, long time"

"That's what you say, but I'm not convinced in the least. I certainly can see that you're avoiding whatever the problem is. And, to be honest, I don't believe you. I think you're dwelling on the past and thinking way too much about it. Either get over it or get some help!"

"Fine, I'll take care of it today – just as soon as I get to the office! I slammed the door and stalked out of the house. I resented the hell out of being told what I was thinking; particularly when I knew I had spent a fair amount of my life *not* dealing with the past!

After a few discreet inquiries and a long, embarrassing conversation with a doctor friend of mine, Dr. Joan Foster's name kept coming up as one of the most highly regarded psychologists in Indianapolis.

I called her office that afternoon. Initially, the receptionist said Dr. Foster was only accepting new patients by referral. It took a call from my doctor to get an appointment with her. It was scheduled just two weeks later. I was very thankful for that. The intervening days, especially the nights, were filled with uncertainty, uneasiness, and an element of dread, but the voice did not return. There were no panic attacks, but I was terribly afraid another would come! The melody I had heard seemed stuck my head. I caught myself humming the tune several times a day. It was as though it had been indelibly imprinted on my consciousness...

My relationship with Connie during that time was strained. The tension between us was palpable; neither of us spoke about what had happened. Neither of us spoke very much at all. The day of the appointment with Dr. Foster finally came.

I left early to make sure I wouldn't be late. I needed someone to understand, someone who could help...

Her office was in a new three-story brick office building on the near northside of Indianapolis. The sign outside read "Professional Offices," no other identification except the street name and number, much understated, a little too cryptic, frankly, for my taste. Just inside the doorway was a thick glass-topped coffee table with a vase of fresh cut flowers on it. An oriental rug was carefully centered on the highly polished marble floor, but the lobby was relatively small. I looked at the building directory, Psychological Services, Dr. Joan Foster, Suite 350, all very formal. "Psychological services," what was I doing there? I felt uneasy, almost didn't push the "up" button next to the elevator door. Just then a smallish woman, well dressed, wearing a business suit, entered the lobby, pushed the button for the elevator, glanced up at me and smiled; then the elevator doors opened. I gestured for her to enter. She didn't see it, walked straight ahead anyway. This lady had been here before, I thought... I would have felt foolish just standing there in front of the elevator and not entering. It's funny about elevators; nobody ever looks at anybody else. We stared at the little lights above the door indicating our ascension.

The doors opened again for the third floor, there was a long corridor in both directions, the woman went to the left. Dr. Foster's office, a sign announced, was to the right, I walked down the hall, checking each number as I went, and I took a deep breath as I reached for the doorknob to suite 350. I turned it and pushed. It was a heavy, windowless door.

I walked into an empty waiting room, was glad of that, "This must be where the nut cases wait," I thought to myself.

I felt very awkward. Maybe I would turn out to be one of the "nut cases." I hoped not.

There was a large aquarium at one end of the room; exotic tropical fish were slowly swimming in and around plastic green plants. A pink fluorescent light in the cover gave the tranquil water a warm soft glow. There were upholstered straight-back chairs all along the other walls, a magazine rack, and a small table with an oversized lamp - that was all - except for an inner door with a narrow panel of glass. No reception desk, no one in sight, I looked for a magazine, noticed that all the mailing labels had been neatly cut off every cover. I wondered why anybody would bother to do that. Glancing at my watch I saw it was about ten minutes until my 2 PM appointment. I assumed there would be paperwork to fill out; there wasn't. I sat down near the table with the oversized lamp and nervously thumbed through a copy of <u>Psychology Today</u>. I glanced at the narrow glass panel, no sign of life at all, I checked my watch again.

Suddenly, the inner door opened. There stood a woman who appeared to be about my age, maybe a little younger, attractive, smiling, long ankle-length print skirt, matching top with poofy sleeves. Somehow I had expected a more clinical look, at least a white lab coat. "Paul? I'm Dr. Foster, please come in." Her voice was gentle, calm, reassuring.

"Yes, thank you." I stood up as she held the door open. We walked into a narrow hallway.

"Last door on the left," she said. I walked into her office; desk, books, a black leather sofa – I sort of expected that - an overstuffed red leather chair, Southwestern art, a single red-orange rose in a bud vase on a smallish end-table, a comfortable look. I stood by the sofa, fumbled with a button on my jacket, not quite sure what to do. "Please sit down; make yourself comfortable."

I sat in the middle of the sofa. "Am I supposed to lie down? I've never been to a....psychologist before."

"You can if you want to," she smiled, "but most people usually prefer to sit up." She sat in the red leather chair, tucking one leg under her, leaned back. "Now, how can I help?"

This was not the classic image I had expected. Here was a young woman in an informal atmosphere, smiling calmly at me, no notebook, just a pleasant expression. She seemed to be genuinely interested in what I had to say. So, I told her about the voice, the song in the waking dreams I'd been having, the rather terrifying panic attack, and the strange, anxiety-producing sensation I had felt when the box of old family memorabilia arrived, which seemed, I told her, to have precipitated all that had happened after its arrival.

"How did you feel in the dreams? What emotions did you feel?" Whoa! I had never thought about that before - how did I feel in a dream? I looked out the window and tried to remember. Took a deep breath and sighed.

"Well, I guess, confused at first, in an odd, disconnected, unreal sort of way. Maybe alone. Maybe helpless and afraid, both at the same time, I suppose. Terrified of the feeling of loneliness, of losing something...I don't think I really know. Does any of that make any sense at all? It's very difficult to put into words." I felt really stupid; what sort of inarticulate non-answer was that?

"Of course, it does. What you're describing isn't all that uncommon. Why don't you tell me a little about yourself, your childhood?" OK, I expected that type of question. I went through the litany about the loss of my parents, about being raised by two old-maid great aunts, my grandfather, having been fearful a lot as a child growing up. Time passed; I rambled on. But Dr. Foster listened intently to what I had to say. She leaned back in her chair, but looked at me directly. "I think, Paul, we're talking about a loss of something much more precious than you may realize. Most people don't have to face that magnitude of loss. What do you think it means?"

I wasn't sure what she meant, although I should have been. "What, about my parents or about the feelings of loneliness during the panic attacks?" I told her I didn't remember either of my parents - my stock answer - so, I supposed, it must have been about something else.

"Your dreams about the voice you heard seem like a natural reaction to me. You couldn't face losing any more of your security. I think it's still probably terrifying for you to contemplate losing any more of your past, that's what the box seems to represent – the past. Don't be critical of that. Even though you don't have any conscious recollection of it, losing your parents had to be devastating. It would be to anyone. You were so young; there was no way for you to store, in a cognitive way, any recollection, especially of your mother, any sense of the security that is critical to young children. I think the loss of a psychological and physical attachment to your mother affected you profoundly, as it would anyone who experienced that magnitude of loss. I also think it created significant terror for you, at an unconscious level, which you would have felt, but not known what it meant. I suspect you've been repressing very deeply held feelings for a long time and the arrival of that box was something like pulling an emotional trigger."

"Does that mean I'm trying to live in the past or something, in terms of these recurring dreams? I've never wanted that, but my wife seems to think so."

"No. Not at all. Learning how to live *with* the past isn't the same as living *in* the past."

"But I don't remember either of them! How can something I don't remember have affected me in the way you've suggested?"

"How old were you when your mother died, Paul?" she asked gently, compassionately.

"About 17 months, I think."

"In children that age, as I said, cognition wouldn't have been there, but the sense of loss certainly would have been profound. No wonder you've been having panic attacks and strange, disturbing dreams. There's only so much to lose, especially for small children."

I sat there, stunned, trying to absorb what Dr. Foster was saying. I could feel tears welling up; she was reaching further down into my soul than anyone ever had before, and further than I had ever wanted to go. I fought back the tears, trying to stay in control, objective.

She leaned forward, looked intently, compassionately, at me, and said, "There are several things we can try, but I think you ought to start by trying to make a connection with your mother, get to know more about her, if you can. There must be people you can talk with who still remember her. Try to get to know her." She paused, looked away for a brief moment than back at me. Gently she placed her hand on mine and said, very softly, "The essential problem, in my opinion, Paul, is you still miss your mother very much."

Her words went through me with the power of a laser beam, intensely clear, like a blinding pencil of light penetrating down a long dark hallway. The impact of her words was instantaneous, devastating, and intensely moving. Their power pushed me, literally, back against the sofa. In less than a heartbeat, my world had changed. I sat there overcome by what she had said. Tears ran down my face. I could not help it. Never before in my life had anyone, in a single sentence, touched such a hidden, imprisoned emotion so deeply buried within me. I had no idea it was even there – or existed at all – until that very moment in Dr. Foster's office.

On the drive back home, I tried to internalize what Dr. Foster had said. The world *had* changed. It was as though a door at the end of that long dark hallway had begun to open, just a little. While I could not see it all with total clarity yet, the possibility of finally coming to terms with the past I had tried to shut out for over half-a-century was thrilling, tantalizing, and terrifying – all at once! But where would I begin? How could I get to know a woman who had died over fifty years before? My next appointment with Dr. Foster was scheduled for the following month, so I, at least, had some time to try.

Chapter Six

I decided to try and search out people who knew my mother, people who could help me understand. The first and most obvious choice was my Uncle Bill, her brother, her younger brother, by about eight years. In many ways, he had been a surrogate father figure. During all the time I was growing up, I had always looked up to him for his advice, experience, and good judgment.

In his early 70s at the time, Bill Winship looked younger than his age. About six feet tall, he was a slender, well-proportioned man. Still ram-rod straight, he had graduated from Culver Military Academy in 1939 and served as an officer in the Army Air Corps in England during World War II. He had always been my gold standard for style and proper behavior. He was always impeccably dressed, crisp shirts and razor sharp creases in his trousers. I remembered the summer before leaving for college: "Paul, you need a new wardrobe for school!" So, off we went to a relatively exclusive men's clothing store in Indianapolis. It was the summer of 1963; and I was not prepared for striped ties, cuffed khaki slacks, oxford cloth buttoned-down shirts, wing-tips, and herring bone sport coats. These were not the type of clothes that boys wore in Rushville, Indiana. But, when I got to campus, I quickly learned that his choices for me had been the right ones. I fit right in!

Over the years, we had gotten into the pleasant habit of having lunch together, along with a small group of friends. It was a nice break in the day, a time to talk about sports, politics, and local gossip, but asking my uncle about his late sister was something to be done privately. I waited until the day came when we were the only two at lunch. I had carefully considered how to ask him. Like other family members, he seldom spoke about my mother. He told stories about his father, my grandfather, but I couldn't recall ever hearing him talk about his sister. The moment finally came one day at lunch. It was just the two of us. Now was the moment. I swallowed hard, took a deep breath.

"Uncle Bill, I've never asked you this before, but I'd really like to know...what was my mother like, what kind of person was she?"

He hesitated. The question had caught him off guard, but it was almost as though it was a question he somehow knew, perhaps dreaded, he would be asked one day. I could see that this was not going to be an easy subject for him to talk about. He leaned back in his chair, sighed, looked away to a distant place only he could see, and said, "Shippy was a wonderful girl...my sister. I never knew anyone who didn't like her."

"But what was she like?"

"She was fun to be around, a wonderful sense of humor. She was kind to everyone, always for the underdog. Very popular in school." That was all well and good; but who was she, what were her dreams, her fears, her hopes? What did

she care about? What made her happy, sad, angry? I wanted
to know more. So I asked.

"Well, you have to remember, Paul, that Shippy was eight
years older. She hung around with an older group of friends,
and I was the little brother. But my childhood memories of her
are all happy, warm, good memories. We became much closer
when I was a cadet at Culver and she and your dad were
married and he was teaching there. I've never known anyone
with such an optimistic outlook on life." He looked away again
to that distant place to which I could not go. Almost wistfully,
he added, "Everyone loved her...because she had so much
love to give..." He paused, caught himself. The emotion of the
moment showed clearly on his face.

He had told me about as much as he could. There was
only one conclusion; the memories were just too painful.
After all, he had lost his sister and his mother within the
space of only four months. He was just 27 years old at the
time. That's why he and my grandfather had been so close;
they both had lost so much so quickly. Clearly, there were
other memories he kept tucked away like precious keepsakes,
the type of memories that bring some comfort just knowing
they're there, I could tell that, but they were memories he
just couldn't share, as much as he may have wanted to, even
after fifty years, I could also tell that. Neither of us spoke for
a very long moment...

"Paul," he said, looking squarely at me, as a warm smile
of recollection crossed his face, "I just thought of something
that might help. Are you busy after work?

"Ah, no sir."

"Why don't you stop by the house for a few minutes," he
said as a wistful smile brightened his face. No one loved life
and laughter more than my Uncle Bill! He had clearly had

one of those brilliant flashes of inspiration or recollection that sometimes come to us when we need them most!

"I'll be there!"

At the appointed time, I drove to his house, 1131 North Main Street. I had been there a hundred times before as a child growing up. The house held warm, pleasant memories for me; cozy Thanksgiving dinners, happy Christmas Eves, sun-flooded afternoons playing in the backyard with my uncle's son, my cousin Bill, three years younger, lovingly known as "Little Bill," much to his everlasting chagrin. I knocked at the back door. For reasons I still don't understand, the family custom was to always go in the back door, not the front. I couldn't remember having ever walked through the front door of that house!

"Paul, come in! You don't have to knock," I heard my uncle say.

"I know, but I just don't want to barge in..."

"Nonsense! Come in! Would you like a drink?" Before I knew it, I was holding a class of Jack Daniels and water. My Aunt Maxine was in the kitchen fixing dinner. She came over and gave me a warm hug.

"How are you, sweetie?" she asked.

"Oh, just fine."

"Family all right?"

"Yes, everybody's fine."

My Aunt Maxine was a wonderful woman. As a small boy, I had a crush on her; she was gentle, patient, pretty and always seemed to be genuinely glad to see me. The fragrance of mint and spring air always seemed to surround her. Best of all, she was never too busy to give me a loving embrace. Nothing seemed to bother her very much or for very long. If an unpleasant subject ever came up, it was quickly dismissed.

"Well, we just won't talk about that," she would say, and that was the end of any further discussion on the topic!

"Your Uncle Bill called me earlier this afternoon and asked me to see if I could find what he wants to give you. I'll bet it took me two hours of rummaging through the bureau in the upstairs hall and through that old trunk in the attic, but I found them!"

"Paul! Come on in here!" I walked into the family room. Uncle Bill was sitting at the large table in front of the big picture window. "Take a look at these," he said with a smile. Before me was a small pile of what appeared to be 45 rpm records. "These are studio recordings your folks made at Culver." He gently removed one from its yellowed paper slip-case. "Look! This one is your mom and dad singing a duet together!" He handed me the record. It was a wax recording on a metal disk, with four holes in it instead of one – a center hole surrounded by three outer holes. This was a master recorded directly on a blank wax disc! The three holes were meant to hold the record securely in place while the needle cut the grooves that contained the original music! I looked at the hand-written label – "Paul and Shippy." "Here's one of your dad doing a piano solo! Until we talked at noon, I'd completely forgotten I had these old recordings. You really should have them – look at this; here's one with Doc Baxter and your parents singing a number together!"

I looked at the treasure trove of original sound tracks my mother and father had made on some long ago day! I hardly knew what to say!

"This...this is more than I could have dreamed of..."

"Well, be careful with them, the wax is old and brittle, they're starting to deteriorate...you can see the bare metal disc underneath some of them. Now, you're going to need to play these at 78 rpms. They were made years before lps or 45s." I could not believe how things seemed to be unfolding; first the box, then the photograph Janet Mosley had given me...now recordings my parents had made!

"I can't wait to listen to them! I'd be happy to return them..."

"Nonsense! They're yours! You should have them! Can't wait to hear what you think. Your folks were very talented people!"

"I promise I'll let you know," I laughed. I finished my drink and started to leave. "Uncle Bill, I can't tell you how much this means..."

He interrupted me with a sweep of his hand.

He looked affectionately at me, with emotion clearly in his voice, softly he said, "I know." Perhaps he did...

I hurried home, the fragile records sitting next to me on the seat. I used my right hand to steady them, so they wouldn't slide with the motion of the car.

Fortunately, we still had a seldom used stereo in the corner of the family room. I carefully placed the old recordings on a nearby table. I gently lifted the top one from its discolored paper dust-cover. On the label, was one hand-written word, "Shippy." Carefully, I placed the record on the turntable, while I adjusted the speed to 78 rpms. I turned on the record player and gently placed the tone arm on the outer edge. For the first few seconds there was nothing but the sound or rhythmic scratches. Then I heard her voice. What I heard next defied all logic or explanation:

"Long ago and far away,
I dreamed a dream one day,
And now that dream is here beside me;
Long the skies were overcast,

But now the clouds have passed;
You're here at last!
Chills run up and down my spine:
Aladdin's lamp is mine;
The dream I dreamed was not denied me.
Just one look and then I knew
That all I longed for long ago was you."

I felt stunned! Totally numb! The voice on the record...was the same voice I had heard in the night! The voices were identical, the same inflection, the same vibrato, the same vocal quality! It had to be, but how was it possible? I felt paralyzed! The song was over, the scratchiness at the end of the record kept repeating, repeating, and repeating. Could the voice I had heard in my dream, or whatever it was, have been my mother's voice? How was that possible?

I decided not to tell Connie about the experience. I was reasonably sure she wouldn't believe me, anyway. The first thing the next morning, I called Dr. Foster's office. I got her answering machine. I left a pleading message. "Dr. Foster, this is Paul Bradshaw; something unbelievable has happened. I know our next appointment isn't scheduled for another couple of weeks, but I have to see you as soon as possible. Please, please call me," I begged.

Within a few minutes, the phone rang. It was Dr. Foster. "Paul, hello? What's wrong? What's happened?"

"I know you're busy," I blurted out, "but I have to see you. Do you have any time at all later today?"

"Well, yes, I could see you at 4:30. I did have a cancellation, but this is very much out of the ordinary..."

"I know it is, but so is what I have to tell you!"

I arrived at her office exactly at 4:30. I burst into her office!

Dr. Foster appeared at the door. "Paul, what's wrong? You look like you've seen a ghost!"

"Well, I may not have seen one, but I could have heard one," I sputtered.

"Come in." I sat down heavily on her couch and took a deep breath. I could see the concern on her face. "Now, what's happened?"

"You told me to try and get to know my mother. Well, I started by having a conversation with my uncle, her brother.

"Yes, go on."

"He really couldn't tell me very much, but he remembered some old studio recordings he had, records my parents made! I took them home and the first one I played...it was my mother's voice, it was the SAME voice I heard in my dreams!!! I could feel myself trembling.

Dr. Foster reached out and gently took my hand. Softly she said, "What you may have experienced is sometimes called a 'memory trace.' Very early memories are stored in the brain. It's possible that the arrival of the box you mentioned released a suppressed longing which stirred up those early memories that were in your dreams. It's also possible the release of those early memories started a chain of events that have been pushing you toward the box that can no longer be ignored."

"I don't want to be too clinical about this, but the Swiss psychiatrist, Carl Jung, referred to it as 'synchronicity.' Put plainly, synchronicity is the experience of two or more occurrences – beyond coincidence – in a manner that is logically meaningful – but inexplicable to the person experiencing them. Such events may suggest some underlying pattern or meaning, according to Jung."

"Dr. Foster, I don't know what you mean..."

"Paul, another way to think of this is that, perhaps…" she paused, looked away, then said, "Without sounding metaphysical, it could mean that this isn't just about you finding out more about your mother. It may also have something to do with her finding…you."

I sat there, unbelieving, trying to comprehend, unable to respond – to say anything at all.

"I know how difficult this may all seem right now, but I think you need to continue searching for people who knew your mother; and, if you can, see what that box has to tell you about her."

Chapter Seven

The box! The contents of which I still dreaded might not be the full answer, but at least it might be a beginning. It was a hot autumn Saturday afternoon. Connie had gone to Indianapolis shopping for the day. I had dutifully cut the grass and done the trimming the evening before, so I had the rest of the day to myself.

I went to the closet where I'd 'buried" the box weeks earlier. It was right where I'd left it, in a dark corner of the hall closet, in an even darker corner of my conscious mind. I didn't know it then, but I was about to begin a quest that would lead down an unseen road to a new understanding of the past – my past. Placing it on the floor of the library, I sat down beside it and carefully opened the lid.

The first item that caught my attention was a pink baby book, entitled, "Our Baby's First Seven Years." Inside the front cover was an envelope with my name on it. I carefully opened the flap and gently pulled out a card. It had a red border surrounded by hearts. In script, were printed the words, "On Valentine's Day." Inside, hand written, I read, *"To my darling, on his first Valentine's Day."* The date on the card was February 14, 1946. My God! My mother had written these words to me! There was also a little two-line verse. It was signed simply, *Mother. "Mother."*

I formed and reformed this strange new reality in my head as I reread the lines a dozen times over. I was only four months old, and she had written a Valentine's Day card to me, even though it would be years, a half-century, before I would ever read it. I looked at my hand holding the card and savored an oddly detached thought: she had held the very same card. My hand was where her hand had once been. I was reading words she had written for me! An emotional appetite overtook what were, at first, reactionary and random thoughts. What had she been feeling as she wrote those words for a baby who couldn't have understood? It was only a greeting card; I understood that, but discovering it now was like creating an umbilical connection to the mother I never knew. A Valentine card! My first real connection to her! I felt as though it had been sent to me only yesterday! For a brief instant, all the intervening years seemed to vanish as I reread her words once again: *"To my darling, on his first Valentine's Day."* Tenderly, I set the card aside.

Next, I reached for a yellowed newspaper clipping, unfolded it. It was from the local paper, the "Rushville Republican."

Margaret Bradshaw Dies At Culver

Monday, March 10, 1947

Culver, Ind. -- Mrs. Margaret Winship Bradshaw, 36, a native and well-known here, expired Sunday, March 9th, at her home in Culver following a prolonged illness. She was the widow of Capt. Paul M. Bradshaw, chairman of the Fine Arts Department at Culver Military Academy.

Mrs. Bradshaw was born April 29, 1910, in Rush County, a daughter of William S. and Florence Newkirk Winship. She was a graduate of DePauw University and received her Master's degree at the University of Michigan. She was an instructor of music and art at Knox and Lakeville. Mrs. Bradshaw was a member of the Main Street Christian Church here.

A son, Paul William Bradshaw, of Culver; her parents here; one brother, Bill Winship; and a grandmother, Mrs. W.R. Newkirk of here, survive her.

Funeral Services will be held at Culver Tuesday, March 11th, at 3 o'clock. The Rev. Dr. Sexton will officiate and burial will be in the Culver Community Cemetery.

A wave of sadness engulfed me just as suddenly as had the joy of discovering the lost Valentine. I read the words again. "Margaret Winship Bradshaw, 36, a native and well known here, expired...." Another even more unpleasant emotion surfaced as the sadness became mixed with anger. So that was all there was to it? A brief news item was all there was to her life? A cold statement of facts? There had to be more. I would FIND more. The sadness mixed with anger was still in the forefront of my emotions, but they were beginning to be framed by something more constructive -- that odd aforementioned *appetite*. I wanted more. I wanted to *know* more. Now, for the first time in many years, since my first summer at Culver when I was twelve, I wanted to know more about my mother and her life. What was she like? Why did she die so young? What happened? The Valentine card and the newspaper clipping were only a beginning. Dr. Foster was right. I needed to make a connection with my mother!

Another emotion washed over me. It was one I didn't relish, but it was there just the same. On an intellectual level I knew it was a childish reaction, a selfish tantrum, in fact. But it had been hidden and unexpressed for most of my lifetime. Now it surfaced with a vengeance – demanding to be heard. It was resentment. If my mother could have only known how my life had been changed by her death, the fears of abandonment, the loneliness, the profound feelings of insecurity, the gut-wrenching anxiety that I lived with for so long! How could she have done that to me? I needed her! God! What a price I had paid! No one should have to go through the childhood I had!

As those powerful and painful resentments surfaced, it was like an emotional boil had been lanced and a sense of relief came over me almost immediately. Clearly, the box from the closet held some powerful information that was going to change my life in any number of ways. This wasn't going to be just an idle Saturday afternoon alone in the house with some old family scrapbook sent by a distant relative. I was at a threshold. A doorway. And something told me there were keys inside this box – maybe not traditional keys – but keys nonetheless to questions I had avoided asking myself for a long, long time.

My mother was just thirty-six! What had really happened to her? What was the long illness alluded to in the obituary? What if there had been just a little more time? Perhaps... if I had been older I could have helped her. Questions with no obvious answers swirled in my head feeding energy and determination to my new appetite for truth.

What a strange and unexpected treasure chest this box might turn out to be. It just might change from being something I felt I didn't want or need into a "portal" through which I might glimpse the past. It might turn out to be a lifeline. It looked as if all these photographs, letters, yearbooks, trinkets and....memories (not mine, but my mother's) might bring me closer to her.

There were stacks of snapshots of my mother as a little child, as a young girl, and a teenager, even a set of photographer's proofs of my mother and father taken in their apartment at Culver. They were the proofs from which the one photograph I had of the two of them together had been made! I lifted a small book from the box; it had that distinctive smell old books always seem to have, slightly musty, "The Holcad 1928," the one Betty Brown had asked me if I had – the one about which I had lied! The ragged cover crackled along the spine as I opened it. 1928 – That was the year my mother had graduated from high school – a very long time ago. I carefully turned each page. Then, there she was, hair bobbed in the style of the day, the late 1920s, a mere girl:

"Distinctive Seniors"
MARGARET WINSHIP - We might
remember Margaret as 'activity
roundup girl' from her varied accomplishments

*this past school year. Whenever an able person in any
line was needed, they came to Shippy in the first
seat inside the library door. She will be remembered
for her enthusiasm."*

Toward the back of the book I found the "Senior Rogue's Gallery."

The prediction was that in twenty years she would either be an actress or a lecturer. *Twenty years*, the words rolled around in my head, I put the book down, stared out the window. Who could have imagined, in those youthful days of happiness, full of hopes and dreams about the future, that twenty years later, just twenty years, she would be dead.

I put the high school annual aside and reached for "The Mirage 1932" the yearbook of DePauw University. It was bigger by far, over 350 pages long; I let the pages slip by. There was her picture as president of the senior class!

During the 95 years the school had existed prior to that time, she was the first woman to win that honor. She looked so happy, large bright eyes, hair done in finger rolls. She had been involved in lots of activities; but, as I looked at the pictures of her, the one feature that burned itself into my memory was her smile. It was a beautiful, happy, self-assured, loving smile. As I looked at group pictures, I found her in an instant - by her smile. That's what my aunts had been talking about so long ago! I could almost feel the warmth of that smile - almost. How I longed to know more about her. The pictures and books were all about the surface, what was behind that smile? I had to know! Then I came to another yellowed newspaper clipping; it shouted at me:

"Faculty Member Dies Suddenly"
Heart Attack Fatal to P.M. Bradshaw of Arts Dept.
Wednesday, October 17, 1945

"Culver, Ind.--Funeral services were held Tuesday for Capt. Paul M. Bradshaw, chairman of the Fine Arts Department at Culver Military Academy, who died Saturday, October 13th, shortly after a heart attack. The short rites, conducted by Dr. Sexton, Director of Religious Activities at the Academy, were held in the Music and Arts Building on campus. Members of the faculty, the Company C football team, representatives of the corps, and local friends attended the service. The remainder of the corps served as a Guard of Honor while the funeral procession moved through the campus on its way to graveside services.

The 41-year-old faculty member was stricken while coaching his company team during an intramural game Saturday morning. Death was attributed to a coronary thrombosis.

Capt. Bradshaw was known to the corps as coach of a winning football team, composer of the First Class Song and originator of first class sings. At the time of his death he was also director of the Chapel Choir, instructor in piano, voice, and organ.

In 1934 he married Margaret Winship of Rushville, Indiana, a prominent public school music teacher. His wife, his parents and two sisters, and a son, Paul William, who was born in South Bend's Memorial Hospital only a week previous to Capt. Bradshaw's death, survive him."

That clipping closed the circle. They were both gone. After collecting myself, I looked deeper into the box and started reading some of the fragile letters. The first, on thin airmail paper, was from my father to his sister, Dorothy:

June 2, 1945

Dearest Dorothy:

I received your wedding announcement today and it looked like the real thing - so formal and everything. I would truly give a good deal to be there for the wedding, but I just can't. The most important thing my Glee Club does is at Commencement time and that particular day falls on Sunday, June 8th. I am glad that Grace will be there. I would like very much to hear more about Frank, but I suppose you don't know so very much about him yourself. I didn't know a great many things about Shippy nor did she about me. Still we are getting along better than ever and need each other even more than ever. We will have been married eleven years next Friday at four o'clock.

I'm up a stump about seeing the folks between winter school and summer school. If I could fly out there to Montana with some Santa Claus I would be happy. Boy, I just dream about that beautiful place, the hills and streams. I honestly would like to live there someday all the year long. I would read and practice and chop wood during the winter and hike and climb, fish and loaf during the summer. We really want to learn to live that way, but with the baby on the way it may be a while before that dream comes true for us.

Love always,
Paul and Shippy

It was a light, airy, conversational letter, but he had written how much he and my mother needed each other and knew, to the hour, when their anniversary was. It was a clue to their lives together, a tantalizing glimpse of who they were. "Shippy," I knew had been her nickname since high school, an adulteration of her maiden name, Winship. As pretentious as it might sound a half-century later, "Shippy" was what everyone called her. It was a very natural term of endearment for the times in which she had lived.

The next letter was short, but its poignancy was staggering. When my father wrote these words he had just three days left to live. I was five days old:

Wednesday, October 10, 1945
Dear Colonel Gregory:

I am sorry not to have acknowledged your note regarding our First Class Sings sooner. I am glad you are pleased with the progress we have made in making the "Sings" a first-rate tradition. Speaking of "sings," these days I have an uncommon interest in lullabies. When Shippy comes home please come up and see our new quarterback!

P.M. Bradshaw

His relaxed style was engaging. Phrases like "first-rate," were dated, but still sincere for the times. "I have an uncommon interest in lullabies...come up and see our new quarterback!" He was talking about me! I wondered what my life would have been like if, well, if tragedy hadn't struck us all. Struck us all? The words echoed in my mind over and over again. *Struck us all.* For the first time in my life, I had thought of "us," the three of us, as a family! It was a unique sensation, a unique thought, and one that had never occurred to me before, one that I had never felt before. "Us." What a beautiful, warm, reassuring feeling that little word gave me. I felt a slender thread of connection to the events, and the people, that were so much a part of the past that had been hidden. For just a little while there had been an "us." We had been a family, even if it was only for a few short days...

There were other letters from my father to his mother written while he was a college student and after, letters about everyday events, letters urging my grandmother to see a doctor about the pain in her chest. Then I found an extraordinarily poignant letter from my father's sister, Grace, to her sister, Dorothy. It was about my father's funeral. It was a haunting letter filled with emotion, evoking images that took me to a time and place of long forgotten sadness:

Wednesday, October 17, 1945
Dear Dorothy:

I started to write to you last night, but couldn't quite find the right opportunity. Mother's train arrived in Chicago on time Monday night, and she stood the trip about as well as could be expected. I'm so glad you saw to it that she had all the conveniences possible while traveling. She met a minister on the train who helped her considerably. We drove straight to Culver - about a three-hour trip - and stayed at the club.

Yesterday morning mother and Shippy spent time with the baby. Later we took mother down to see Paul. It was dreadfully hard on her, but it was something she wanted to do. Paul looked very peaceful. I hadn't wanted to see him, but I'm glad now I did.

The services were at 3:00 PM at the Music and Arts Building. The academy minister spoke, not really a sermon, but all the things about Paul we wanted to hear. His choir sang one number very beautifully and that was all. When we came out of the building the cadets were lined up on either side of the drive through the campus to Logansport Gate. The cars drove between the two lines of cadets standing at attention. It was the finest thing they could have done, and it made me feel so very proud to know that Paul had been so much their friend that they wanted to do this for him.

The cemetery is out of town down near the lake, a beautiful little spot, the sort of place Paul would want to be. The hardest part for mother and Shippy was when Paul's choir sang and when we left the cemetery.

The baby is a little darling and very good. He has Paul's head, the same shape exactly. He has been a source of extreme comfort to Shippy and Mother, too.

This is an awful thing, Dorothy, something we can't understand or find any reason for - but I guess the only thing is to accept it and try to go on. It is so very hard for Shippy. Her anguish tears at my heart. I see her and try to realize what she's going through. She's so brave most of the time and there's nothing anyone can do to help.

Mother and I are staying on until Saturday or Sunday. We'll call you when we get home. I know there are lots of things I haven't said, but what I've written are the most important details. I thank God that I came to Culver when I did so I could spend a little time with Paul before he died. It was almost as if it was planned - just last Friday he was talking of the family - mother, dad, you and me, and everything he said showed how great was his love for all of us and how much he missed us.

Love, Grace

There were more letters, letters my mother had written. They made it clear to me that something terrible was happening. They weren't letters, really, just notes. But they showed just how much the world had changed for "Shippy." I began to feel the torment, the anguish, and the sense of unreality that must have filled her life as I read the words:

Margaret Winship Bradshaw
Culver Military Academy
Culver, Indiana

March 2, 1946

Dear Mother Bradshaw,

Your offer, to make me a dress came at the most opportune time for I am badly in need of summer clothes and haven't much to buy them with. My job as Social Secretary at the academy pays me just half enough to live on, but dad is supplying the remainder and I hope to make more in the fall. I am sending you patterns for a playsuit for little Paul, a dress, and a pair of slacks and if you can possibly make one of each for me I'll be so glad to pay for the material.

I took the baby to the doctor in South Bend a week ago Monday. He was so pleased. He weighed 16 lbs, 4 oz. We had him vaccinated for smallpox and the past two days he has been a little restless. I have taken some more pictures and I will send you some.

Love,
Shippy and little Paul

Margaret Winship Bradshaw
Culver Military Academy
Culver, Indiana

April 7, 1946

Dear Mother Bradshaw,

Your sweet letter came today. I am sorry not to have written sooner. I spend the morning with our darling, making formula, singing to him, bathing him and playing with him. I go to work at 1:00 PM and get home at 5:00 PM and I am with him the rest of the evening. He is wonderful, mother - so healthy and round. He is eating vegetables, cereal, and fruit now. His doctor is so pleased with his progress.

I am usually too tired in the evening to write but I shall try to do better. I hope you will keep writing to us. You must not worry dear, for I know that Paul will come back to us - just remember - Paul will come back. I know it and you must believe me.

I am enclosing some snapshots that you will love and cherish.

Our best love to you,
Shippy

My God, what had she written about Paul coming back? I looked at the date on the letter again. No, this was April, 1946. My Father died in October, 1945. This was no mistake. I re-read her words, blinking at the page. "Paul will come back..." What could she possibly have thought? "I know it and you must believe me." What was this? What had happened to her? Did she really believe that my father was somehow coming back to her? Had his sudden and unexpected death caused her to lose touch with reality? Was the shock and loss so painful she couldn't or wouldn't accept it?

All those euphemisms I'd been told by my aunts about my mother dying of "a broken heart" replayed in my head. Was it possible that she had intentionally ended her own life? Was that the event from which I had been shielded all these years? The possibility was almost too horrible to imagine, but it still could turn out to be a reality I might have to accept... Was this what they really meant? Had she suffered some kind of mental breakdown? Had no one ever been willing to say those words to me all these years? Was this their way of being "kind"? Feelings of anger came again. Right in the pit of my stomach. Only this time, a sense of betrayal had been added to the uncomfortable mix. And if it turned out to be true that living had become too much for her to bear, what about me? What did she think would become of me? Anger mixed with sadness. Suddenly, I felt very, very alone.

I looked up from the letter; all around me were things of the here and now in my life. The library was the same room Connie and I had planned and furnished when we built the new house. My desk was where it was supposed to be. The photos and books were in their same familiar places on the shelves, including the one formal portrait of my mother and father, sitting together at a grand piano, the only photograph I had of the two of them together. There, also, was the new photo of my mother as a young girl on the table next to the little slipper chair – right where it was supposed to be. The landscape out the window was the same. Nothing around me had changed, but I was not the same! I had disturbing, new information I had never known before. New questions, new and terrible possibilities. And I would have to learn to understand and cope.

I knew there was something called "post-partum depression" that affected new mothers quite frequently. I'd heard of it, even if it wasn't something I knew about personally. Connie sailed through three pregnancies like a trouper – better than I did, I almost said out loud -- smiling at my memories of those long-ago days. We talked about the "baby blues"; but, if she had them, they weren't serious and they never lasted long. But our children were born during the 1970s in a more enlightened time of feminism and medical science (including mental health).

Looking back at my mother's letter, I asked myself, "What was her world like in 1945 and 1946?" She (and the country) had been through the most destructive war in the history of the world. It had ended only a few months before, in August 1945. The lives of American soldiers and sailors were being snuffed out by the thousands on foreign soil in nightmarish violence beyond most people's comprehension. Life on the home front was strained by worry, rationing, and other shortages of all kinds, plus the constant dread of a telegram from the War Department being delivered to the door at any time. If the telegram didn't come for a brother, or a son, or a father, it arrived next door for a neighbor, a cousin, or an old school chum. There was tremendous loss everywhere.

Where was the room to think about an obscure disorder (not even commonly known back then) such as the post-partum blues of a healthy young mother? My mother would have been especially vulnerable; her husband was _not_ away at the war, he was safe at home and strong and well...teaching music and coaching boys' football at a military academy in northern Indiana! His sudden death must have been a devastating shock to her, just days after giving birth...with hormones and other physical changes running riot through her mind and body. Today it would probably have been called post-partum psychosis.

As quickly as they had come, the feelings of anger and betrayal turned to a profound sympathy for this woman who was my mother. I didn't know it then, but it was coming from a place in me I had never explored before. It was a place called love; the love I had begun to feel for my mother that had been sleeping quietly, hidden deep within me for five long decades.

Chapter Eight

The box with its letters and pictures had been a starting point. A few small pieces of the puzzle of my past had been given to me, but there was still so much I didn't know or understand, so many important pieces missing. I needed to find some of her contemporaries. Surely that would be possible – or so I thought. I went back to the old high school yearbook, looked for names I might recognize from the Class of 1928. Why hadn't I thought of that before? I returned to the box and my mother's high school yearbook. I scanned through the names and senior pictures. Faces and names I knew well jumped off the page at me, all looking eerily youthful and innocent. I recognized the photos of Ruth Moran and Francis Richards. They had both been in the class of 1928 with my mother! I *knew* these people! They were both in their late 80s, but I was so energized by this possibility of a breakthrough that I overlooked the possibility of a soft and gauzy filter of time and memory affecting the recollections of those in the twilight of their lives.

My odyssey in search of my mother's contemporaries was incredibly naive. I see that now. But at the time I was thrilled to find these people alive and willing to talk with me about this vitally important and, in many ways, enigmatic character in my evolving life story – my mother, Margaret Winship, the bright, vivacious, and witty girl they all called "Shippy."

One way or another, I had known both these people most of my life! Why had it never occurred to me to ask them about my mother before now? Well, the answer was obvious after a moment's reflection; I didn't really want to know - until now. But this new appetite I had developed was nearly insatiable.

Ruth Moran had never married, but she had been like my surrogate mother in many respects, but only on a part-time basis! She had been the secretary to the local attorney who had handled my grandfather's estate back in the sixties, so I was in his office frequently. I was just a teenager at the time and had never quite understood her lectures about economy and proper behavior.

"Well, you're just spending way too much money on gas! (Ruth, unfortunately, saw the gas receipts.) You don't have any business wasting your time driving up and down Main Street with the other teenagers. You need to be home studying. You'll never amount to anything just driving up and down Main Street! I just don't know what to do with you," she would scold.

Francis Richards had been the "Welcome Wagon" hostess when I was a kid. She had a bundle of energy, always happy to talk to anybody about anything. She had married, not long after high school, a young man whom, she said she would have run away with after their first date - if he had asked her. They were still together after nearly sixty years.

Here were these two wonderful women who knew my mother so well, and I had never made the connection during all the years that had gone before! Now it was important!

I talked with Ruth Moran in her living room on a bright and beautiful early October afternoon in 1997. In her late 80s, she was a tiny, frail-looking, white-haired woman, but looks were deceiving with Ruth. Tiny though she may have been, she was a tough little Irish woman who was proud of her heritage and ready to defend it!

Her living room was an airy pleasant place. There were family pictures on the mantelpiece and on the piano, lace curtains at the windows, and crocheted doilies on the arms and backs of the upholstered chairs. She served martinis! "Well," she smiled, sipping her martini with one hand and slapping her other hand on her knee, "I'm proud of you! You turned out much better than I thought you would." Ruth did not mince words. "Your aunts just spoiled you terribly. I can remember them bringing you by the house in a little stroller when you were small. They treated you like a breakable porcelain doll! But you made it! Now, kiddo, what's on your mind?"

"Ruth, I've never known very much about my parents; and, well, I've reached the point in life where I'd like to know more. You and my mother went to school together and I'd like to know more about her."

"Oh, honey, your mother...Shippy, was just a doll!" Apparently nobody _ever_ called her Margaret, except my great aunts. "She was just a lot of fun to be around. She was always on the go, always involved in some kind of activity. She was, well, always the life of the party." Ruth's eyes sparkled as she shared memories from nearly seventy years before. "We had such good times. Life was still ahead of us then, and we all thought we were pretty hot stuff at the time. Everybody thought Shippy would really go places. I never met your dad, but he must have been a special guy."

Ruth took another sip of her martini, looked at the floor, her mind traveling back in time. She smiled. "I remember how she used to get in trouble for chewing gum in Miss Madden's senior English class. Instead of parking her gum behind her ear like everybody else, she'd pop it! Of course Miss Madden knew who it was. 'Miss Winship,' she'd say, 'Take that gum out of your mouth this instant,'" Ruth laughed. "Then there was the time a gang of us helped Shippy sneak your grandfather's car out of the garage and we all went for a joy ride around town. We had to push the car nearly a block before anybody dared start it. We finally got the car stuck in the mud out in the cemetery east of town, of all places! We all had to walk back! I'll bet there were nine or ten of us kids in that old Model T. Your grandfather was fit to be tied when we got home – one of the neighbors heard all the commotion and told him what we were up to! He had to get out of bed, get dressed, and walk all the way out to the cemetery, and then get the car un-stuck. When he came back in the house, he tracked mud on your grandmother's carpet; and she made him clean it up before she'd let him go back to bed! I don't think Shippy was allowed out of the house for a month!" she laughed.

"But Ruth, what was she like? What..."

"Oh, honey, that was such a long, long time ago. So much has happened over the years, so much time has passed..." There was a long pause; Ruth leaned forward in her chair, her face softened, her eyes looking intently into mine. She reached out her pale, slender hand and gently brushed my cheek. For a brief instant time seemed suspended. "But when I look at you," her voice was sweet, penetrating, gentle, "when I look at you...I see her. I see...." Ruth looked away, gathered herself, and leaned back. The moment had passed. "Honey, all I can tell you is that she was a wonderful person and a great friend.

How are Connie and the boys?" It was strange; it was as though Ruth and my uncle could only go so far before hitting some kind of emotional wall. Or, sadly, perhaps it had all been too long ago. I hoped not. What had she seen? Where had she been during that brief moment? The rest of the afternoon was idle conversation and at least two more martinis each!

Before I left, Ruth said, "Honey, sometimes it's best to leave the past alone. Your mother was a wonderful person, and she was my friend. And she would have been very proud of you." Ruth gave me a gentle kiss on the cheek. "Come back and see me again sometime. I love to fix martinis!"

What had she meant, "...leave the past alone?" Was there more to this than anyone was willing to tell me? I thought about the disturbing letter I'd found in the box. "Paul will come back..."

I remembered the feeling of frustration, coming so close, and yet being held so far away. I knew Ruth could see my mother in her mind's eye...had actually seen her! She had a living memory, a vivid image, when they were all young together, but it was an image I could not see or feel or hear, except in my dreams. Something special had happened in that brief moment, as if a distant door had opened just slightly. I wanted more. Somehow I had to find that door for myself.

My visit with Frances Richards was equally frustrating. Poor Frances suffered from severe crippling arthritis. So severe, in fact, that she lived in an extended care facility. I had to call to set up a time to go see her. Francis and her husband had lived in a beautiful white-pillared Greek-revival house for most of their sixty years of married life together. They lived on Harrison Street, the same street where Ruth Moran lived, just about five blocks north.

The assisted living facility was nice enough, but it was nothing like the home on Harrison Street I remembered from my childhood. I walked down the bright corridor to the nurse's station. There was an empty, hollow sound to my footsteps as they echoed down the hall...the passageway to God's Waiting Room, I thought.

Francis was in a wheelchair. The nurse asked me to wait in a pleasant little reception area, filled with plants and sunlight and institutional-looking furniture. "Francis will be out in a few minutes. She wanted to look her best for your visit."

The two metal doors swung open mechanically. There was Francis! Slowed by age and infirmity, but still vital and alive. She had on a beautiful dusty pink dress with a pleated skirt. Her snow-white hair had just been done, and she was wearing a single strand of pearls.

"Oh, Paul, how nice to see you!" Her arms reached out to me. We hugged. It felt very awkward. The nurse steered her to a cozy corner of the reception area, near a window.

"Francis, you look great! How have you been?"

"Oh, all right, I suppose, I can't get around the way I used to. I can't even use my cane anymore. I'm happy enough here, but I miss our home so much." The nurse left, but returned quickly with a large scrapbook. "They're so kind to me here," she continued as she adjusted the scrapbook on her lap. "I've been able to bring a few special things from home...."

"Francis, the reason I came to see you..." I started to say. But she interrupted.

"I want you to have this." She reached for a brown envelope inside the scrapbook. "It's a photograph I've had since high school. We had a girl's quintet and we sang for all sorts of occasions. Here." She handed it to me.

I carefully opened the flap and removed a mezzo-tint photograph. It was of five young girls. In the second row, I instantly recognized my mother. She was beautiful with a smile that, again, almost seemed intended for me. The memories of her smile were not just fanciful recollections made up by people who were trying to be kind. I also recognized Francis - she was wearing a strand of pearls.

"Are these the same pearls as the ones in the picture, Francis?

"Oh, yes! My husband gave them to me before we were married. We've had many happy years together." Her voice faltered with emotion. "He'll be here later this afternoon. He comes to see me every day."

"Francis, I'm trying to learn a little bit more about my mother. The two of you were in high school together, right? What was she like?"

"Oh, she was a wonderful person. We were in the first girl's choral quintet at the high school...ever! I played piano and sang. Shippy sang alto. I can't play the piano any more because of my hands." She looked down at her arthritic fingers, nearly frozen in a half-clenched position.

I tried to change the subject from her painful hands. Leafing through her treasured scrapbook, I noticed the first few pages seemed to focus on the late 1920s. "Here's another picture of the quintet," I said. What else do you remember about her?"

"We had such fun in high school," she said wistfully. "Your mother had a beautiful voice. I thought she was good enough to become a professional singer someday. Your mother and I; we hit it off right from the start. You look so much like her. Of course, we all knew Shippy and your dad were living at Culver and that you had been born but..." her voice trailed off.

"What sort of person was she?"

"Oh, she was very popular in school. She was one of the few girls I knew who could whistle. We would walk to school together when we were in high school, and she would be whistling some new tune she had heard on the radio the night before. I almost had to run to keep up with her; she had a very long stride, and I was much shorter, short legs." Francis looked down at her legs, sighed, "I certainly couldn't keep up with her now, though. It's all I can do to get from this awful chair into my bed without help..."

Frances seemed to change gears in her mind. "Do you remember the day I came out to visit you with a Welcome Wagon basket when your own little Paul was born?" She was now talking about a generation later and the birth of my son, Paul, Jr.

"Shippy's little boy with a son of his own!" she added with a warm smile. I realized her mental visit to the 1920s was over for today. And I was no closer to gaining any real insight into my mother's true self.

I leaned back in my chair. "It's so obvious," I thought, looking at the strand of pearls around Frances' neck, "People live out their own lives, have their memories, joys, and heartaches close around them like the pearls of a necklace." Bits and pieces strung together. It was better than nothing, but that's all I was getting about my mother -- little bits and pieces seen through the rose-colored glasses of time and life's frailties. What had happened to that carefree happy girl? How could such a promising life have become such an unbearable weight to carry?

Awkwardly, I said good-bye to Frances. I didn't know when, if ever, I would see her again. Time must be very precious to those of her generation.

"I hope you come see me again soon," she said. "I have so few visitors, except my husband." I told her I would, but I wondered if I really meant it. I stood and smiled as the nurse wheeled Frances back down the corridor.

As I turned to leave, I noticed another elderly lady sitting alone in a wheelchair in the far corner of the reception area. I hadn't noticed her there before. At first, it looked as if she might be waiting for someone, I genuinely hoped so. This seemed like a place where far too few comings and goings awaited the elderly residents. As I walked past her toward the door, she reached out and gently touched my arm. As I turned, I noticed she was looking intently up at me. "You know...you need to go there."

"What an odd thing to say," I thought to myself, still numb from my conversation with Frances. "I'm sorry," I said. "Go where?"

"Go back to Culver and see what you find." I chuckled -- almost automatically -- and I replied, "You know, you're probably right." Having been raised in the gentle company of kind-spirited old ladies, I'd learned long ago to agree with their unexpected remarks _first_ and process what they were saying _later._

When I realized that she had been listening to my entire conversation with Frances – overheard the whole thing – I was a little embarrassed. But of course she had. I was so focused on what Frances could tell me about Shippy, I had been oblivious to everyone else in the room. But, somehow, it was all right. Lonely people are more than eager for any distraction from their often-dull routine. This kind old soul was past the age where social politeness would restrict her, rob her of an opportunity to contribute to our conversation. I could understand that; even respect it on some level. Her need to be helpful was still young and vital -- totally alive. Her interruption came from a sincere desire to help, to contribute to my quest. A spark of recognition passed between us when she touched my arm.

"Go back to Culver...!" she said. I really hadn't thought of that.

Chapter Nine

On the way home, I thought about what the elderly lady had said at the conclusion of my visit with Frances. "Go back to Culver..." Her words rolled over in my mind. Soon, my thoughts wandered back to the long summers I had spent there in my youth.

When I was twelve, my grandfather had taken his sisters' overindulgences about as long as he could. I think he knew, at some level, that something fundamental and vital had been missing from my life, something he knew he was unable to give. We were watching a baseball game on the large, wooden-enclosed console black and white TV in the living room one late spring afternoon. Suddenly, out of the blue, he said, "Bud," (For some still unknown reason, my grandfather always called me "Bud"), slapping his knees with both hands, "I think it's time for us to get you out of the house."

What! Out of the house! "But, Granddad, I don't want to leave!"

"Oh, not for good. Just for a few weeks this summer. I think it's time for you to learn how to swim. Every boy should know how to swim. Best place to do that will be at Culver. You'll like it there. You're Uncle Bill went to school there."

"How long will I be away from home?"

"Not long. I think the summer session lasts only about eight weeks."

Eight weeks! Eight weeks sounded like a lifetime! Within a few days, however, I had received a full-color catalogue from Culver, full of pictures of boys who appeared to be having a great time. I had heard of Culver before, but I had no idea of what the full import of that name was – or the meaning it would have in years to come. Perhaps, I thought, going to Culver wouldn't be so bad at that, and learning to swim would probably be fun!

In late June, during the summer of 1958, I was on my way to the "Woodcraft Camp" at Culver Military Academy.

I remembered my first day at Culver, Uncle Bill, my Aunt Maxine, along with my two great-aunts, drove me to the lakeside campus, just under three hours from home. It was a completely different world for me, as much as I had looked forward to going - I had practically memorized the catalogue showing boys having fun - I recalled the terrible fear that swept over me as we neared Logansport Gate, one of the main entrances to the campus. Up until just a few minutes before we arrived, it was going to be a grand adventure, and then the reality of it struck me like a hammer blow. It was the first time I had ever been away from "home" in my life. Suddenly, I did not want to be there the least little bit, but it was too late to back out; somehow I had to find the courage to "stick it out." Granddad wanted me to go, and I didn't want to let him down.

"Well, sport," my uncle said casually, "We're here. I haven't been back to campus for years. This is going to be a great experience for you…wish I could go with you!" I sat glumly in the back seat, my anticipation having turned to foreboding. At that moment I also wished very much that he could go instead of me! My uncle had graduated from "winter school" at Culver in 1939, almost twenty years before. He knew the ropes in this strange new world.

Our first stop was a very large and imposing tent, just inside the entrance to the Woodcraft Camp. It was the headquarters tent. My uncle led the way. "We'd like to see Colonel Leland," he said to the receptionist.

Before she could say a word, a voice from the next room said, "Come right on in, Winship. I'd recognize that voice in a minute!" We walked into the next room, where Colonel Leland extended his hand to my uncle and shook it enthusiastically. White-haired, Colonel Leland had a kind, grandfatherly look about him, but he was as straight as a ramrod! He was wearing freshly starched khakis, silver eagles on each shoulder, and a tightly knotted khaki tie which was tucked inside his shirt between the second and third buttons. "Good to see you again! It's been a long time." He looked down at me. "So, this is your nephew – Paul and Shippy's boy?"

"Yes, sir," my uncle replied as he patted me on the shoulder.

"Here, please sit down, ladies," he said to my aunts. "It's good to have you back at Culver," he said quietly, looking at me intently. I didn't feel all that good about it at the moment. "Well, let's get the paperwork out of the way and get on with it!"

After signing in, I was sent – by myself - to the Recreation Building for uniforms, (relatives were not allowed to interfere in uniform fittings). Young men, also in crisp khaki uniforms, officers, were there to give us directions. "Keep that line moving, boys. No talking there! This isn't church camp," one of them said. Perhaps there was going to be more to this than simply learning to swim...

The uniforms were very much like the old Boy Scout summer uniform except they were sky blue instead of olive-drab. I was given six sets. The dress coats were dark blue, long-sleeved, with a gold aiguillette for members of the Woodcraft Drum & Bugle Corps to which I had been assigned. It was all very orderly. I was handed two laundry bags which were quickly filled with uniforms, blankets, a standard issue bathrobe, raincoat and hat, overshoes, socks, underwear, and more. The next stop was a series of tables at which were seated several ladies from the tailor shop, marking every item with a laundry number with pen and indelible ink.

"Over here, mister," one of them called out to me. I hefted all the equipment I'd been issued and stepped up to the nearest table. "Where are you from?" she asked without looking up.

"Rushville," I replied.

Slowly she looked up at me. "Never heard of it," she said with a faint smile.

From the Recreation Building, I lugged the overstuffed laundry bags of Culver equipment back to the entrance of the Woodcraft Camp. Thankfully, it was a short walk.

Another man in crisp khaki, with an air of serious professionalism about him, was waiting at the entrance, standing with my uncle. My aunts were seated on a nearby bench. He extended his hand as I let the overstuffed laundry bags drop with a thud. "I'm Major Kurtz, senior counselor of the D&B," he said as he firmly shook my hand. "Your boy, Mr. Winship?" he asked my uncle.

"No, sir. My nephew. Bradshaw, Paul Bradshaw. This is his first summer."

Major Kurtz scanned his official-looking clipboard. "Ah, here's his name. He's been assigned to Tent 421. Shall I have one of the older boys give you a hand?"

"No, thank you, sir," my uncle said, "We'll find it. Come on Paul. Maxine, you help the girls along." The "girls" he was referring to were my great-aunts who, at that moment, looked almost as uncertain about all this as I felt.

The Woodcraft Camp was literally a tent city all laid out in strict military-looking rows. As we walked past each row, I wondered how I would ever find my tent among so many that all looked exactly alike. After putting things away, according to the sheet of rather precise instructions I had been given, Uncle Bill helped me make my bed and line up my "footwear" beneath it. There were instructions for that, too. Uncle Bill knew how beds were supposed to be made at Culver, square corners, the top sheet folded back over the blanket exactly eight inches, an extra blanket folded neatly at the foot of the bed. There was even a sheet of instructions specifying the order in which hang-up items were to be placed on the hooks attached to the rear wall of the tent! My roommate was a kid from Missouri, smaller than I, but a lot more worldly. His older brother had gone to Culver, so he knew what to expect. Clearly, I did not.

When the time came for everyone to leave, Uncle Bill gently ushered my aunts, who by this time were distraught, toward the car. Aunt Maxine lingered. She gave me a gentle kiss goodbye, and I was by myself in this strange world. I sat on the rough-hewn hickory chair outside Tent 421 and felt terribly alone.

"Hey, kid!" It was my new roommate's voice. "Ya wanna play some ball?"

"Sure," I replied absentmindedly. I grabbed my ball glove and was off on the first great adventure of my life.

It didn't take long to discover that at Culver I was responsible for myself. We were expected to make our beds every morning, keep our tent clean, keep all our uniforms neatly folded and shoes shined. For the first few days, I was very homesick.

We lived in those wood-framed, concrete-floored, canvas-covered tents just north of the Recreation Building all summer long. After a couple of weeks, my tent actually became a warm, cozy place, especially on a rainy evening. "Hey, Foster," (my roommate's last name – we all called each other by last names, except, of course the officers who were always, "sir"), "Do you know how to swim?"

"Sure. Why?"

"That's one of the reason I'm here, to learn to swim."

"Come on, Bradshaw, you don't know how to swim? How do you get to be twelve and not know how to swim?"

"Nobody ever taught me how."

"Well, ya gotta learn to swim so you can earn your swimming "C." Can't swim in the lake until you do that." Learning to swim was another life experience from which I'd been protected at home! My grandfather wanted me to learn to swim, but I think he understood that what I needed was the companionship of other boys, discipline, and some male authority figures in my life.

Culver, even in the summer, was a military school. I learned important lessons about responsibility, honesty, self-discipline, teamwork, getting along with other kids and, at least in my case, discovered I could actually do things that would otherwise have seemed impossible - like learning to swim!

Culver was also a beautiful place...still is. The main campus would have been the envy of many small colleges: the lake, the collegiate gothic architecture of the buildings, the memorials, and the chapel with its majestic spire reaching toward the sky, the playing fields and the vast expanse of green lawn that was the parade ground.

I was there a full week before I actually saw the lake! That first summer there were nearly 1,600 boys between the ages of eight and eighteen at Culver. I learned to march at Culver. We marched everywhere. Three times each day we marched down past the Music & Art building to the Dining Hall, which was big enough to accommodate all 800 Woodcrafters at one sitting.

I knew my parents had lived at Culver. I recalled one large color photograph of my mother holding a tiny baby. Color photography wasn't all that common in the mid-1940s. She was standing in front of a brick building with a large picture window; bright red tulips were blooming all around her. I had looked at that picture a thousand times. My aunts had told me the baby she was holding was me; still, I felt no connection to my mother, wished terribly that I had. I wanted to feel something when I looked at her image, but nothing came.

I realized the picture had to have been taken on the Culver campus! And I wanted to find the spot where it had been taken. It might make a difference!

Exploring the campus near the lake one Sunday afternoon, I turned the corner down by the Administration Building; this was where the older boys lived, the midshipmen of the Naval School, in large impressive, turreted brick barrack buildings. Off to my left the lake was blue and beautiful. I glanced to my right, and suddenly, there it was! There was the picture window from the photograph! I would have recognized it anywhere! Finally, part of the image from that photograph was real!

There were evergreen bushes where the tulips had been, but this was the place! I stood, staring at that spot, praying I would feel something, remember something...anything...but nothing came. No connection. No emotion. No recollection. Nothing...

That was the day during my twelfth summer when I quit trying to remember, didn't want to remember. During that long first summer, I walked the same paths, passed the same barracks, competed on the same playing fields, and marched on the same parade ground my parents had known so well - just twelve years earlier - it might as well have been a century.

Learning to swim turned out to be the crowning achievement of that first summer. I didn't know I was afraid of the water until I was in it! Major Dunning was the swimming instructor. "Mr. Bradshaw," he said, looking at me squarely in the face, "In all my years at Culver, I have never failed to teach a student of mine how to swim and you, sir," he told me emphatically, "are not going to be the first!" I begged and pleaded, all to no avail. Major Dunning had seen plenty of kids like me before. He knew how to handle me. He was patient, but firm. Little by little I overcame my fear of the water and gradually gained sufficient skill to earn my swimming "C." Earning that "C" meant being able to swim 250 yards, and with it came the privilege of swimming in the lake.

The day finally came for me to swim that distance. All my lessons had been in the academy pool. Major Dunning's words were reassuring, calm, "You're doing fine. Keep your chin up. Kick. Chin up. Steady, steady. Keep going. Keep going. You're doing just fine." Lap after lap, I concentrated, kept going, until finally he said; "You're done!" Trivial as it may sound, up to that moment it was the happiest day of my life. "I'm proud of you, Mr. Bradshaw," Major Dunning said! He was proud of me! After class I ran to the Tailor Shop to have the little "C" patch sewn on my swimming trunks; I couldn't wait to tell my friends! I had never felt more proud in my life. I had accomplished something that had seemed impossible only a few weeks before.

"Foster, guess what? I earned my 'C!' I swam my 250 yards! I made it!"

My roommate was lying on his bunk reading a comic book. Without looking up, he said, "Big deal."

Chapter Ten

The next three summers were spent attending Culver's Summer Naval School, which was even more military than Woodcraft Camp. We wore white ducks and middy blouses, tightly folded black neckerchiefs, leggings, and traditional sailor caps. There were inspections every morning, roll calls before every meal, and, again, we marched everywhere. There were privileges, rank, and leadership positions, all very structured. I loved it. I was in a world of boys, all of us parentless, at least for those eight weeks each summer. There was a certain equality about all that, I felt I belonged; the experience brought a balance to my life. There were crew races, track meets, classes in seamanship and navigation, retreat parades, and Sunday afternoon band concerts.

Years before, back home, my aunts had wanted to encourage what they supposed was the musical ability inherited from my parents. So, through no particular desire on my part, I took up the cornet in the fifth grade. By the time I was in high school, I had discovered that I did seem to have a natural flair for that little ancestor of the trumpet. It was only natural, therefore, for me to be in the Naval School Band, as I had been in the Drum & Bugle Corps two summers before.

I remembered the first day of band practice as a lowly Third Classman at Culver. Colonel Edward Tilden Payson, a fixture at Culver, was the director, a no-nonsense sort of man, dressed in a crisp summer tan Army uniform, with a brilliant silver eagle on each shoulder. He called the roll. Each member of the band, by sections, in turn, jumped to attention and spit out, "Here, sir!" as his name was called. With each response Colonel Payson would glance up quickly and go on; there were nearly a hundred of us and there was a lot to do. He hesitated as he read my name, but pronounced it correctly which not many people did. He looked up slowly. He looked intently at me, and there was a strange sadness in his eyes. I have never forgotten that look. For an instant it was as though time stood still. I felt embarrassed, as though every eye in the room was on me. "Here, sir!" I answered quickly.

After that first practice, he told me to wait. I waited, scared, wondered what I had done wrong. He walked slowly up to me, hands clasped behind his back, "Mister Bradshaw, I knew your father very well." I swallowed hard. "We worked together for years until, well, until the day he died so unexpectedly. He was quite a wonderful musical talent, you know." He glanced away, "Together, they made such a perfect match, your mother and dad, so sad..." He seemed to catch himself, said, "Well, how are things going for you so far?"

"OK, sir,"

His stern bearing returned, "Never say 'OK;' answer 'Very well, sir.' Work hard. Practice. I expect the best from Captain Bradshaw's son. That's all. You're dismissed." Colonel Payson worked with my father! Knew my mother! For an instant, I wanted to ask more. I could remember the sound of Colonel

Payson's heels clicking against the cold tile floor as he strode out of the rehearsal hall. Perhaps on another day there would be time to talk. It never came.

Colonel Payson demanded a great deal, especially from his summer school bands. If we didn't measure up to his expectations, he called us a "kid band." We worked very hard to measure up. No one wanted to be thought of as being in a "kid band."

By my First Class summer, my musical skill was good enough to fill in for the regular bugler, Bill Barkley, on dance nights. Bill played lead trumpet in the academy dance band. One day I overheard Colonel Payson mentioning to the Company Tactical Officer how impressed he was with whoever had played the bugle calls the night before, I wanted to tell him it was me, but couldn't muster up the nerve. I was very proud nevertheless. It was a wonderful feeling. Colonel Payson had been impressed by the skill of that unknown bugler. "Work hard. Practice."

We were one of nine Naval Companies, nearly 600 boys, during the summer of 1962. I must have passed that huge picture window from the photograph hundreds of times, I never thought about the color photograph of my mother holding that tiny baby during all those summers; I didn't want to.

There was, however, something very strange about Culver – when you were there, it was the whole world, your whole existence; but, when you left, it was as though it ceased to exist. It was a place out of time and space where traditions were like slender cords that bound one generation of cadets to the next. The four summers I had spent at Culver were some of the best, and most difficult, times of my life. I had discovered I could survive in a very different world; it felt good, and going there had been a very good thing for me.

My grandfather was there the day I returned home after that last summer at Culver, back to the house on Perkins Street. As I walked in the kitchen door, I saw him. There were tears in his eyes; he didn't say much, just shook my hand, the first time he had ever done that. "Welcome home, Bud," was all he said. I never understood the memories, the sorrow, and the pain he kept locked deep inside, but it was there and would always be a barrier that kept us apart.

As I look back on it, he was the truly tragic figure in my life, and I had never realized it. He had lost so much more than I had. But he had to live on, having loved and lost both a daughter and a wife. My sense of loss was just as real and just as profound; but, for so many years, it was an unknown loss that I was trying to rediscover. He knew the source of his private pain. I did not.

There was so much to say and so much left unsaid. That moment was as close as I would ever come to hearing him say he loved me...as close as he let anyone ever come. It never happened. Love. What did I know about love? The love I felt for him and my great aunts was bountiful enough and certainly real - but it passed through a dark Victorian veil. The natural stirrings of adolescence were certainly present, but those feelings were far too immature and hormonal to be instructive. It would be many years before I would find a love that gave me any insight to what my parents must have felt for each other. Years would pass before I would become a parent myself, and be able to identify with the love and the wonder they had known.

Chapter Eleven

October 30, 1997: Connie and I were sitting on the deck. It was a beautiful late October afternoon. The trees were awash with fall color; bright red was shimmering in the sunlight from the top of the big sugar maple near the house. Gold sparkled from the tiny yellow leaves that fluttered, spun, and floated gently down from the nearby thorn trees. We weren't talking about anything in particular, just enjoying the warmth of the afternoon sun. I hadn't said anything to her about the encounter at the nursing home. "You know, the strangest thing happened a couple of weeks ago during my visit with Frances Richards. There was a little old lady across the room who overheard every word of our conversation. As I was leaving, she said I should go to Culver to see what I could find."

"Oh, for Heaven's sake! Who was she? What was her name?"

"She didn't say and I was so struck by her comment that I didn't think to ask. I know this is going to sound totally weird, but I've been thinking a lot about what she said and I have the feeling that she was right, that I ought to go there."

"I'll bet you do! Well, you go right ahead! If it'll put an end to all this nonsense, do it! This is all just silliness!" Connie didn't understand. But why should she? She knew her parents, had a connection with them. Her mother was still living. I was entitled to a connection, if somehow I could find one. Too much of my life had been twisted, turned, and thrown out of balance by events over which I had no control.

I had been invited to Culver's annual alumni reunion, but hadn't paid much attention to it. It would be the 35th anniversary of my graduation from Culver's Naval School, and it had been years since I had been on the campus. So, I could justify a weekend visit, although I knew the reunion was just an excuse. I would go back to Culver.

"How would you like to go with me?"

"Nope! If this is something you need to do, then I think you should do it by yourself. Don't drag me into any more of this foolishness!"

It was the last weekend of October 1997. I left the office at noon, drove home, packed a few things in a bag, and headed back for the car. "I'll be home no later than Sunday evening. I'm just going to see what happens. I think I really need to do this, but I have no idea why."

"Well, I still think its all nonsense," Connie said. "You've talked to people, you've gotten letters, and that box of stuff which, by the way, is still sitting on the floor of the library... Get over it! What's past is past! Oh, well, never mind, I hope you find whatever you're looking for...or whatever it is you think you're supposed to find. Sounds like 'The Twilight Zone' to me, but you love that sort of stuff." We kissed. I tossed my bag in the back seat of the '97 Olds Cutlass. "Be careful," Connie said softly.

"I'll be careful; I may even be home sooner. Who knows?" I knew Connie thought this was all absurd, I could hear the disdain in her voice, but it didn't matter. Perhaps it was, after all, just sentimental nonsense, but this was something I felt I should do...for me.

It was another perfect autumn afternoon, so I decided to drive up to Culver the "old way," the way we used to go when I was a kid. A new four-lane highway had been built since the 60s that bisected the state north of Indianapolis, a straight shot to South Bend. Culver was about thirty miles south and a few miles west of South Bend. The "new" four-lane road hadn't been there in the 1960s, let alone in the 40s. I took the old two-lane state highway that led through sleepy little crossroads towns like Waugh, Kirkland, and Middlefork, on through Logansport - the only town of any size along the way.

It was a very pleasant drive. The autumn colors were at their peak, even more brilliant than at home. Shades of red, orange, yellow, and purple all accented by an unusually bright blue sunny afternoon sky. I listened to CDs as the miles rolled past.

The last few miles were still the longest. I never knew why, but that's the way it seemed when I was a kid, and it still seemed that way. I had planned to drive through the town of Culver and then the last mile or two to the Main Gate. Not much had changed along the way; the little towns looked the same, the farms, and the recently harvested fields stretching nearly to the horizon. There were no signs like you'd find on the interstate highways telling you which exit to take. You had to intend to go to Culver, and you had to know the way. There was nothing to suggest that the place even existed at all.

Finally, the town of Culver! As I drove toward the little lakeside village, I noticed that the sky in the west was growing overcast. The gray pallor of an impending storm muted the brilliant reds of the sugar maples. I drove past familiar landmarks, the movie theater, and the little drive-in restaurant. The sky continued to darken; bad weather was definitely on the way, like one of those roiling thunderstorms that used to drive all the boats from the lake during sailing class back in the 60s. They came on quickly and violently, with such speed that sometimes it was difficult to make it back to the dock before they hit. There wasn't much traffic on a Friday afternoon. I checked the digital clock, just a little after 3 PM; I hadn't made bad time considering the route I had taken!

As I turned the corner on to Academy Road, the storm hit. It was a real cloudburst, the rain came down in torrents, thunder crashed and boomed, the sound rolling and re-echoing in the thick air like the sound of old fashioned field artillery. Lightening flashed across the sky in jagged blinding streaks. I turned the wipers to the highest setting, hoping it would help. I could just barely make out Logansport Gate in the distance. I flipped on the headlights. There was only one way to go at Logansport Gate, left. I could see the chain that was always stretched between the two large brick pillars, capped with ornate lights that defined the Gate. I made a slow left turn. I could hardly see the high brick walls of the dining hall on the right, but I knew exactly where I was; things at Culver just don't change. The downpour was so heavy and intense that it was hard to see, even with the wipers going full blast.

Off to my right was the faintest outline of the old Music & Art Building, where my father's office had once been. I could just make out the bare wooden tent frames of the old Woodcraft Camp, their canvas covers stored away for the winter. Strange, I thought, the Woodcraft Camp had been moved to the other side of the campus years ago.

It was only a few hundred yards and one more right turn to the Main Gate on the north side of the campus. I lowered the window just enough to make sure I wouldn't miss the turn. Rain poured in, but there it was! The Main Gate. I was back at Culver!

I couldn't have been going more than five miles per hour. The ghostly image of the campus infirmary, an impressive two-story brick building, barely visible through the torrential sheets of driving rain that swept across the road, was just where it was supposed to be. Now that I was on the campus, extra caution would be required; cadets could be anywhere, and I obviously didn't want to hit one of them. I made the slow turn toward the Administration Building... Suddenly there was an enormous crack, I pulled the car over and stopped. A deafening, ear shattering blast of sound rocked the car and, at the same instant, a flash of lightning turned everything to blinding white!

Chapter Twelve

I found myself sitting on one of the old carved stone benches down by the lake. This particular bench had a high curved back and a natural spring-fed water fountain that divided it into two sections. An inscription by the fountain said it was donated by the Class of 1927, in memory of the Culver graduates "lost" in "the Great War." Chiseled in stone for all time -- they had assumed there would be only one Great War. How innocent and naive they were to believe that! How justified, though, to cast in stone their deep sense of loss for the lives cut short by the folly of war -- the war to end all wars.

Sunlight danced and sparkled on the water of the lake... how beautiful it was. There was a paved walk just in front of the bench. It bordered the length of the campus shoreline by the lake. To the left was the stark white Naval Building, headquarters for the Summer Naval School, where I had spent so many hours as a youth. Off to the right was the library, one of my favorite buildings on the campus; it resembled a Norman castle with twin turrets on either side of massive oak doors. As I looked out across the lake, my mind flooded with memories of young friends I had known at Culver and the great experiences we had shared.

"Excuse me, sir," came a young voice from over my shoulder. I looked up and saw a slender apple-cheeked cadet standing near the bench. He must have been walking across the lawn behind me. "Sir, could I be of some service? You seem lost: are you familiar with our campus?" I stood up. "Well, actually, yes," I heard myself say -- a little surprised at how calm my voice sounded. "I graduated from summer school here, but... uh...that was a long time ago," I added, shaking my head. "I haven't been back in years. Caught up in the moment, I suppose. It's still a beautiful place, isn't it?" -- talking to myself as much as to this polite young boy.

"Yes, sir, it is that."

"How old are you, son?" I asked bluntly.

"Seventeen, sir, going on eighteen."

"I see."

I tried to think back to when I was at that age -- where a seventeen year-old cadet might be under the old Culver system. But I simply asked, "What year are you in school?"

"Second classman, sir. Company C."

"Well, then, I'll bet you're looking forward to next year and graduation."

"Yes, sir. Very much so."

This kid was so friendly and eager to please -- I was strangely calmed, even felt acclimated to this new, yet old, situation. I decided to draw him out a little more, to ask him about his background, his life here at Culver.

"What's your name, son? Where are you from?"

"Cadet Joshua Billingsly, sir, from Cincinnati, Ohio."

"Oh yes, Cincinnati. Great town. I know it well," I added -- eager to establish some common ground.

"Well, Cadet Billingsly," I continued, "if you have the time, could you accompany me to Main Guard so I can sign in and make this visit official."

"My pleasure, sir. I'm headed that way for a rehearsal anyway."

Together, we walked back across the broad green lawn, through the old grove of Sycamores, to Pershing Walk, and on toward the Dining Hall. Cadets in all manner of dress were walking in all directions; it was a late Friday afternoon. Some were just lounging on the grass, others were throwing a football. A small group was gathered on the front steps of one of the brick barracks. It was a typical Friday afternoon, a timeless Culver scene, I thought to myself.

"Do you like it here at Culver?"

"Culver's a swell place, sir. This is my third year. I'm hoping to get an appointment to West Point next year."

"West Point? Then military life must agree with you."

"When I first came to Culver, I didn't like all the rules and regulations, the uniforms, and all the regimentation, but now I can see the value in it. You can't lead others if you don't know how to follow. Once you get used to it, you begin to appreciate it, I guess."

This was a very mature young man. "So you don't mind making your bed, shining your shoes, and all the rest?"

"Not at all. Once you get into the routine, it seems like a natural way to live, and besides I'm getting a great education here. Going to West Point seems like a logical next step."

"Well, I hope you make it. I'd think you're chances of being admitted would be pretty good after four years here."

"I hope so," Cadet Billingsly said with a smile.

We walked up the wide stone steps dividing South Barrack from West Barrack and headed toward the dining hall. To my right, I recognized Sally Port, a famous spot on the Culver campus, a wide open-ended passageway through the Administration Building leading to The Oval, as the name suggested, a wide, circular, green, open space where retreat parades were held. A kaleidoscope of memories was carrying me away. Beyond that was the vast expanse of green Culver playing fields. Just inside of Sally Port was the Main Guard post and, on the opposite side, the entrance to the school's administrative offices and, farther within it's tradition-steeped recesses, the infamous door to the superintendent's office, the one portal through which no cadet ever wanted to be sent! Invited, yes. Ordered to go, no!

As we came to the interior of the campus, I felt I should let this youngster go. I could handle things from here -- however strange my circumstances. "Well, Cadet Billingsly, it was very nice meeting you. I'll bet you're heading up to the Music & Art Building, the M&A, for your, ah, rehearsal, right?"

"Yes, sir. There's an extra practice today."

What a fine young man -- I was thinking. Any father would be proud of the way he carried himself, his self-confidence, and his manners.

"What kind of rehearsal is it?" I asked -- for no particular reason.

"Glee club, sir. I'd better hurry; Captain Bradshaw always starts on time!"

Chapter Thirteen

My thoughts went reeling. "Captain Bradshaw" the boy had said. I had heard the words as clear as a bell. And yet, I hadn't heard them. I couldn't have! Captain Bradshaw. *Captain Bradshaw?* My mind replayed those two words over and over -- trying to take in what they might mean. Was this some incredible coincidence? Had I misunderstood? Was my visit to Culver so focused that I had heard only what I subconsciously wanted to hear? Cadet Billingsly waved as he turned and started back toward the Dining Hall. "It was nice meeting you, sir!" he called out.

"Wait son!" I called to him -- noticeable urgency in my voice. "Who did you say...? 'Started on time?'" Several cadets suddenly turned and looked at me. I suppose I called out louder than I had intended.

"Captain Bradshaw," Billingsly called back, now halfway past the Dining Hall. He's Glee Club director. So long!" He smiled, and waved as he slipped out of view.

In that instant, I felt strangely detached, unaware of myself, my own being -- I was somehow reassured of reality by the familiar sense of the place. I looked around, stunned, embarrassed. Confused more than anything. Surrounding me was the Culver campus I knew and loved. The campus looked the same, yet somehow now different, strange. There was something unnatural about it. "Captain Bradshaw," he'd said. "Director of the Glee Club." My heart pounded. I ran toward Sally Port! Cadets I passed looked at me with something like alarm, but I didn't care. I WAS alarmed. Inside Sally Port there used to be a bulletin board...all of the important information of the day. Rounding the corner at a dead run, I slipped and fell to one knee -- the trick knee that had bothered me since high school. Odd, I felt no pain. Scrambling to my feet, I saw that, YES -- the bulletin board was still there, just as it always was. That's where I'd find some explanations for all this nonsense! Bolting past a couple of cadets, I quickly scanned the notices posted there. Cadets and conversations completely out of sync! Captain Bradshaw! What the HELL was going on here? Adrenalin pounded in my ears, my eyes suddenly focused on the signature written under a "Special Order" about alumni weekend. At the bottom it read, "by order of Brigadier General Leigh R. Gignilliat, Superintendent." Then I saw the date: 28 October 1944. 1944! My God, that was nearly a year before I was born! My God! Oh, my God!

Just across from the bulletin board was the Main Guard post manned by a couple of cadets and the Officer of the Day. I rushed over to the window. Inside I could see a cadet sitting at the desk, feet propped up, casually reading a copy of Life magazine. I stumbled forward, out of breath, grabbed for the sides of the window to avoid falling. The cadet inside was startled. His head snapped up, and he stared at me with wide eyes. He jumped to his feet. "May I help you, sir?"

I tried to collect myself. Took a deep breath. "What year is this?" I blurted out without thinking.

"What year? What do you mean, sir?"

"No, no, I mean what day is this?"

"It's Friday, sir. Friday, October 30th. Are you all right, sir?" He looked at me quizzically as if I might not be in my right mind. I wasn't at all sure I was! I groped for a more rational question to ask, still breathing heavily. Nothing came, my thoughts were racing. What could I ask this boy that wouldn't sound insane?

"I, ah, just got here a little while ago. Just a little out of breath from, ah, walking so far." I could see this boy's expression had turned from curiosity to suspicion. "Came up for alumni weekend. It's been years since I've been back to campus. Too bad you've got guard duty today, Friday afternoon and all." My head was still spinning. I steadied myself against the window frame. Still out of breath.

"Sir, you don't look well. I'm going to call the Officer of the Day." Before I could say anything, he turned his head, called out, "Lieutenant Watkins!" I had to get away! Something was terribly wrong!

I ran through Sally Port out to the wide grassy expanse of The Oval. Started walking again. Over my shoulder I could see a young officer, not a cadet, standing outside the door to the Main Guard post, hands on his hips, looking at me, but he didn't follow. Cold perspiration ran down my forehead. I gasped for air, felt lightheaded, pressed on. Tried to look nonchalant. My heart pounding. I looked around, the green grass soft beneath my feet. There was the lake, the Naval Building now off in the distance, and the riding hall far to the west, and then I glanced up the gently sloping hill where the big Academy Chapel stood. It was there, but somehow it didn't look right. It shimmered like a mirage in the desert, indistinct, hazy, and almost transparent. I blinked my eyes hard and looked again. It was gone! Nothing, just a...barren hillside! How could that be? What had just happened? I had just seen the chapel, but it wasn't there! There was no sign of the huge chapel, capable of holding close to a thousand people, with a spire soaring nearly 150 feet into the air! What had I seen? Now I felt fear for my own sanity! Wait a minute, I thought -- the chapel had been built in the late 1950s! The date on the order said 1944.... Something here was very, very wrong!

"Captain Bradshaw," the kid had said. The words kept pounding in my ears! I ran as fast as I could to the curve in the roadway where I last remembered being in the car. Incredibly, the road was lined with classic vintage cars! There was an old Packard, a Hudson, even a Pierce Arrow -- looking used somehow, some spattered with ordinary road dirt and...I stood there staring, half in shock...there were ration stickers on the windshields! I sat down heavily on the grass by the side of the roadway. I felt stunned. Tried to make some sense of what I was experiencing...

Slowly, I began to comprehend what seemed to be happening to me. I'm not saying I understood it -- at first -- but somehow the fear was gone and I began to feel a strange sense of wonder at this...dream! Or whatever it was. This place was Culver, but apparently as it once was, as it used to be, over fifty years ago! Strange warmth spread over me as I began to accept this "visit" to the Culver of another time as a *gift*. A blessing. A chance to continue my quest to understand the one critical element lost to me as a child -- my parents.

By some strange power beyond my understanding, I seemed to have been given this chance. A chance...to revisit, perhaps to actually know, to hear, touch, see, and most importantly, to finally understand! The realization was overwhelming.

Could it be possible that I was in their world? By whatever power this moment in time had been given to me, it became crystal clear to me that I was meant to pursue it. I was going to pursue it! This was the chance I had been searching for... all my life.

Accepting this gift, emotionally, was one thing; taking it into my head was another. At first, I thought it might be a dream. But was this just a dream, or even an illusion? It didn't feel like a dream. Dreams always have a peculiar blend of reality and distortion, familiar people in odd, not-quite-familiar places. I had none of the feeling that I was just an observer amid some strange subconscious mental wanderings in an imaginary world. In a dream, frequently, even while you're experiencing it, you somehow know you're dreaming. This was not like that at all! This was too clear, too sharp, and too tangible. Besides, I had spent too many summers at Culver not to be able to tell the difference between a dream revisited and reality. Every one of my senses told me this was a real place and I was somehow here! Had the lightning strike, in an instant, torn the fabric of time? Perhaps. It didn't really matter... I seemed to have been given a chance. That meant I had a job to do; and, if was going to accept this for what it seemed to be, I was ready to get started. My breath had returned. I drew in a deep breath, slowly let it out, and tried to think what to do next.

This was the last week of October 1944! The air was still warm, and the smell of the grass that covered The Oval was familiar and, at least for the moment, reassuring.

The thought of what was happening was overwhelming, but I needed to accept it as fact. I walked slowly back to Sally Port, looked again at the bulletin board, "by order of Superintendent Leigh R. Gignilliat." General Gignilliat, had been the force behind Culver's rise to national prominence as a college preparatory school; he was superintendent from the time of the Great War until the late 40s, long before my summers there. I had only seen a cold flat painting of him in the academy library. I sat down on the worn stone steps at the entrance to the Administrative Building. How long would this last? How much time did I have? I felt a surge of energy, combined with the fear that it could all end in an instant; I had to make the most of this precious time.

I stood, looked down at my clothes - a brown herringbone jacket, striped tie, pleated flannel trousers, and a pair of worn brown wingtips! At least I looked the part, but what part?

Out across the playing fields, the sun was just beginning to cast long afternoon shadows across the playing fields that stretched far to the east. Obviously, I couldn't tell anyone who I was. Nobody would believe me. If this weren't happening to me, I wouldn't believe me either!

OK, come up with a story. I remembered that my grandmother's maiden name was Newkirk. I could use that as a last name, if anybody asked. But what was I doing at Culver besides coming back for a short reunion weekend? Then it came to me! Looking for a job! It would make sense, I could be a distant cousin of my mother, one she wouldn't be likely to know, and I would remember that name, Newkirk, when pressed -- I hoped. I saw my reflection in the tall glass doorway, and I looked the same, despite the clothes. A "middle-aged" distant cousin - looking for a job! That would make me far older than either of my parents in 1944, I calculated. Paul Newkirk, distant cousin, looking for work, but what kind of work? Since the war was still on, there probably was a manpower shortage. I looked again at the reflection in the glass, too old for the war, that would help, but still....

Then, behind me, the unmistakable sound of a door opening. I quickly turned around, and there, standing before me, was Colonel Gregory! I stumbled backward! He caught me by the arm! I felt the power in his grasp! His eyes looking into mine. "May I be of some service, sir? You look a little pale. Do you feel all right?"

Colonel Gregory had been at Culver when I was there in the early 1960s, but a much older man then, gray and stooped, who shuffled when he walked. Behind his back we called him Gramps Gregory. Here, now, was this man in his prime, a young man, straight military bearing, trim mustache, dark clear eyes. He had on a crisp brown uniform blouse, khaki riding trousers, and highly polished brown riding boots. Silver eagles were on each shoulder, Dean of the faculty.

"Ah, no sir. I mean, yes sir. I'm fine. I, uh, didn't know any members of the faculty would be around this late in the afternoon."

Colonel Gregory released my arm from his strong grasp, stepped back, looked me up and down, and cocked his head to one side. "Somehow you look familiar. Do I know you?"

"Ah, no sir. But I've seen you before, sir...your picture in the yearbook. I have a...distant cousin who graduated in the class of '38, Bill Winship. His...sister and, ah, her...ah, husband are here I believe."

"Of course! I remember Winship! Company A, I think. Overseas now with the Army Air Corps, an officer! Paul and Shippy! Yes, of course! Dear friends of mine!" He reached out, grabbing my hand and shook it warmly. "So, you're related to the Winships. How are Mr. and Mrs. Winship? Where do they live again?

"Rushville. Rushville, Indiana, sir. I, uh, I've just come from there. They're fine. Just fine." My grandmother had died in 1947, my grandfather in 1962. This was going to take some mental gymnastics - not to mention more acting ability than I anticipated. I needed to get a grip!

"What brings you here, Mister....? I didn't get your name."

"My name? It's...ah.... Newkirk.... Paul Newkirk...and... it's.... a pleasure to meet you, Colonel." I hesitated, looked down. "To be honest, sir, I'm out of work and my.... that is, Mr. Winship, *cousin* Will, thought, ah, his daughter – Shippy – might be able to help me find something here at the academy."

"I see. This is a little out of the ordinary." He paused, looked at me more intently, and then added, "I wish you knew how many times I've had requests like this. During the Depression, it was all too common. Those were very hard days -- especially for a school like ours. But what with a war on, I'm sure there's something you can do. I'll be glad to try and help. In the meantime, I was just on my way to watch the Lancer Platoon drill over in front of the Riding Hall. Would you like to go along?"

I looked toward the Riding Hall. Already people were beginning to fill the green benches on the terrace in front of the long castle-like riding hall, in anticipation of the exhibition. More period cars were coming down the hill, parking on either side of the road. People walking across the green expanse of lawn. "Thank you, Colonel; I'd like that very much."

We started across The Oval. "Tell me a little about your background, mister.... what was it again, Newkirk?"

"Ah, yes, sir. Well, I have a degree in, ah, business from Indiana University, major in marketing." That was true, but not for another twenty-three years!

Colonel Gregory looked at me curiously. "Really? That could be a piece of damn good luck for us.... and for you. We're short-handed in the academy business offices, publications to be specific. I'm afraid it doesn't pay very much but, ah, considering your present situation, it might be better than nothing. We need somebody to work with our admissions people on marketing, develop new brochures, write copy, come up with new ideas to help attract the best students here, that sort of thing. Think you could do that?"

This was almost too good to be true! "Yes sir, I'm sure I could!" We continued to walk toward the Riding Hall. More people, men in fedoras and women wearing elbow-length gloves and wide-brimmed hats, were making their way to the riding hall terrace. It was fantastic, like living in a full color movie made in the 40s!

Red and yellow leaves swirled gently, pushed along in the late afternoon breeze, tumbling toward the lake in colorful billows. "About the pay.... even though it's not a princely sum, you would be allowed to take your meals in the Dining Hall and, I think, there's a vacant room on the top floor of West Barrack you could use. Of course it will be up to the general. He personally interviews everyone employed by the academy. Perhaps he will be at the exhibition, I'll introduce you."

"Thank you very much, sir." There weren't many cadets in the crowd in front of the Riding Hall, mostly civilians, parents and faculty, I supposed. The Lancer Platoon was the elite unit of Culver's famous Black Horse Troop. Even during my summers at Culver, the Lancer Platoon had been part of the summer cavalry program.

During winter school, cadets were either assigned to infantry, the artillery, the band, or the cavalry. The Black Horse Troop had brought fame to the school because of its participation in Presidential Inaugural Parades. The Lancer Platoon was the best of the best in the troop.

We arrived at the walk in front of the Riding Hall. Several hundred people were either sitting on the rows of benches that sloped down to the level of the parade field or standing along the crowded walk in the rear. Bandsmen were busily setting up folding chairs and music stands to provide the music for the Lancer Platoon. They didn't look all that pleased about losing part of their Friday afternoon to provide musical accompaniment to a bunch of horses.

"We'll watch the performance from the walk. No point in taking up space intended for parents and visitors," Colonel Gregory said. "Nasty rain storm earlier. Did you get caught in it?

"No, sir. I sat it out in the car over by the Administration Building."

"Do you know Paul and Shippy well?"

I turned my head quickly toward Colonel Gregory. His words almost startled me as they bounced around in my head – did I know Paul and Shippy... "Ah, no sir, I can't say that I know them at all, to be honest...but I'd like to know them...very much." I turned away, looked at the ground. Felt embarrassed by the surge of emotion I could feel rising up inside.

"Hmmm. Well, we'll see if we can't fix that...Mr. Newkirk."

It was almost as though he knew! But how could he? Slowly, Colonel Gregory put his hands behind his back, right over left, and looked out over the green parade field, slowing rocking back and forth on his heels.

Soon, from the east end of the Riding Hall, the members of the Lancer Platoon made their appearance. Each cadet, mounted on a coal black horse, carried a long steel-tipped lance with a small red and white pennant at the top. They looked like throwbacks from the age of Napoleon. On each saddle blanket was the word "Culver." Everyone in the stands stood and applauded wildly as the band struck up the famous old tune of the US 7th Cavalry, "Garry Owen."

"Outstanding!" Colonel Gregory said admiringly. He leaned slightly toward me, but continued to look ahead. "Paul and Shippy, you know, are two of my favorite people.

I looked around at the crowd. Admiring parents, intently watching the exhibition, various members of the troop staff - old-timers from the days of the army's regular horse cavalry watching every move - prancing horses, ram-rod straight cadets, proud, moving in unison, pennants fluttering gaily.... then, from the corner of my eye.... far off to the right, perhaps fifty yards away, I saw a tall man, taller than most around him. The crowd of people ebbed and flowed around me blocking my view, many with old box cameras, trying to get just the right shot. I stepped back; I had to see the man again.

People were moving in every direction, I strained to see beyond the milling throng. Where was he? If only I could see over these people.... then, for an instant, there he was! I could see him, standing with his arms folded, watching the exhibition. Standing next to him was a woman, her arms around his waist, looking up at him, saying something to him. He turned his face toward hers.... even from where I stood I could tell...could sense.... this man was.... my father! There was no mistake, I had seen that one picture of the two of them a thousand times, and it was burned into my memory! Gently, slowly, he put his arm around the woman with him, smiled at what she was saying. I couldn't see her face, but I knew.

I had to see her, had to see her face! I started to move toward them, but was held up by the crowd watching the Lancers do an intricate maneuver, I struggled to force my way through the mass of people, so close, yet so far away! I had to get through! Suddenly, there was a strong hand on my arm, pulling me back! Back away from them! Annoyed, I turned quickly, "Mr. Newkirk! Allow me to present General Gignilliat." It was Colonel Gregory!

My God, it WAS General Gignilliat. This man only lived in Culver legends, but here he was! Narrow face, looking at me directly over the top of his pince-nez glasses, silver-gray hair, ramrod straight, dress blue uniform jacket, triple row of ribbons above his left pocket, brown cross-belt, one silver star on each epaulet, a commanding presence! I snapped to attention, an old habit learned at this very school, felt foolish.

"Good afternoon, sir," I said nodding my head. The general just stood there looking sternly at me.

"Newkirk here is related to Paul and Shippy..." Colonel Gregory hesitated, caught himself, "I mean, sir, Captain and Mrs. Bradshaw."

The general continued to stare at me. Slowly, he reached out his hand. "Glad to meet you Newkirk. You must be a fine man if you're related to the captain and his fine lady. What brings you to our school?" His voice was strong, resonant.

Before I could answer, Colonel Gregory spoke up. "Mr. Newkirk is seeking employment with us," the Colonel glanced quickly at me; "he's a graduate of the University of Indiana, business background, thought he would be a good candidate for that vacant marketing spot in publications, sir." I smiled weakly at the general, his expression didn't change, I felt nervous, it was like being inspected. A long silent pause.

"Well, Newkirk, be at my office at 900 hours Monday morning. We'll talk. Have you had time to find Captain Bradshaw?"

"Ah, no sir." I looked back over my shoulder to the spot where I had seen him. Oh, no! Gone! "I, uh, thought I saw my.... that is, I thought I saw him over in that vicinity, sir," pointed vaguely to the spot where I had seen them, looked quickly back at the general, brought my arm down quickly, felt awkward.

"You'll have to excuse me Newkirk. Duty calls." The general nodded, I returned it, almost saluted, old habit. He and the other members of his reviewing party started down the terrace steps to accept the salute from the commander of the Lancer Platoon at the end of their exhibition.

"The general's quite an impressive man, isn't he, colonel?"

"One of the finest I've ever served with," Gregory said in almost a reverent tone. "Too bad you missed Paul and Shippy. But don't worry about it, there's a faculty and staff cocktail party at the Culver Inn this evening. Why don't you accompany Mrs. Gregory and me? I'm sure they'll be there."

I hesitated, the clothes I was wearing looked mussy, my shoes needed a shine, but I was determined to see this through. "Thank you, I would love to."

Chapter Fourteen

It was fully dark when the three of us arrived at the Culver Inn, Colonel and Mrs. Gregory and I. The campus was bathed in the soft amber glow from the decorative lampposts that lined the walks and pathways. A large ornate electric brass lamp shone brightly above the entrance to the Inn. I held the door open for the Colonel's wife. "Shippy is such a dear, so much fun, just full of life," she said, gesturing broadly with white-gloved hand. I had heard that before. Mrs. Gregory was a bundle of energy, an attractive self-assured woman who, I concluded, was not the type to be told "no" easily. Clearly, she was aware of her husband's position at Culver, and she basked in the reflected influence and deferential treatment that came with it. We walked into the lobby of the inn, already congested with faculty members, many in uniform, and their wives.

The Culver Inn was a wonderful place, the only place, really, for any large social event on the campus. The second floor was all guest rooms, but they were tiny places, Spartan at best, with barely enough room for a twin bed, a dresser and a sink; the solitary bathroom was at the end of the hall.

The main floor had a reception area and long "L" shaped lounge, thick pale blue carpeting, and a baby grand piano near a large picture window overlooking the lake. It also had a well-appointed dining room that was often used for parties. Outside was a long screened-in porch where smaller parties could be held. The rest of the porch was lined with white wicker rockers. In the lobby Culver memorabilia was displayed amid comfortable upholstered chairs and sofas. A wide brick walk led up to the door. Above the entrance were the words "Culver Inn" in gilt letters.

"Now, tell me how the two of you are related," Mrs. Gregory asked.

"Mrs. Winship, ah, Shippy's mother's maiden name was, ah, Newkirk. Her grandfather and, ah, my grandfather were brothers. So, that would make us...let's see...second cousins, I believe." So far so good, I remembered my "cover story," not too bad considering that I was making up every word of it!

"So, do you know Shippy well?"

"To be honest, Mrs. Gregory, I don't," which was painfully true, regardless of time or space, "but her father.... Cousin Will.... thought she might be able to help me find employment here. Actually, your husband may have already taken care of that for me. I met the general at the Lancer Platoon exhibition this afternoon and I'm to have an interview with him Monday morning."

"Don't be too over confident, Newkirk," Colonel Gregory cautioned, "the General is a kind man, but he'll expect results from you, so don't take anything for granted."

"No, sir. I certainly won't do that."

"Oh, now, dear, don't scare this gentleman off before he's even had a chance. Besides, this is a party. Not a time to talk business, come along." Colonel Gregory shrugged his shoulders at me and smiled.

As we walked through the lobby to the lounge where the cocktail party was being held, I saw familiar faces, some I remembered from my summers at Culver, most I had only seen in photographs or on canvas. Not far away I saw Commander Fowler, Director of the Summer Schools, gleaming in his dress whites, Colonel Henderson, Director of Admissions, and Colonel, then Major, Whitney, Tactical Officer for the troop, all talking together.

Colonel Whitney was as much a part of Culver as anyone could be; he was the living embodiment, at least for me, of everything Culver Military Academy stood for. He had been at Culver during my summers there. All of us were afraid of him. He was a no-nonsense, hard-bitten old horse cavalry officer. Pity the poor midshipman or trooper who passed Colonel Whitney without a crisp salute! I could still hear his voice: "Head and eyes straight ahead! Keep those hands cupped along the seams of your trousers! Chest out! Heels together! You're at attention!" This was like walking through the pages of Culver history!

"Oh, Captain Payson!" Mrs. Gregory called out, "I'd like you to meet someone!" Suddenly, walking toward me was Colonel Payson, director of the Naval School Band when I was at Culver! I was startled; would he recognize me? Wait! Of course not! How could he? My time as a midshipman at Culver was over fifteen years in the future!

"Good evening, Colonel -- Mrs. Gregory." It *was* Colonel Payson! He looked so young, but there was no question about who this man was. No question at all - "I expect the best from Captain Bradshaw's son," he would say to me on one far distant day.

"Captain Payson, I'd like you to meet Shippy's cousin, Paul Newkirk. He may be joining our staff, if he can pass the general's inspection," Mrs. Gregory laughed. "Captain" Payson almost looked stunned as he reached out his hand. "A pleasure Mr. Newkirk. You somehow remind me of someone I've seen before. Have we ever met?" It was that same sad expression I remembered from my first summer as a member of the Naval School Band.

"I don't see how, sir. This is my first visit back to Culver in years."

"Oh, you were a cadet here?"

"Naval School, sir. Just during the summers...right after the war."

"Really? What organization?"

"The Naval School Band."

"A bandsman, then? Outstanding! Culver wouldn't be much without the band. But you do look vaguely familiar somehow. Well, perhaps there's a tinge of family resemblance. You remind me of.... well.... of Shippy. I believe she and Captain Bradshaw are here somewhere."

I laughed nervously. "Well, Colonel...I'm sorry.... that is, Captain...Payson, family characteristics sometimes do seem to pass from one generation to the next, sir." Colonel Payson looked at me curiously, as if he knew! But that was impossible.

"Let's join the others," Colonel Gregory interrupted.

"Yes, let's do. I think I hear the piano," Mrs. Gregory said. "That's probably Paul."

"It's an honor to meet you, Captain Payson," I said. "I hope.... I hope we'll have the chance to talk again, perhaps later."

"An honor returned, Mr. Newkirk," Colonel Payson nodded, "I shall look forward to it."

We walked into the part of the lounge that led to the main dining room. There were people milling around everywhere. It was a warm evening, small groups were sitting around the candle-lit tables on the porch, others were standing near the temporary bar, laughter, talk of the war, cigarette smoke hanging in the air, the clinking of glasses, gin martinis being poured, faces moving in front of mine, smiles, nods. In the background I could hear music.

Over by the picture window a crowd was gathered around the piano. The familiar melodies of Hoosier composer Cole Porter drifted across the room, "*In the Still of the Night*", "*You'd Be So Nice To Come Home To,*" "*My Heart Belongs to Daddy*"...

"There's Captain Bradshaw," Mrs. Gregory said, tugging at my sleeve, "I would recognize his style anywhere! Why don't you go over and listen, Mr. Newkirk, I'm sure Shippy is somewhere nearby."

Without speaking, I walked, as if transfixed, toward the sound of the piano. The crowd obscured my view. Cigarette smoke drifted in the air, like wispy clouds on a late summer afternoon. I politely worked my way around toward the far end of the piano, looked over the crowd, tried hard not to be rude, finally, he was there.... my father.... my father...smiling... as the intricate melodies flowed effortlessly from his talented hands. The music stand was down, he was playing from memory, and I could see his face...alive, animated, and full of life.... He looked at the keys, and then at the faces around him, glancing back, smiling, at someone I could not see.

As the last chords faded, the crowd burst into energetic applause. My father.... my father, looked embarrassed. He looked back and called out, "Shippy, how about doing a number with me?" I strained to see! Had to see! All my life seemed to have come down to this one moment! There was motion over by the window, a slender form moving, a floral print party dress, mutton-leg sleeves, shoulder-length auburn hair; still I couldn't see her face! Applause!

"How about..." she leaned forward, I couldn't hear, she nodded. My father played the introduction; slowly she turned around, and a lifetime passed by in an instant.... my mother! It was my mother! She was young, mid-30s.... beautiful...just as I had always dreamed, just as I had tried to see her in my mind's eye a thousand times! I was glad to be at the far end of the piano; my eyes were welling up with tears. The first four bars of introduction drifted from the piano, my father's face beamed as my mother lowered her head, looked at the faces surrounding her, began to sing...."Easy To Love,"

"I know too well that I'm just wasting precious time
in thinking such a thing could be,
that you could ever care for me..."

she looked back at my father,

"I'm sure you hate to hear - that I adore you dear...."
they were looking directly at each other...
"For you'd be so easy to love,
So easy to idealize all others above..."

I would describe the feeling, the emotions I felt, if it were possible.... it was not, is not, possible. Her voice was rich, clear and full, smooth as silk....

As the song continued, she looked at the various faces in the admiring crowd, her elbows resting on the piano. Slowly, as the song neared its end, her face turned toward me, her eyes met mine....

*"It does seem a shame that you can't see
your future in me 'cause you'd be oh...so easy to love..."*

Time stood still. I wasn't sure I could contain myself, tried not to gasp for air, tried to smile pleasantly, her eyes still focused on me. Then she looked away, bowed, acknowledged the applause, looked up at the crowd around the piano, then back at my father.

The last notes ended. The crowd around the piano continued to applaud... I tried to restrain my emotions, applauded politely. Felt a tug at my arm, looked around. "Isn't she something?" It was Mrs. Gregory.

I took a long deep breath. "Yes, she certainly is," I said softly, carefully wiping a tear from my eye."

"Would you like to meet her now?"

"Now? Right now?" I ran my sleeve over my eyes, hoped Mrs. Gregory didn't notice. This was what I had dreamed of, longed for, all my life, but I felt a strange reluctance.... almost fear.... that this would end if...if...

"Well, of course right now, silly. I'm sure she'll be happy to meet you" Mrs. Gregory laughed. She held my elbow, pushed me gently through the crowd. My mother was standing just a few feet away, talking with a small group of people; I could only see her profile. It was as though I was being magnetically drawn to her; despite Mrs. Gregory's gentle urging. "Shippy! Shippy, I want you to meet someone!" We moved closer.

She turned. Her face was no than a foot or two from mine. She looked up at me.... a smile.... the smile.... everyone had talked about. For the first time, it was intended for me...it belonged to me. "Shippy, I'm so excited. This is Paul Newkirk, a cousin of yours on your mother's side. He's just come from Rushville. There's a chance he may be employed here, has an appointment with the general on Monday!"

"Well, Mr. Newkirk, its swell to meet you." she said. Her smile, her face...I was enchanted, thrilled, felt a surge of emotion like nothing I'd ever known before. She reached out her hand. I held it, felt a warm glow sweep over me, a sense of oneness hard to describe. She looked down at our clasped hands, looked back up at me.

"It's wonderful meeting you, too.... Mrs. Bradshaw." It was all I could do to say the words. "I've always.... I mean, I've heard so much about you...I, uh, your parents have told me... this is a special.... you have a lovely voice." I felt like a fool, stumbling for something to say. I let go of her hand.

Chapter Fifteen

The room was a mixture of light and shadows. Odd indistinct shapes, unfamiliar, a strange silence. Everything seemed out of focus, hazy; my eyes felt heavy, like slowly awakening on a lazy Saturday morning after a long winter snowfall. There was heaviness in my chest and arms, then.... a stirring.... a tingling sensation. I rubbed my eyes; a reddish-orange shape came slowly into view. Slowly the haze faded, and the room came into sharper focus. My gaze came to rest on a single red-orange rose.... Southwestern art on the far wall...books... a desk...this was Dr. Foster's office! I was in Joan Foster's office...

"I'm so sorry, Dr. Foster, I guess I've been under more strain than I thought, must have dozed off for a second. What were you saying?"

"How do you feel," she asked quietly.

"Well, embarrassed! I told you I haven't been sleeping all that well, I'm sorry. Anyway, what were we talking about?"

"We weren't talking, Paul. You were," she said calmly.

"What do you mean I was talking?" I tried to focus my thoughts. "Weren't we discussing the Culver reunion weekend thing? Being back on campus, seeing some of the guys I was in school with back in the 60s, the storm?"

"Do you remember talking about the different ways we might approach this problem during your first visit? Remember we said hypnotherapy was one of the options we decided to try?"

"Are you telling me I was...hypnotized? That's not possible. I've never believed in all that power of suggestion stuff. Are you telling me that's what's been going on? Wait a second; let me get my bearings," I rubbed my forehead, felt confused.

"Take your time. It's perfectly natural to feel disoriented after a session like this. Sometimes it comes as quite a surprise...the first time."

"Wait! I remember now! Dr. Foster...Joan...I was there. I was at Culver and it was 1944!"

"It sounds as if it might have been effective. Was it?"

"You don't understand! I was there! I saw... It wasn't a dream! It couldn't have been.... it was too real!"

"You sound excited. What did you see? What did you feel?"

"I SAW my parents." My voice broke, I tried to stay calm. "I looked into their faces, and it was them! My mother and my father! We were all at a party. They weren't just images in black and white photographs. I heard her sing. I can hear her voice! I...I touched her hand. Colonel Gregory and Colonel Payson where there! Young men! We talked! They were...all of them...REAL!"

My mind was reeling. It was euphoric. I had never believed in hypnosis, just a magician's trick. I had gone to Culver for that alumni weekend, had seen friends I knew, older, less hair, more weight. I had seen the painting of General Gignilliat, stern as always, hanging in the library, had gone to chapel services, saw the Sunday evening parade, remembered driving home. But now there was more....

"Dr. Foster. I don't care about the details or mechanics of hypnotherapy or how it made my visit to 1944 possible. If it means I could actually see my parents again, I want to go there. It was so real.... they...were so real."

"I'm glad for you, Paul. It sounds as though this was a place you needed to go. This is progress...movement in the right direction, at least. But that's about all the time we have today, and this has been a good first step. I'm pleased. But we do have to wrap up for now and think about trying again in - shall we say, two weeks?

Would that be convenient for you?"

"Convenient! Of course, it would be convenient!" I felt exultation, but still in shock. One thing was certain, however. This was one of the most intense and amazing experiences of my life. I knew I wanted to do this again - as soon as possible.

The drive home was an odd experience. Every imaginable emotion was washing over me like waves on a storm-swept ocean. It was as though I had been sent to a totally new and separate reality. It had not been a dream! It had been too real, but rationality told me that what I had experienced could not have happened. As intriguing as the notion was, I understood that it was not possible by any science mankind was capable of understanding to travel back and forth in time. I had been in Dr. Foster's office the whole time.... and yet I hadn't been, at least by the definition of reality with which I had always lived. Perhaps there was more to hypnotherapy than I understood. Was it possible for your body to be in one place and your consciousness in another place, even another time?

As I pulled into the driveway, I concluded that perhaps there was more to heaven and earth than could be understood in my philosophy. I decided not to tell Connie about the experience. She was even more of a pragmatist than I _thought_ I was.

Our house had taken on a festive autumnal look, something between Halloween and Thanksgiving. Connie had red and purple Indian corn, orange pumpkins, colorful gourds and, of course, burgundy, lavender, yellow, and white mums carefully placed in the garden, on the deck, and around the house. The maples had taken on a crimson hue. I walked into the house.

"Well, how was your session with what's-her-name?"

"Actually, it was very good. Dr. Foster calls it a process... a journey."

"Sounds a little melodramatic to me."

"Maybe. But to the extent that it's producing some beneficial results, I don't really care what she calls it. Hey, the point is I'm getting help! That's the point."

"You're right. I'm glad that it seems to be making a difference. What did you talk about?"

Well, that would be a little hard to describe. I wasn't sure I could honestly tell Connie what went on. "We talked a lot about my trip to Culver a few weeks ago. We talked about the dreams, about feelings, stuff like that."

"What did she say," Connie asked with more emphasis.

"Oh, you know, things like 'what do you think this or that means?' I did most of the talking, I guess. By the way, the house looks great! I can tell you've been working hard!"

"Thanks. When do you see her again?"

"Two weeks." Connie had been more understanding than I thought she would be. Her view of the world didn't allow much room for sloppy sentimentalism, but she was trying very hard to understand. That meant a lot.

Chapter Sixteen

The next two weeks flew by. The warmth and color of autumn had given way to the chilly days of early November. They were uneventful weeks. I was edgy and a little anxious, but the nightmares seemed under control. At least that was my hope. Dr. Foster had not promised overnight results, no miracle cures. If this was a "process," I was willing to go the whole mile - an extra mile, if only to get back there and see them once more....

The tropical fish in Dr. Foster's waiting room aquarium seemed oblivious to the changing seasons, slowly swimming in and around their plastic plants, warmed by the incandescent pink glow of the light on the top of the tank, watching, never passing judgment on life outside the tank...just watching.

In a way, I envied those fish as I sat waiting for my appointment; their world was simple, safe, warm, no cares, no worries, none of the harsh realities of life, (at least none as far as I could tell). Just peace and tranquility. The thought stuck me - I had missed that stage in life. As long as I could remember, I had equated security with a caring father and the warmth of a loving mother. These fish were enveloped in protection, it seemed to me. It was just a lousy aquarium, but the contrast between their environment and my childhood was glaring.

I had deliberately arrived early for my appointment with Dr. Foster, but she didn't see me until my designated time. She was utterly professional, and I could respect that.

"Paul, come in." We exchanged pleasantries and got down to work. We discussed my "visit" to Culver and how real it was, about recalling every detail, about how the experience had settled over me like a gentle embrace in the days that followed. I wanted to talk about another try at hypnotherapy, but was almost afraid to ask. She brought it up first, asked if I had any more interest in returning to the world of my parents' time. I answered with a wisecrack that I immediately regretted. "About fifty year's worth."

"Then let's get started."

A gentle snow was falling. I found myself walking past Main Barrack next to the Administration Building. It is the oldest building on the Culver campus. It wasn't cold enough for the snow to stick to the pavement, but it was clinging to the trees and shrubs, glittering in the morning sun. Two cadets passed, wearing their traditional dark blue greatcoats, "Good morning, Mr. Newkirk." At first it didn't register that they were talking to me, but then it came to me...I was Paul Newkirk! They've recognized me! I'm back! I knew where I was, but the question was *when*!

Almost automatically I said, "Good morning, gentlemen." Then I turned north along the path between Main and the Administration building. A copy of the front page of the *South Bend Tribune* was posted on the bulletin board inside Sally Port. The headline screamed "Nazis Counterattack In Ardennes." The date was December 18, 1944! There were also notices about the upcoming Christmas leave from General Gignilliat.

I glanced out toward The Oval. There, just coming into view was a slender woman, walking with long confident strides, full of youthful exuberance, her auburn hair parted on the left, bouncing from side to side with each step. She was wearing a knee length plaid overcoat. I knew, almost instinctively who it was...my mother! She glanced toward me, stopped, waved, and started to walk toward me. I didn't know what to do. I froze. What would I say? What had gone on since the cocktail party? I felt panic!

"Well, Paul Newkirk isn't it? Cousin Paul? Where have you been keeping yourself these last few weeks? It looks as if you passed the general's inspection and got a job, but *you and I* haven't had a chance to get acquainted. I've had a few letters from Mother and Dad, but they didn't mention you.... we really should have a cup of coffee and talk." She looked up at me. A playful smile danced across her face. "Say, I've got an idea. If you're not too busy, let's go now! How about it?"

Oh, my God, what would I say next! There was so much I wanted to know, but at that moment I couldn't think of a thing we could possibly talk about! I chastised myself, thinking "I've had a million conversations with you, Mother, but you were never there. Now that you *are* -- I don't know where to begin."

Just then Colonel Gregory came through the double doors of the Administration building. "Ah, Newkirk! Shippy! You two finally getting a chance to talk. The general tells me you're off to a fine start...very pleased with your work so far, Newkirk!"

"Thank you, sir."

"You know, Newkirk, Shippy's awfully popular around here.... on the go every minute! If you've got the time to get better acquainted, I would take it if I were you, before she gets away!" Now, there was a comment that could break your heart.

"Well, yes sir, I don't doubt that. Mrs. Bradshaw's just invited me to have a cup of coffee with her...catch up on things, but...."

"Well, go ahead then! The general is meeting with the Faculty Council all morning down at the library. He won't miss you. Why don't you? I'll tell the people in the business office you'll be late. It's close to the holidays, time for family! Perhaps you can finally meet Captain Bradshaw, the other Paul that is..." Colonel Gregory laughed. He slapped me on the back, and I instantly understood I didn't really have a choice. That was OK; I didn't really want one.

I was suddenly afraid it wouldn't take her long to discover my deception. I wanted my mother to think of me as someone who could be special and not some kind of liar. I took a deep breath and heard myself say. "Well, if you think it would be OK, sir."

"Ah, ah, Newkirk! Don't let Captain Payson hear you say that! He has a strong aversion to faculty and staff using any slang terms. Ask any cadet."

"Yes sir. I should have known that."

Colonel Gregory looked at me, somewhat quizzically. "Well, anyway, you two go ahead. Spend some time with Shippy and Paul."

Spend some time? That's all I had ever wanted to do...all my life. I glanced at my mother; she looked up at me, another smile swept across her face, her eyes wide and sparkling. "Come on! We'll go to The Shack for coffee and meet Paul for lunch." She clasped my hand, it was as though a feeling of warmth flooded up my arm and surged through my body and

I was whisked away, figuratively and literally. I felt strangely light, like a toy balloon tied with a string, pulled along by a happy child. The snow was slowly, gently, swirling around the two of us.

"The Shack" was the cadet hangout on campus. Actually, it was part of the Culver Inn, but it seemed like a totally separate place. It had a soda fountain, paneled walls, a wonderful view of the lake, a jukebox, big stone fireplace, and Culver pennants and banners everywhere. It was the one place where cadets could get away from the routine of academy life. I held the door for my mother, making the mental note to be sure and call her "Shippy." The music coming from the jukebox was Glenn Miller's "American Patrol." Its easy rhythm filled the room. A few off-duty cadets were there. We ordered coffee and sat at a table near the fireplace.

She looked at me. Smiled. Rested her head on her hands. I struggled not to look enraptured by her. "You have a beautiful voice," I stammered.

"You told me that at the cocktail party a few weeks ago. You're very kind to say so." She tilted her head toward me. Before I could think of anything else to say, she acknowledged my awkwardness.

"You seem a little on edge...nervous...family characteristic, I suppose. All the Winships are high strung, even me!"

"Oh, I'm fine. This place just takes some getting used to. So many rules and regulations to remember. And, well, I've heard so much about you over the years, it's...it's exciting to finally meet you."

"How sweet! So tell me, how are things at home?"

"Well, I, uh, was only there a short time. Your folks are fine. I suppose it's a stretch to say it, but Cousin Will, your dad - that's what he wanted me to call him - said I should come here, thought you might be able to help me, you know... find work."

"I can sure understand that. Mother and Dad are wonderful! I love them so much. I know how worried they are about my brother, Billy. Did you know he's stationed in England with the Army Air Corps, 306th Bomb Group? I think he's pretty safe there, but you never know, especially now that the Germans are on the move west again. What's happening in Rushville?" The abrupt change of subject told me she didn't want to think about the danger her brother was in. I understood that.

I was going to have to fake this big-time. "Oh, you know Rushville. Nothing much changes there, except on Saturday nights when everybody's downtown. I saw some of your friends while I was there. Let's see, I saw Francis Richards and Ruth Moran." I had to build some credibility. "Everybody wants to know how Shippy's getting along."

"Did you happen to see Judith Mosley? I haven't seen Pearl since she stopped for a visit here two or three years ago. She was another one of our crowd. She's married to Hunter Roberts now. He graduated from Culver back in the 30s."

"Pearl?"

"That's a nickname I gave her. I don't tell many people this, but my middle name is Ruby.... I absolutely hate it. Judith used to tease me when we were in high school by calling me 'Ruby,' so I decided to call her 'Pearl' just to get even...and the nickname stuck. She got what she deserved for teasing me, don't you think?" she laughed.

"I didn't have the chance to see her before I got here, but I've certainly heard the name Mosley before." Now I had a chance for some real believability. I tried name-dropping. I *did* know Janet Mosley – she had delivered the photograph of my mother as a young girl, and she had told me that her sister, Judith, and my mother were close friends. "Doesn't Judith have a younger sister, Janet?"

"Oh, yes! She's five years younger than Judith and I. She's just a doll. Lots of fun. Not bad on the church organ either. Do you know her?

"We've met. It would be more accurate to say I know *of* her." It was time to change the subject. This was getting dangerous. "I can't get over how beautiful this campus is. There isn't an eyesore in any direction, no matter where you look. It must be wonderful living here. So, what's life like for you and, ah, Paul is it? Apparently he's made quite an impression with the home folks!"

"Isn't it funny that the two of you have the same first name?"

I laughed nervously and said, "Yes, I guess so."

"Well, *my* Paul and I have been married nearly nine years. Can you believe that? Are you married, Paul? I hope you don't mind if I call you by your first name - it's been a favorite of mine for - almost nine years," she laughed, too. Her smile, my God, her smile was the most beautiful thing I had ever seen. Through all the years, everyone who had seen it, commented on it, remembered it - and they were right! I wanted so much to tell her who I was, wanted to hold her hands, embrace her, and say, quietly, "Mother, I'm your son. The son you'll have someday." I wanted to tell her so much, but I couldn't...she wouldn't have believed me anyway. Still, I wanted so much for her to know!

"Well, yes, I'm married, Connie, a wonderful girl, I, ah, hope to be able to afford to have her join me here one day soon and, no, I don't mind at all if you call me Paul. So, tell me -- how did you and Captain Bradshaw meet?"

"Well, it's the funniest thing," she smiled and sipped her coffee. "I wanted to study piano when I was teaching music at Knox High School, not far from here. Some friends told me there was this old professor who taught piano here at Culver. They said he sometimes gave private lessons. They told him there was an old-maid schoolteacher who wanted to learn piano! Well, they arranged for us to meet and, I know this sounds corny, but it really was love at first sight. Oh, I dated boys in high school and college, but I had never met anyone like Paul, so sensitive, so kind, so talented, good looking...so wonderful." Her eyes sparkled even more than before.

I could feel tears welling up, looked out the window toward the lake, and took a deep breath. "That's a great story. I'm truly happy for you."

"I don't think it's possible to be happier than we are right now. We don't have a lot yet; his academy salary isn't a princely sum. But we have been able to save enough to buy our new piano," she smiled. "It's a Steinway baby grand! Paul is so proud of it. It makes our apartment a little cramped, but music is a great part of our lives." She leaned toward me; a sly little grin swept over her face, she whispered, "What I'm really hoping for now is a child. I'm ready to start a family. After nine years together, we're ready; it's time. Our apartment has two bedrooms; the spare one will be a wonderful nursery. I already know how I'll decorate it!"

"What are you hoping for, a boy or a girl?"

"Oh, I don't really care. A healthy baby is all that matters. Everybody says that I guess." She looked at me with a little embarrassment. "I hope I'm not being too personal."

"Not at all. I'm glad you feel comfortable enough to share that with me." I heard myself say, "Your dad actually mentioned that to me." Now I was intentionally faking it! "He thinks it's high time for a grandchild. To be honest with you, that's what some of your girl friends back home were wondering, too. 'When are Shippy and Paul going to start a family?' they asked me. Not that it's a hot topic of conversation back on Harrison Street," I laughed.

"But, you know, that's really all I've been thinking about for the last few months. I think women reach an age where the desire to become a mother sort of kicks in or something. He's almost forty. It's time, past time. It will be so much fun! Watching a little life unfold, I remember all the happy times I had growing up. I just hope I can do as good a job as my mother did. She was the one who kept Billy and me in line. Dad was a softy. All I had to do was hop in his lap and whine a little, and he would let me get away with anything. Paul's a little nervous about it, I think. But he'll be a great dad, I just know it!"

"You don't really care, then, whether you have a boy or girl?"

"Nope! Just a healthy child!"

"Well, suppose it is a girl!"

"Oh, I'd put her in frilly little dresses with ruffles and bows. Paul would teach her to play piano. We'd go for long walks by the lake together. I still have some dolls at home in Rushville. We'd sit on the lawn and have little tea parties. We'd go to Sunday School. We'd try not to spoil her too much."

"And what if it's a boy?"

"If we have a boy, I hope he looks like Paul! I'll rock him and sing to him and tuck him in at night, but he'll be all-boy, like my brother. I suppose Paul will teach him the piano, too. We'll run and play tag and sing songs together. I would have to think about all the things little boys like to do...maybe Paul will even teach him to play football someday...."

"Football? Why football?"

"Oh, it's the most unusual thing; they've asked Paul to be the coach of the Company C intramural football team next fall. I don't think he knows very much about the game, let alone how to coach it, but he's already studying a book on the rules of the game. I believe he's actually excited about it," she laughed.

I felt my stomach tighten. I knew what would happen next fall. "Are you sure you want him to do that? Coaching takes a lot of time...there's a lot of...stress, you know, pressure, coaching a sport like football." I felt sick. Almost without thinking, I said, "Perhaps I could help, be his assistant. I know a little about the game."

"Oh, I think that would be swell! Paul loves tennis and handball. He plays golf; he's just never played football, that's all. But he loves watching the academy team. I honestly think he'll enjoy it, and it would be wonderful if you wanted to help."

Just then the door of The Shack swung open. My mother looked past me. "Paul's here!" she exclaimed joyfully. If it was possible, her face actually seemed to brighten as she waved at him. I turned in my chair. In he strode, smiling and waving back at her. My God, he was tall! About 6'4" I guessed. Slender, high forehead, thinning hair, the delicate, almost feminine hands of a musician. He was wearing a tan trench coat with the unfastened belt streaming behind him as he walked to the table. I stood up.

"Hi honey!" he said. "How's my best girl?" He swept by me and bending low, gave my mother a slightly lingering kiss.

"Paul, I want you to meet someone." He turned quickly and looked at me with a warm smile. He had clear, gentle eyes and I perceived in him the look of a man who knew he was very lucky. "This is Paul Newkirk. He's a cousin of mine on Mom's side. He just started working over in the business office. We've been getting to know each other. Catching up on the news from home!"

"Well, Paul, it's nice to meet you!" He reached out a long arm and shook my hand enthusiastically. His hand was soft, but the grip was firm and confident. He pulled out a chair, tossed his overcoat over a nearby table and sat next to my mother. "So, what have the two of you been talking about?" He leaned back casually in the chair, putting his arm around my mother's shoulders. She seemed dwarfed by his size.

"Oh, nothing much. The folks, friends at home, starting a family!" she laughed.

"Now, Shippy." He looked at me a little embarrassed. "Golly, that's all she talks about these days." He smiled and gave her a gentle hug with one arm. "So, Paul, how did you end up here?

"My, this could get confusing, two Pauls!" Shippy interrupted, almost thinking out loud.

I was sticking to my story. "Well, Cousin Will, Will Winship, thought Mrs. Bradshaw, ah, Shippy, might be able to help me find a job here. As it turns out, I ran into Colonel Gregory and told him about my background in business. He arranged an interview with the General and the rest is, well, history," I smiled.

"Guess what, honey? Paul says he'd be happy to help you coach football next term."

"Really? That would be great. I'm going to need all the help I can get, never played or coached football before, as Shippy probably told you."

"I would consider it a privilege," I answered.

"Well, I don't know how much of a privilege it'll be; but, if you're game, we'll give it the old college try!" He turned to my mother. "And what new mischief have you been up to?" I could see the warmth of his smile as he looked at her. For an instant, they seemed to be lost in each other's gaze. These two people were clearly in love. I could almost feel the warmth glowing from the other side of the table. It gave me a warm, secure, comforting sensation just to see them together.

"Oh, not much, running a few errands, looking at baby furniture..." she giggled.

"Shippy!" He frowned at her with mock irritation and ignored the remark.

"Let's get some lunch before I have to get back to the M&A." We stood and I left some change on the table for the coffee. My father helped Shippy on with her coat. I stood back, in awe, watching the two of them together. In one sweeping move, his trench coat was back on and they were headed for the door. My mother was so much smaller than my dad that her head reached barely to his shoulder. She looked nestled against his body as they went outside. I stood there transfixed. Then, suddenly, my father looked back over his shoulder and called to me. "Paul! Why don't you join us? We're just going up to the Dining Hall for a bite to eat!"

"Fine by me!" I grabbed my coat and hurried out the door. They had just passed the corner of The Shack as I closed the door behind me. They were, by then, perhaps ten yards ahead of me. Just then, a gust of wind knocked some loose snow from a tree branch nearby. The mini avalanche distracted me for an instant. The distance from my parents and me seemed to grow enormously while my attention flagged. My father looked back, smiling, and with a broad sweep of his arm, motioned me onward. It was snowing harder. I glanced over toward the lake where swirls of snow were sliding across the frozen surface. When I looked up again they were gone! I ran ahead, but they were nowhere to be seen through the curtain of blowing snow!

"Well, Paul, our time is just about up for this session." I looked up. Dr. Foster was smiling at me. Her office came sharply into focus. Another "visit" was over.

Chapter Seventeen

A cold and bitter wind swirled around the building as I left
Dr. Foster's office. My car was covered with a glistening coat
of ice. I struggled to get the frozen driver's side door open;
finally it broke free and ice flew in all directions like a small
explosion of glass shards. I had to rummage around under
the front seat to find an ice scraper. It was dust-covered
from lack of use. I felt a strange new sense of frustration as I
chipped away at the quarter inch of ice on the windshield. I
really hadn't wanted the session to end. There was so much
more to know...so much to learn! Still so much unknown...

The drive home was tough. Freezing rain continued to fall.
The sound of the windshield wipers grated back and forth on
the accumulating ice, pounded out a monotonous rhythm,
and I was nearly out of washer fluid. Despite the roar of the
defroster, the wiper blades could only slap away part of the
distortion that blurred my view. I swiped at the fog forming
on the inside of the windshield with my sleeve, trying to see
where I was going. Traffic had slowed to a crawl. I replayed
the images swirling around in my head from the session. The
people who mattered most to me, the parents I had never been

allowed to know, had been there. It had all been so real! Why couldn't the damn session have gone on longer? It seemed as though I was just beginning to know them, starting to feel a slender thread of connection for the first time...to finally understand!

The freezing rain intensified. The road was coated with a glare of ice, slick, hard to see. The hole defining my vision of what lay ahead was gradually shrinking, and yet my mind still wandered back to this most recent "visit." Had I imagined all that I experienced during the session? Was Dr. Foster somehow creating the world to which I was being allowed to go? How could she? How could it be possible? Was it all in my imagination? Had I completely lost touch with the prospect that this was all coming from somewhere within me?

No! There was more to it than that! I had *been* there! Something surreal was going on. Perhaps Dr. Foster was just the facilitator, the "gatekeeper" to my past through this new experimental form of hypnotherapy. She had said it was possible to physically be in one place and experience a separate reality in another place. So, perhaps it was possible....

The windshield wipers continued to blink away the freezing rain. It helped that the road was familiar. My emotional dilemma, on the other hand, was far less clear. I tried to understand, to internalize, in some sort of rational way, what was going on. Making progress, she had said! Making progress...how could she say that when I already *knew* what was going to happen? As I drove on through the freezing rain, it was as if a small flame had been ignited within me, I began to feel an overwhelming urge to go back to their world again and try to change it.

What if I could save my newly discovered parents...rescue my father...from the terrible destiny I knew was waiting for him? What if I could change his past, alter their history...for them and, perhaps, for myself. What if I could do that! I felt strangely compelled, obligated to try! I knew the day when it would come. I knew the place. It didn't matter by what power the chance had been given to me. Perhaps this was what I was meant to do. Perhaps I had been given this time to save my father and, thereby, also save my mother. I realized I had to try! If I understood it intellectually and emotionally, then Dr. Foster would surely understand it, too!

My mind wandered back to 1945. I began to consider ways to keep my father away from that football game on that horrible day when the world changed. But to do that, I had to know him better, had to earn his trust, had to....

Suddenly, through the rain-spattered windshield I saw onrushing headlights coming straight at me! I swerved to the right; the rear of the car side-slipping out from under me, there was a prolonged blast of an air horn!! I hadn't been paying attention to the road ahead...the car had drifted into the other lane of traffic! I jerked the wheel back to the right, struggled to keep the car under control! A semi-trailer rig flashed by on the left, just inches away!! I pumped the brakes, again and again. The car was still fishtailing from side to side down the slick road. In an instant I was sideways, half on, half off the pavement. The tires finally caught in loose gravel along the shoulder. I looked both ways. Thank goodness no other cars were coming!! My heart was pounding!! Carefully, I eased the car forward, back onto the road. My hands were shaking!! God!! That had been a close call, too close.

I eased off the slick pavement and stopped. I grabbed the scraper, scrambled out of the car, and frantically hacked away at the ice-covered window until it was free of ice. Damn! How stupid! I looked around in the gathering twilight. For the moment there were no cars coming in either direction. I swallowed hard and got back into the car...terrifying experience...reckless!! Foolish!

Finally, just down the road, our driveway, home, a safe haven from the storm. I took a deep breath as I got out of the car. It was nearly dark. With a still unsteady hand, I opened the front door. The house was warm. Connie called out, "Is that you, Paul? I've been worried about you."

"Well, this time you had a good reason to worry." I sat down heavily in the recliner. "I need a drink, a stiff one."

Connie quickly entered the room. "What on earth happened? Are you all right!"?

"Yes, I'm fine. Just a little shaken. I wasn't paying attention and nearly got sideswiped off the road by a semi."

"How could you not have been paying attention in weather like this?"

"Oh, I was thinking about my session with Dr. Foster. I'm afraid I let my mind wander, stupid thing to do. I was just damn lucky nothing happened."

Connie handed me a drink that was more Scotch than anything else. I took a large swig, could feel the warmth of it flow all the way down my throat. "Thank God you're all right. What in Heaven's name went on during your session with what's-her-name that would take your mind off your driving like that?"

I hesitated. "Oh, you know, the usual stuff. She, ah, says we're making genuine progress, though."

"What sort of progress?" I could hear impatience in Connie's voice.

"Well, in the process...the journey."

"Paul, are we partners in this life...or are we not?" Connie was clearly irritated, and I couldn't really blame her.

"OK...look, maybe it would be best if you knew what's going on. This is all very new and _very_ strange to me; and, to be honest, I'm not sure I know how to handle it."

"Handle what?" Connie's tone was more sympathetic.

"I know you're not going to believe me. I'm not sure I believe it, but in these sessions with Dr. Foster, I seem to be going...someplace. Everything I understand about reality tells me that this...someplace...has to be inside my head, but...."

"What do you mean you go someplace? That doesn't make any sense at all."

"I know it doesn't. What's going on, clinically speaking, I think, is hypnotherapy. Maybe it's possible to somehow be in one place, physically, and to experience another place mentally...like an out-of-body sort of thing. Maybe it has something to do with genetic memory, but it's very, very real to me. And to tell the truth, I'm having trouble sorting out what's real and what isn't."

"I don't get what you're talking about at all!"

"I'm drawn to this like a magnet, Connie. And whatever this is, wherever it goes...I think I've got to follow it through. Somehow, I think I'm _supposed_ to follow it through."

Connie put her hand on mine. "Help me understand, honey. You're starting to frighten me!"

I took a deep breath. "I know this is going to sound very strange, but this place I go...is back in time...to 1944! And I'm _with_ them...my parents! I see them and I seem to be getting to know them. I talk with them as real people for the first time. Ever. Do you have any idea how powerful that is for me? Can you imagine how much I've longed for that all my life? I'm not sure, but I'm beginning to think...if I do this right, assuming there's any right or wrong to it, I'll come out on the other side of this...more complete as a person, more at peace with myself than I've ever been in my life. Do you understand what I mean?' Hell, I'm not even sure if I do!"

"Honey, are you dreaming all of this? That's what it sounds like."

"No, no, this is nothing like any dream I've ever had. I've never experienced anything like this before. All I can tell you is...it's happening. I, uh, think it may be like a special gift I've been given somehow, but a gift that could be taken away at any minute. But I really think I'm *meant* to see it through!"

Connie held my hand more tightly, looked intently at me. "Is there anything I can do to help?"

"Connie, there's nothing you can do, nothing I need from you...except your support and, if you can, your understanding while I make this...journey, if that's what it is. The terrible, painful thing I'm struggling with is this awful feeling that I may have somehow been given the chance to save them from what I know is coming in their future...in their time. The feeling is as irresistible and just as real for me as it would be if either you or I darted out in traffic to save one of our boys. We'd do it without thinking. And, honey, I'm sorry if this all sounds crazy or if what I'm trying to say frightens you...it's as close to a description of what I'm going through as I know how to give you. Can you understand any of this at all?"

"No, I don't think it's possible for anyone to understand. I understand what you're saying, but to really understand what you're feeling, no, I don't. But I love you and I do agree this is a journey you have to finish...for yourself, maybe even for us." We stood; Connie gave me a long lingering hug. "Let's have some dinner."

Chapter Eighteen

The holidays passed quickly, filled with shopping, decorating, parties, and all the special family traditions that give meaning to that festive season. My visits with Dr. Foster had been interrupted by the swirl of holiday events, both for her and for me. My next appointment wasn't until the end of January, but the time passed quickly enough.

It was a brilliant winter afternoon when I left home for my next appointment. Snow covered the ground, but the sky was a cloudless bright blue. The low angle of the winter sun reflected off the snow like a spotlight hitting a million tiny mirrors. As I turned out of the driveway, I put on sunglasses to reduce the glare that seemed to come from every direction. The highway was clear. There would be no difficulty seeing on-coming traffic on this trip! I was anxious to reach Dr. Foster's office for the next step in my "journey."

My thoughts were about my last visit to the past, or wherever I was going. If this was a place I was somehow meant to go, then didn't it make some sort of sense that I was being given this *gift* for a reason? What would be the point of passing back and forth through this window of time just to be a passive observer? Perhaps I was meant to intercede, to be there, at least in that reality, to give my parents the chance to live out more of their lives together? Perhaps that was my mission in all of this, to give them more time - *within* their time! Yes, I could believe that! And it could be done, because I knew what the future held and they did not. With just a little manipulation, I could change what I knew was coming!

The miles passed quickly. In my mind I again began to consider different ways that I could alter their past. Then the thought struck me.... if I could alter their past, could I be altering my future as well? Could it mean that there would be no Connie, no sons, no career? On the other hand, perhaps my intercession would only alter their future together in their own time, and not mine.... my mind swirled with a hundred possibilities!

No! Wait! That was all nonsense! The gift I had been given was the chance for me to fill in the missing pieces of my past, my childhood.... my life! Besides, there was no way of knowing how much time I might have with them and, more importantly.... how much time there was to overcome the sense of loneliness and loss I had carried deep within me for so long. What reality was I dealing with anyway? The real point was to savor every minute of this gift of time with my parents.... to fill that void, not to change history, or whatever this was! As I pulled into the parking lot of Dr. Foster's building, I made a promise to myself that I wouldn't waste precious time trying to manipulate the events of the past when I could be getting to know this man and this woman who had once existed, who had been taken from me so long ago.

Dr. Foster's waiting room was now a familiar place. The tropical fish in the aquarium still swam slowly in and around the plastic ferns that defined the limits of their world, their reality. What must they think of the separate reality beyond the boundaries of their calm and tranquil existence? What an intriguing thought! Right before me were two separate realities co-existing side by side. Maybe there was something to all this...

The door opened right on time. It was Dr. Foster. "Hello, Paul," she said warmly, "I hope the holidays were a happy time for you."

"Hectic but, yes, happy." We walked back to her office. I took my customary seat on the black leather sofa.

"How are you feeling?"

"Excited, I think. Anxious to see where this 'journey,' as you put it, takes me this time. I'm ready whenever you'd like to start."

Long shadows were being cast out toward the parade field. Patches of snow still covered much of The Oval. I found myself walking down the stairs that led from the gymnasium which faced the lake. Obviously, it was winter, but when, what month, what year? I clutched the wide lapels of my overcoat close to my neck against the harsh wind sweeping down from the north. I headed for Sally Port to check the news on the bulletin board. Sally Port had become more than just a portal from one part of the campus to another; it was like my own personal gateway to the identification of the time to which I was being allowed to travel. At least I was out of the wind as I looked at the newspaper posted there. "Big Three Meet At Yalta" the headline shouted. Yalta! Remembering my American History, I recalled that Roosevelt, Churchill, and Stalin had met at Yalta in the Crimea to plan the final defeat and occupation of Germany in February 1945. I looked more closely at the paper; saw the date, February 14, 1945! Valentine's Day!

Behind me, I heard the familiar sound of a door opening. "Well, well, Newkirk! Haven't seen much of you since the Christmas break!" It was Colonel Gregory. "And it seems like this is the spot where I most often find you. Odd." He fastened the top button of his trench coat against the winter wind, silver eagles shining on his shoulders. He straightened the tilt on his OD garrison cap and looked me up and down. "On your way, I suppose, to Paul and Shippy's party."

"Uh, yes sir." What party? I wondered.

"I'm on my way to their apartment myself. Care to join me?"

I tried to collect my thoughts. I might as well go along. There seemed to be a strange inevitability to all this, but perhaps this was the way it was supposed to be. "Thank you, sir, it would be my pleasure."

We walked quickly past the rear of Main Barrack in the gathering twilight. I looked at my watch, nearly 6:15 PM. Then, suddenly I noticed something different. I looked more closely at the watch itself. Instead of the battery operated Accutron Connie had given me, I was wearing a square-faced "Lord Elgin" with a tiny second hand and a leather band - and it looked new! Colonel Gregory noticed me inspecting the watch. "Christmas gift, Newkirk?"

I glanced up quickly, startled. "Yes, sir. Ah, from the.... folks."

"Nice present." There was a long pause as we walked past the front of the Dining Hall. Suddenly Colonel Gregory stopped and said, "Newkirk, is that a Culver ring on your hand?" Oh, my God, he had seen my Culver summer school ring with my initials, PWB, and the year...1962 on it! How odd! The watch was from this time, but the ring was from a time yet to come.

"Ah, yes sir." I twirled the ring nervously with my thumb. "I thought I had mentioned going to summer school here... guess not. Perhaps I told the general during my interview." Why had the watch changed and not the ring? Would this be my undoing? The initials didn't match and the date on the ring was a full seventeen years in the future! I could feel the perspiration on my forehead, what if he asked to see the ring? How would I explain..?

"When were you here? What organization?"

"Oh, years ago. Naval School, Band Company, in the, ah, just, ah, after the Great War...." I kept moving my hand, twisting the ring so Colonel Gregory couldn't get a good look at it. World War I had been referred to as the Great War; I smiled inwardly at that fortuitous bit of recollection!

"Hmmmm. Before my time. Well, no matter. Just makes you more a part of the family, I suppose. Don't remember you saying anything about being a student here, though." Another pause. Thank goodness he hadn't asked to see the ring up close! "You know, Newkirk, I think we're in for a surprise this evening. I can't quite put my finger on it, but I think something's up." I could see that he was eying my ring curiously. I shoved my hands into my overcoat pockets.

"Like what, sir?"

"Well, I don't really know. Paul's been acting a little strange lately, almost like a kid at Christmas. Giddy...that's it, giddy." We arrived at their three-story brick apartment house. We went in the south doorway, up the dimly lit stairs to the second floor. Colonel Gregory knocked. I could hear laughter, the tinkle of glasses, and the unmistakable sound of a Bing Crosby record coming from behind the door. The door swung open flooding the hallway with a warm yellow glow. There, towering above us was.... my father...

He smiled broadly at us. "Colonel! Newkirk! Welcome! Come in, come in!

As we walked into the apartment, my father casually put his hand on my shoulder. I felt a tingle go through my body; a warm feeling of security engulfed me. I wanted to turn and embrace him, but knew I could not. About two-dozen people were in the living room and adjoining dining room. I recognized several of them, faculty and faculty wives mostly. They all looked so young! Mrs. Gregory was already there. Tobacco smoke hung thickly in the air. Nearly everyone smoked; no one knew the risks back then. It was still socially acceptable. Strands of red cardboard hearts were draped from a chandelier and taped to the windows. The room was full of light and love and laughter.

"Oh, hello, dear," Mrs. Gregory called out. She came over and kissed him gently on the cheek. "It is Valentine's Day, you know. A time for kisses!" He frowned. She turned to me. "Paul, how nice to see you here. I'm sure all this is new to you...all this socializing and partying. But it's like one big happy family." My father took our coats and offered us a cocktail. I looked around the room. Colonel Payson was there. So were Colonel Whitney, Coach Oliver, and Dr. Baxter. I had also known "Doc" Baxter as a student at Culver myself. He looked so much younger than I remembered him. He and my parents had been the best of friends, almost inseparable. On a small table, near the piano, was a photograph of my aunt and uncle together, taken when he was an Army Air Corps flying cadet! I had seen the photo a hundred times as a child on the mantel in my grandfather's bedroom on Perkins Street. It was now in the library at home. But here it was, in this time and in this place....

My father returned. "Newkirk, the more I've thought about it, the more I'm looking forward to you helping me coach intramural football next fall." Thanks Dad!

"It would be my pleasure, if you wouldn't mind."

"Mind, hell, I don't know the first thing about football!" Coach Oliver, who had coached nearly every varsity sport at Culver, including football, came over. Coach Oliver had been a genuine star athlete during his cadet days at Culver and, later, at the University of Michigan.

"Sorry Bradshaw, couldn't help overhearing. Do you mean to say they want you to coach an intramural football squad and you've never played the game or coached it before?" He laughed sarcastically at the absurdity of this "music teacher" coaching football.

"That's exactly it, but I'm reading a book about the game and Newkirk here has volunteered to help"

Coach Oliver looked me up and down with an air of unspoken condescension. "Well, if you want my opinion, I'd run the offense from a straight T formation if I were you.... can do lots of things from the T and you don't have to pass the ball much from it. What to you think, ah, what's your name again?

"Newkirk, Coach, Paul Newkirk." He was obviously testing me to see if I knew anything about the game at all.

"Oh, right."

"I think the T would be fine, coach; but, without a passing game, the linebackers can come up to play the run on every down if they know you're not going to throw the ball."

"Hmmm. Good point, Newkirk. Anybody in Company C who can catch the ball, Bradshaw?"

"No idea, coach, but if there is, perhaps you could give us some advice on the passing game."

"Well, yes, I'd be happy to. You just let me know if I can help," he said with a smile. Coach Oliver looked me up and down again; I knew he was wondering how somebody my size could possibly know anything about football. If the truth were known, I really thought I could help with an intramural squad, but that would be about it! At least I'd gotten past Coach Oliver's initial scrutiny.

I excused myself and walked into the dining room. Off to my left, I heard familiar laughter...it was my mother! I was drawn to her like a magnet. She was talking with Mrs. Payson and another woman I didn't recognize.

"Happy Valentine's Day," I interrupted.

My mother turned to me, our eyes met, she smiled sweetly at me and, almost in slow motion, she put her arms around me and held me close. I thought I would melt! Her lips touched my cheek with a soft kiss, and then she moved back, "Oh, Paul, how wonderful to see you." There was an extraordinary glow on her face I had not seen before. I wanted the moment to last forever. "I'd like you to meet two dear friends of mine. This is Mrs. Payson, the Captain's wife. And this is Jane Somers, my best friend from college."

I nodded. "It's a pleasure meeting both of you. Mrs. Payson, I admire your husband very much." I turned to Jane Summers, "and you and Shippy are both sorority sisters, Kappas?"

"Yes, how did you know that?" my mother asked.

"Oh, you both just look the part. Actually, I've seen a copy of your yearbook. I think it's called 'The Mirage,' isn't that right?"

"Why, yes. How flattering. I'll bet I don't look much like the skinny girl in that annual."

"Well, to be honest, you're more beautiful now, if that's possible." My mother blushed, looked at Jane and back at me, I had embarrassed her. I had gone too far! A totally inappropriate thing to say. I tried to recover. "Your husband, Paul, is a very lucky man."

"How sweet of you to say that."

"I'm very sorry, that was much too forward of me."

"Oh, not at all! Every woman likes to think she's pretty. Isn't that right Jane?"

"Shippy, it's the strangest thing. I feel like I know this fellow from someplace. Were you ever at DePauw, Paul?"

"No, no, I went to Indiana University."

"It'll come to me; you look so familiar. Does he remind you of anybody, Shippy?"

"Well, now that you mention it. There is something familiar about him; I felt that the first time we met last fall. I don't know..."

A long arpeggio sounded from the piano in living room. I heard my father's voice. "Shippy, could you come to the piano for a minute?"

"Oh, I hope he isn't going to ask me to sing...the neighbors," my mother laughed.

We walked back into the living room. Everyone moved closer to the piano

My father spoke. "Since this is Valentine's Day, I've got something special for Shippy and I want to share it with all of you, our dear friends." My mother stood facing him, her hands folded in front of her. "Shippy, I've written a song for you and I want this to be the world premier. It's called 'Love Once Again.'" My father looked around the room. "Now, some of you may be wondering about that title. Well, I came up with it because I didn't think I could ever love anyone more than I love Shippy, but I'm afraid she's going to have to share whatever love I have...because sometime this fall we're going to have...a baby!" An audible gasp went up from the crowd. My mother smiled warmly at my father. He continued, "Doc thought it might be so a few weeks ago; then the doctor in South Bend confirmed it. So, we wanted all of you to be the first to know. I haven't even written my mother about it yet. If I've been acting funny lately, it's because Shippy and I are so thrilled that we're going to be adding a new member to our little family." The applause was instantaneous and enthusiastic! There were hugs and laughter and tears and congratulations all around! The women hugged my mother. The men were shaking my father's hand and clapping him on the back. Colonel Gregory proposed a toast. "To Paul and Shippy on this wonderful day. May you have a healthy baby with Paul's talent and Shippy's *joie de vivre!*"

I knew this was a moment I was meant to see. I lifted my glass with one hand and wiped my eyes with the other, hoped no one saw. *I* was the child they were going to have in the fall!

My father stood. "You all know how special this is for us, how we've longed for a baby. If I could have your attention, please, I'd like to share with you the little song I've written for Shippy." The crowd became silent. My father sat at the piano. My mother stood facing him, her eyes filled with love and tears. Effortlessly, my father's hands moved across the keyboard. The melody filled the room. This was no ordinary ballad. This truly was a love song, a lullaby. There was no sound, save for the music engulfing the room. The melody swept along. I moved a little closer. My father's hands could easily reach two keys over an octave as he played. It was as though I was watching a scene out of time and space. My father looked only at my mother as he played the music she had inspired. I stood transfixed.

Chapter Nineteen

"Well, Paul, that's all the time we have time for today. Suddenly, I was back in Dr. Foster's office! "What are you feeling?"

"Oh, my God, you have no idea where I've been! It's so real! I was at a Valentine's Day party at my parents' apartment in 1945...and it's as though the people in that place, in that time, seem to miss me when I'm not there. My father...my father announced that they were expecting a baby...they were expecting me!"

"But what were you feeling, Paul?"

I tried to tell her. "I don't know exactly, happiness, amazement, fascination, and, well, fear, I guess."

"What do you think is causing the fear?"

I knew instantly. "I think there are two reasons. I know what's going to happen, and I don't know if I'm supposed to try to prevent it or not. I'm also afraid that I won't have enough time with them before all this ends; and, well, that's scary because I don't want it to end."

"I can understand why you'd feel that way, but remember this is a journey, and it's the journey we're most concerned with now, not the destination. Shall we set our next appointment for, let's say, a month from now?"

"A month from now? Why so long?"

"I think you need time away from this. It's obviously very intense for you, very emotional. I want you to have time to reflect on what's been happening, to internalize it, to think about what you're feeling in the here and now. That will take some time. It takes time for deep emotional wounds to begin to heal. I'll see you in a month."

Early signs of spring began to show as the weeks passed. The days were getting longer, and there was freshness in the air. Beneath the brown blanket of last fall's leaves, the pale green tips of daffodils were just beginning to break through the moist earth. Time, again, had passed quickly. I stood looking out the kitchen window. Connie came into the room. "Isn't your appointment with Dr. Foster this week?" she asked.

Absentmindedly I answered. "It's this afternoon."

"I'm not sure all this isn't some sort of a dream you're making up in your own head.... something your subconscious wants you to believe." Connie was not an easy sell on things that, to her, seemed outside the boundaries of common sense reality.

"You know, you could be right, but I don't think I really care at this point. All I can tell you is it seems very real to me. And, well, if it helps bring some closure to everything I.... everything we've been through, then it will have been time well spent." I had given Connie an overview of what was going on, but I hadn't told her very many of the specifics. It was just too personal, too emotional, too strange, and too unbelievable to share. I knew she thought it was all a dream, a subconscious wish that I was somehow trying to fulfill. I really didn't blame her for that, but I had to see this through, dream or not. Whoever I was, whatever I had become, had come from all of this, and I was determined to see where it led, even if it meant traveling this strange path for a while longer. Although I didn't tell Connie, I had the hazy indefinable sense that.... somehow.... whatever this was, was _meant_ to happen. Real or not, this was a very old locked door through which I was finally being given the chance to go. There was more at work here than just the concurrence of random events to produce some predetermined outcome...too much of my life had been bound up by what had for so long been locked away behind that door for it to be...well, for it to be just a dream.

Chapter Twenty

I watched the tropical fish gliding gracefully beneath the warm glow that illuminated the aquarium in Dr. Foster's office. The "inner voice" we all hear when thinking said, "When you stop to think about it, our reality isn't all that different from theirs. Fish tanks. Perhaps that's what we do -- make fish tanks of our lives...."

Dr. Foster opened the door; as always she greeted me warmly. "Paul, it's good to see you again. Come in!" As I got up, I couldn't help thinking how much I had come to admire and respect this woman, for her insight, her compassion, and the skill with which she was helping me to understand... "Have you had time to think about your feelings since our last session?"

We walked down the corridor to her office. I thought about her question as I took my usual seat on the black leather sofa.

"Well, yes and... no. I know I feel very good about what's going on, but there's a sort of awkwardness to it as well. During these 'visits,' the conversations with the people there, even the conversations with my parents, well, upon reflection, which is what you wanted me to do – reflect, have seemed a little flat and ordinary, I guess."

"What did you think would happen"?

"When I'm there, there's this overwhelming sensation that I'm supposed to be there; but, at the same time, I know what's going to happen...and yet, somehow I think I can change it for them, not for me, but for them. Does that make any sense at all?"

"Yes, it does make sense, but just remember why we're doing this, Paul. We're doing this for you, not for them."

"Oh, I know that, but I can't help thinking that I can make a difference for them."

"How will you know that?"

"I don't know, but I do have the advantage of knowing what's going to happen and maybe I can change...."

"Paul," Dr. Foster interrupted, "This isn't about them. It's about you! It's about you in the here and now - in the present, in this reality. Are you ready to begin?"

The shrill sound of a referee's whistle startled me. I found myself sitting on a long green bench. I shook my head. In the distance sunlight sparkled off the surface of a lake. Not far off was a grove of large shade trees, green with dense foliage. It was a sunny afternoon. I sat up. Looked around. This was the parade field! Partially hidden by the trees was the Naval Building! I was back at Culver again! But when, what year?

About 25 young men were running toward me. Kids of all sizes, dressed in a rag-tag collection of football gear. Most were wearing old leather helmets with no facemasks, just a chinstrap! Some had no helmets at all. They looked like shabby extras from the old movie "Knute Rockne, All American!" This is where football games used to be held in the 40s!

I heard a voice behind me. "Well, Newkirk, let's see what we've got to work with." I looked up. It was my father! He was wearing a maroon sweatshirt and a pair of baggy, khaki-colored football pants. Suddenly, I realized...these were kids from "C" Company, out for intramural football. "All right, men," I heard him say. "You've all been back on campus for about a week, now. Today is the first day of practice for the upcoming season and we're here for only one reason: we want to win football games!" His demeanor was commanding and yet gentle. These were, after all, a bunch of growing boys, a tangle of innocence, energy, unchanneled emotion and youthful honor -- suited up and ready for battle...for Culver and everything holy! I was transfixed. This was my father in a role I'd never imagined before -- being parental with boys just like when I was a midshipman at Culver in the 1960s! This was an example of his style of fathering...the fathering I would have had if only...

Suddenly a ground swell of dread washed over me. This was an intramural football field. This was the team he was with at the time of his.... Was this the day? Would I be asked to be a witness to this? My mind reeled with conflicting emotions as I tried to accept the possibility that what had, until now, been a mysterious blessing -- a magical return to an unrealized past -- was descending on me in another form. As a nightmare...as the death of my father? I wanted to reject that thought with every fiber of my being. And while I struggled with all those emotions, on the very edge of panic, I was suddenly aware of his voice as he continued talking to the boys. I managed to turn my urge to escape into a hard-won focus on what he was saying.

"Winning is important, men. We all know that. We've just won a terrible war in Europe. We had to win it. Some of your friends' fathers and uncles paid for that victory; some of the cadets who, just a year or two ago, marched with you on this very parade field laid down their lives..." I could hear the emotion building in his voice. "All of us, in our own way, made the sacrifice to win this war. It's a sacrifice you won't fully understand, I expect, until you're older. But we're here to win another kind of victory...in the game of football." My father collected himself. "And that's another kind of winning altogether, another kind of goal. Before we're through, I hope you'll know the difference. And I hope we'll have many opportunities to talk about it as the season progresses. I know I'm looking forward to it. I hope you are, too."

We'd won the war in Europe! I thought to myself. I tried to get my bearings in this football field scenario so filled with poignancy and dread. My father had said that the war in Europe had just ended; that meant that this had to be sometime in late August 1945. Dad would have just about two more months... I swallowed hard when I heard myself mentally calling him "Dad" for the first time. Ever....

"For many of you," he went on, "I know this is your first experience playing football. Well, I have a little confession to make: this is my first experience coaching football, so we're all in this together." He looked over at me and smiled. I felt like a friend, an insider. Immediately, I stood up and looked away, fighting a growing tightness in my throat (and through sheer determination) forbidding tears from even daring to form in my eyes.

Then I heard him say, "Men, this is Coach Newkirk. He's going to be my assistant. You may have seen him on campus. He works in the business office, but he says he knows football, and between the two of us -- and all of you -- I think we have what it takes to have a winning season if we all work hard and stay together as a team. What do you say? Any questions?

There were blank stares coming from the young faces freckled by the Indiana summer sun. Not a particularly encouraging sign; but it was a start.

"Conditioning, men, that's the key. Are there any first classmen here?" A couple of hands went up. "Good. You two take the squad for a jog around the parade field! Two laps. Double time!" The two boys just looked at each other. "That way." My father pointed to the left, and off they went at a half-hearted trot. "Well, Newkirk, what do we do next?"

I had managed to gain control of myself by that time. And I was almost looking forward to this exchange. And, yet, I was uncomfortable with it, too. I knew we should be talking football. But football was the least of the topics on my mind. He took a pack of Lucky Strikes from his hip pocket. "Smoke, Newkirk?"

"Ah, no thanks, gave that habit up a long time ago. We probably should start with some basic calisthenics, don't you think? Then, we need to find out if anybody has any, ah, skill. You know, how fast they are, who can throw the ball, who can catch it, that sort of thing."

"Swell, how do we do that?" he laughed. My father lit a smoke and took a long drag. God, I hated to see that.

I mumbled something about jumping jacks and tackling drills. "The most important thing, at this early stage, might be to see if anybody has any talent and then send them in for a good supper." He smiled and agreed that I might just be right for the first couple of practices. We'd have to see who was willing to put up with the contact part of football and who had the heart to win before we needed to talk strategy. "Maybe it's a little too early to start talking offense and defense," I said, looking down and taking my seat on the bench in front of him.

He chuckled as he squinted into the late afternoon sun. Then, in one long step, he was over the row of benches that separated us and sat beside me.

That was easy, I thought to myself. And, yet, it was also very hard. I found it difficult to look him in the eye. No one "here" seemed to notice it but me, but there was an uncanny resemblance in our physicality. The timbre of our voices, his hands on the keyboard at the Valentine's Day party when he played the song he'd written for Shippy -- my mother. They were my hands. Built the same way -- long narrow fingers. I looked down at my own hands. The same!

"You know, ah, Captain Bradshaw, I really appreciate this opportunity to work with you and help out with the team." I went on. "I spend most of my time in the business office, and I don't get to see much of cadet life. I miss that. I loved my time here as a kid, and I feel the need, somehow, to give something back to them, now that I'm older and in a position to do so. Know what I mean?"

"You bet! I can understand that. I didn't know you went to school here. When?" he asked.

"Oh, ah, just after the end of the First World War. I was in the Naval School band; I'll bet you didn't know that?" I heard myself blurt out.

He passed over the comment. His mind was clearly on this group of young men. "No, but don't you think this is a fine group of young men. It's rewarding to watch then grow and mature, as a result of all Culver has to offer. It's a process... a fascinating one, but time-tested and very worthwhile. But I suppose you know that...." Then he looked at me and said, "So you were a musician? What instrument?"

"Trumpet, but I never quite made it to first chair...there were a lot of very good players here then." I heard a note of pride leap into my voice, in spite of myself. On another level, an older internal voice was saying, "My God, we're relating to each other.... across time and miles and all the acknowledged rules of what we know of life and death."

"I didn't go on with it, afterwards, really. I guess I got caught up in other things in college. The fraternity, law school for a while, but I love music," I countered -- almost as an apology. "Always have."

My father seemed huge sitting beside me on the bench. He was at least four or maybe five inches taller than I, but no broader in the shoulders. Still, he loomed over me like a giant. Or was it that I felt small in his shadow? Somehow unworthy of his precious, fleeting time.

Then, he filled the silence on his own. I heard him say, "You know, Shippy and I are expecting a baby this fall. Wait a minute! You were at the Valentine's party! I remember seeing you there! You know about it already! The time's getting close, and I'm so excited, have been since we heard -- don't remember who was there or what was said. It's all pretty much a blur, but I remember seeing you at the party. Odd. We're going to be as new to parenting as I am to coaching football!" He laughed and looked down at me, to be sure I was listening. He needn't have bothered.... I was listening. "And while part of me wishes we had more to give a child right now than our small apartment and our inexperience raising babies, another part of me says this is all so right. The time is perfect! The war is nearly over and the world is about to be free again. Shippy and I love each other deeply and the future couldn't be brighter -- that's basically what inspired me to write "Love

Once Again." What a great time to really start living. This is going to be one lucky kid. A great kid, I just know it!"

Suddenly, he seemed much younger to me, almost boyish as he dreamed about the mystery of the baby about to be born. "If it's a boy, maybe he'll have some musical talent." He looked down at his own expressive, talented hands. Paused, thoughtfully. ".... Maybe a keyboard man," he added, half-smiling as he looked over at me.

The sound of shuffling feet and heavy breathing came into my consciousness. The fledgling football team had taken their laps around the parade field and were breathless as they gathered around us for further instruction. My father, Captain Bradshaw, stood up to his full height and said, "OK, men! That's just a taste of what's ahead for the winning team I expect you to be! Right, Coach Newkirk?"

I stood up and looked him squarely in the eyes and said, "Yes, sir!" A keyboard man would be good. Yes, a good keyboard man.

Chapter Twenty One

It was nearly dark by the time I left Dr. Foster's office. The sun had already dropped well below the horizon. I flipped on the headlights as I pulled out of the parking lot. What a trip this visit had been! I was really interacting.... getting to know this man...my father, the way fathers and sons are supposed to, even though he was unaware of it. I tried to think about what I was feeling. Dr. Foster had told me to do that as we set the date and time for my appointment the following month.

Guilt.... that was the primary emotion... that I had failed to measure up to my father's hopes and expectations. Had I let my father down? He had hoped for a child who would be a musician. Was that what this was all really about? Assuaging some sort of deeply felt guilt?

I was aware; had been for a long time that a fair amount of my motivation to accomplish anything in life had come from the desire to, somehow, make my parents proud of me. For them to know, in some celestial way, and be proud of what I had done with my life. Now, strange though it seemed, I was filled with a nagging doubt about whether or not I had or even could have done that. How odd, I thought, wanting my parents, so long gone, to be proud of me, of trying to live up to their unspoken and unknown hopes and dreams.

Perhaps this really was all just some kind of hypnotic dream, but then again....

The highway connecting Rushville and Indianapolis passed through a half-dozen little towns, not much more than wide spots in the road. The actual highway was so familiar that I sometimes thought I could drive it blindfolded. I knew every landmark, every turn, and every dip. But on this trip I noticed something I had not seen before. But there they were, a scattering of shabby little taverns and seedy bars, dives really, with gaudy flickering neon signs. Inside most of them were none-too-successful "musicians" living out their lives for tips in smoky, dim, obscurity. Then the thought struck me.... perhaps it was OK that I had taken another road after all. Perhaps my father would have been proud of what I had accomplished, even though he had hoped for a musician. Perhaps.

I thought about my own sons. Had they always followed the path I wanted them to follow? No. Was I proud of them anyway? Of course! Had I been disappointed with them when they found their own paths? No! Why, then, I wondered, would my father have been any different with me? No matter what this separate reality was all about, wasn't my father entitled to his own fantasies.... even ones that wouldn't come true? Yes, of course, he was, just like other fathers and sons who have each other in their lives all along the way.

It was fully dark when I turned into the driveway. I could see the lights from the house shining through the pale green leaves of the shade trees in the front yard. It was a warm evening. There was that special freshness in the air that only comes in spring. I parked the car and started for the front door. I took a deep breath. What would I tell Connie about my latest session? I could hear her in the kitchen as I walked through the front door. "Hi, honey! I'm back!"

"Well, how did it go?"

"Let's have a glass of wine and sit on the porch for a while. Then we can talk about it."

"That bad, huh?"

"No, not bad at all. Confusing.... maybe. Certainly different." I poured two glasses of wine and handed one to Connie. We walked out to the screened-in porch, my favorite place to be on warm spring evenings.

"Well, how was it?"

"You know, I actually think it's possible for something very positive to come from this experience. I know you think it's all a lot of smoke and mirrors, and I understand why you'd feel that way. But even if it is, I don't think it matters.... if there's some positive outcome for me.... for us."

"For us?"

"Well, the dreams have stopped and I'm getting a much better sense about who I am and that it might be OK to just be me, just as I am, at least the 'me' I'm sort of re-discovering... Does that make any sense at all?"

"No, you're talking in circles again. Why wouldn't it be OK to be you? Who else could you possibly be but you?" I could hear the irritation in Connie's voice. I knew I wasn't doing a very good job of explaining, trying to make it all sound reasonable, logical, and believable. The truth of the matter was that I had entered into a strange realm, too "otherworldly" to explain, even to Connie. And she knew I was avoiding direct answers to her questions.

"When is all this stuff going to end? If this goes on much longer, it will have cost as much as the new dining room table and chairs I've wanted for years."

"I don't know how much longer it can continue, but I have a strong sense that I'm nearly there and I think I can make a difference for them."

"What does that mean? For whom? Your parents?"

I looked away from Connie. "Yes.... I think that's what it could mean." I turned back toward her, "but it also means I love you and all I need you to do is please try to be understanding for a little while longer."

"You're right, honey. It's just that none of this makes sense to me, but, if it's helping, I can be patient.... but not forever!" She smiled warmly at me.

"I really don't think it will take that long." As we sat there on the porch, I became more and more determined to try to change their destiny, even though Dr. Foster kept saying this journey was about me and not my parents. But there seemed to be something almost.... well, timeless.... about the love they shared for each other. Perhaps an unkind fate had distorted time and altered what was supposed to be for them. Maybe giving them back the gift of time together was what I was meant to do.... maybe that was the healing I needed, too. Maybe.

Chapter Twenty Two

I was almost late for my next appointment with Dr. Foster. A minor accident had slowed traffic to a crawl. When I arrived at her office, she was standing in the doorway - looking for me. "I was getting a little worried, Paul. You're usually early for our sessions."

"Oh, I got caught in a traffic jam," I said as I followed her down the hallway, back to her private office.

Ordinarily, Dr. Foster always had a sweet gentle smile on her face during our sessions, this time she seemed much more serious. "Is something wrong?" I asked.

"Paul, I think we're getting close to a critical part of this process. So far I think this has been an emotionally pleasant journey of discovery for you, but I want you to understand that this process may not always be that way. For true healing to take place, you may have to face some of the...well, the grief you've been repressing for a very long time. Do you think you're ready for that to happen?"

"I don't know, but I do know that, at least to me, it seems as though we've come an awfully long way and I know I don't want to turn back now."

"Paul, I'm concerned that you've made the *idea* of your parents into more than they could possibly have been. From all our conversations, it's very clear to me that everyone you've talked to, everyone who knew them has described them to you through their own set of emotional filters, something like looking at them through the proverbial rose-colored glasses. It's important to remember that, even if they had lived, even if you had grown up like all the other kids, the experience wouldn't have been all sweetness and light. It would have been what it was supposed to be.... normal, with all the trials and tribulations that every kid goes through, that you went through anyway in many respects. But your sense of loss is so profound, and understandable, that you've made them larger than life. I have no doubt that they were special people, but that's all they really were, just people, not saints or angels."

"But what about these journeys? They seem so perfect together. They seem to be so.... happy and young and full of life..."

"Paul, I'm sure that's right, but remember that in spite of all that, their lives would have been lived normally, perhaps happier than most, but still normally. And, as you know, life is full of twists and turns, highs and lows; that's life and it's normal. We're not trying to heal them; this is about helping you find healing, and it may be difficult. I just want you to be sure you're ready for that."

"I think I've been ready at some level for a long, long time. You've helped me finally see that. Yes, I think I'm ready."

I found myself walking along North Terrace Drive, the street that led to my parents' apartment. It was a beautiful fall morning. The sun on the sugar maples lining both sides of the street made them glow brilliant red against a cloudless blue sky. The contrast between the leaves and the clear sky always made the colors seem more brilliant somehow. The west side of the street was lined with tidy faculty homes, several of which were bordered with clusters of colorful mums; white, yellow, bronze, gold, and lavender – just like at home. There was already a refreshing briskness in the air, but the warmth of morning sun promised to make it a perfect afternoon. There were no cadets on this part of the campus; just a few faculty wives here and there working in their yards. I thought of Connie, at home, replacing the geraniums with mums. I wished she could be here with me, to share this, to know, to understand... This was the sort of day when you felt you could live forever! It was a day like a cover from <u>The Saturday Evening Post</u>, a scene from the palette of Norman Rockwell.

I strolled up the walk to the entrance of my parents' three-story apartment building. From their sidewalk I could see their open window. I bounded up the stairs, two at a time, knocked at the door. I heard a familiar voice. It was not my mother's voice, but someone else's. Still, it had the warmth and familiar ring of "home."

The door opened and there stood Agnes "Aggie" Cable, my black nurse when I was very small! She was part of my earliest memories as a child! She had the look of safety and security all about her, of someone who, through long experience, knew how to take care of people, to care for them with love and affection that was genuine. She had been a fixture around the academy for years, helping out wherever and whenever she was needed. I had not seen her since I was a summer school midshipman in the early sixties. She looked so much younger now. She was wearing a crisply starched white dress and an equally spotless linen apron trimmed in voile and tied in back with a big bow

"You must be Mister Newkirk," she said as she smiled, looking me up and down.

"Ah, yes, I am. I thought I'd stop by and see what Shippy and Paul were up to this morning."

"Why, Mister Newkirk! You must have been out of town! This is the day Miss Margaret and that new precious little baby boy come home. I'm expecting them in an hour or so. I'm here to make sure everything's ready for them, all spick an' span!"

"Is my...is Paul with her?"

"No sir! He's over by the ridin' hall. He's got the big football game this morning. He left about an hour ago, I expect. Doc Baxter and Missus Gregory drove up to the city to bring Miss Margaret and that precious bundle back home." I stared at Aggie in breathless terror. Oh, my God!

"Aggie, what day is it?"

She looked askance at me with a quizzical expression on her face, wondering, I imagined how I could be so presumptuous to call her "Aggie." For all she knew, we had never met before. "Why Mister Newkirk, don't you know? It's Saturday morning."

"No, no, I'm sorry; I mean what's the date?"

"I believe its October the 13th! Yes sir, saw it on the morning paper."

October 13, 1945!!! This was the say my father would.... die!!! "I've got to find him!" I shouted.

Aggie was startled, frightened by my reaction. "Who do you have to find, Mister Newkirk?"

"My fa.... Paul, I've got to find him right now!!!"

"Down by the ridin' hall. That's where he is," I heard her say as I ran down the stairs, grabbing the banister, hurling myself over as many steps as possible!! There was still time;

there had to be! I ran down the street to Academy Drive. I felt nothing but a passion driven by fear to get to the intramural football field laid out in front of the Riding Hall terrace as quickly as possible! The panic of the realization of this day of tragedy completely masked all the warnings of Dr. Foster and all my self-delivered sermons about the purpose of these journeys. This was a visceral reaction! It had no intellectual component whatsoever! Blind instinct and pure adrenalin had taken over and created a new lens through which reality (even in this warp of time) was oddly skewed.

Oh, this cannot be! It was as though things were moving in slow motion. The faster I tried to run the slower I seemed to be going, as in a dream, but this wasn't a dream! I took the shortest route, in front of Main Barrack, past the administration building, onto The Oval. I could see the Riding Hall in the distance. I could see the temporary goal posts, the crowd of cadets, parents, and kids in football uniforms milling around the sidelines. I continued to run! Closer! Where was he? There, finally, in the distance, among a knot of players...I saw him. Standing a head taller than most of his players was my father. I was not too late!

Here was my last chance to catch myself before plunging into the flaw of logic I had been so warned against. Over and over again, I'd been told: I was not given this chance to travel back in time to STOP my father's fate from happening; I was here to understand it and make peace with it...for ME. Still none of this creased my consciousness in the slightest way.

I pushed my way through the noisy crowd. I could see him. There was less than a minute to go in the first quarter. Company "C" was leading Troop "A" by a touchdown, 14-7. He looked up. "Newkirk! I was worried about you!" Worried about me? That had to be the height of all irony! "Hey, I need your help. See Billingsly over on the bench? He's got a nasty cut over his left eye. I forgot to bring along the first aid kit. It's not serious, I'm sure. But you know how scratches to the head can bleed.... I don't want him to be frightened. It looks much worse than it is. Run over to the Infirmary and see if the nurse can give you a bandage or something for it."

Billingsly! That was the kid I had met during my first "trip" to Culver. I looked over at him. He was sitting there along the sideline with one of the managers holding a towel against his forehead. He looked as if he was on the verge of tears.

Suddenly, I saw myself in young Billingsly - as I never had before. He was me sputtering around in the lake as I struggled to learn to swim. He was me at my first track meet when I took all those cinders in my knee as the price of misjudging a hurdle. That I could be the agent of Captain Bradshaw, offering some kind of nurturing hand to this boy was like having him offer that warm and loving hand to me! Instinctively, I ran over and spoke to the wounded gladiator.

"Billingsly, how are you doing?"

"Oh, I'm fine, coach," he said bravely, "Just can't get this scratch to quit bleeding." He pushed away the manager's hand and towel - pointing to a scratch over his left eyebrow, about an inch long. "Ya think it's gonna be OK?" His eyes searched mine for some sign of reassurance. Then he rushed on with his tale of battle - immune to the pain or fear by the glory of his courage. "Wish you'd been here. I made a great tackle on their halfback!"

"I'll bet you did. Let me see that scratch again." A tiny trickle of blood continued running down the side of his face, and adding drama to the scene. "I think you'll live." I walked over to speak to my father who was huddled with the team. He had just finished a cigarette. As I joined the huddle, he tossed the cigarette to the ground, crushing it out in the grass. He was clearly focused on the game: a look of concentration crossed his brow. He looked fine, excited...but fine.

"All right, men! Let's keep 'em out of the end zone this quarter!" was his advice to the eager young team. "There's less than a minute to go. Don't let 'em score!" The players ran back on the field. "Newkirk, we need Billingsly in the game!"

"I'm on my way, coach." The Infirmary wasn't more than fifty yards away. I could get there and back in a flash. I took off at a dead run. This would only take a couple of minutes. A lousy couple of minutes.

"Newkirk!" My father's voice. I stopped.... looked back. He was smiling at me. "Thanks for being here." I waved, smiled back, and took off, scrambling up the sloping lawn to the Infirmary.

Up the stone steps, I yanked open the door. The hallway was a sterile, white, antiseptic smelling place. I found the nurse in the waiting room, at the end of the hallway. "Nurse! I need a couple of band-aids for one of the kids on our team. He's got a cut over his left eye, not bad, though." The nurse got up without speaking. She walked slowly over to a large glass-windowed white cabinet.

"Do you need to bring him over? Is it near the eye?"

"No, no, above the eyebrow, just an adhesive bandage will be fine. It's just a scratch."

"What's the cadet's name? I'll need to record his name and organization for the log." She was infuriatingly slow. Deliberate. Annoyingly efficient.

"Cadet Joshua Billingsly, Company C," I almost shouted at her, impatient that we be DONE with these formalities. She handed me two band-aids and a small packet of sterile gauze, as she walked to her desk.

"Perhaps you should bring him over after the game. I'll clean the wound and bandage it properly. We don't want to run the risk of infection. What was his name again?"

"Billingsly, "C" Company!" I answered as I headed for the door. I bounded down the steps...

He paced the sidelines. Took a long drag on another cigarette. Exhaled quickly. "Come on men! Dig in! Dig in!" He looked over at Billingsly. "I need him in the game! Watch the ball!" he shouted, coughed. Coughed again. Could feel his heart beating. "Hold that line, men! You can do it!" he shouted. Then he felt the tightness. Cleared his throat. Lifted his arms over his head and stretched. Nothing new. Had felt it before. Just nervous tension. The play was coming in his direction. "Don't let him get outside!" he yelled. The tightness increased. Now pain. Pain gripping his chest like a vise! Tried to speak. Gasped for air. What's wrong? Pain! He clutched his chest. Had never felt pain like this before. It subsided for a second. He stood still. Tried to get his breath. Then the pain stuck again, like a hammer blow, doubling him over. Gasped for air! Hard to breathe now, like having an anvil on the chest! He looked up, vision blurred; suddenly he saw the sky, empty, blue, cloudless. Felt the damp grass against his neck.

He saw his players faces all around him, faces, others.... unbearable pain again!

"Coach! Coach, what's wrong?" Pain in his chest, excruciating, blinding pain! Then, slowly, the voices seemed to be coming from far away. No pain now. Faces and sky swirled above him.

Shippy! The baby, my son.... Oh, God! Not now.... not now! Please, not now! He closed his eyes. Felt someone tugging *loosening his collar. Could feel himself slipping. Like falling from a great height. He opened his eyes once more. Faces. Blurred faces. Tried to raise himself. Could not. Tried to speak, nothing would come, only the distant sound of voices.*

Slowly, quietly, the world became peaceful. Darkness began to surround him. Could feel himself falling, falling, away from the faces. No pain now, felt his strength failing, letting go, darkness surrounding him, a distant light. He drifted far away, toward the light, and was gone.

...I started to run down the hill toward the parade ground, but stopped short in my tracks. I listened...something was strange...no sounds, only songbirds in the overhanging trees! What had happened to the cheering? Where was the cacophony of sound radiating from the noisy football crowd? As I ran past the trees, I could see the chalk-lined football field. Suddenly, my legs felt like lead, as though I was looking out upon a place to which I was no longer allowed to go!

Before me was the playing field, the sky, the lake, the players, the spectators, all motionless! The scene looked like a photograph, a painting. Oh, no! Not now! Oh God! I couldn't have been gone more than a few minutes.... I crushed the band-aid and gauze tight in my hand. I tried to run toward the field again. Slowly, painfully, the world was in motion again. I ran. "What's happened? What's happened?" I shouted - not wanting to hear the answer I knew would come.

"It's Captain Bradshaw. He's passed out I think." I heard a voice say, didn't see who had said it. I stopped hearing at some point; the only voice I heard was my own - speaking to me from some far off place. An older voice, still my own, but perhaps in the here and the now... "Oh, my God!" it kept saying. I struggled to get through the crush of spectators and players. I couldn't see him! Oh, please, dear God, don't let it happen now. Not yet! Oh, God, not yet! I can save him! I can save him! I began to bargain. Give me just a few minutes more...at least time to say.... Please! Please!! Please!!!" The crowd parted.

"Somebody get Doc Baxter," a voice shouted.

"For God's sake, somebody get help!" I looked down. My father's face was ashen. His body motionless. The athletic trainer from the other team was bending over him, listening for a pulse, checking for respiration.

"My God," he said softly, "I think he's.... he's...dead." An audible gasp went up from the crowd. Stunned silence. I stepped forward slowly, stared into my father's face, looked at his hands.... at my hands. I dropped to my knees, sobbing. I reached out slowly to hold his hand. Dad! Dad! Please don't die!! Oh, my God! Please don't...

Before I could reach him, I felt a strong hand on my shoulder. I looked up, tears were streaming down my face, it was Colonel Gregory!

"Newkirk, there's nothing you can do," he said quietly, gently. "He's gone."

I held my head in my hands. "Nothing's changed! I couldn't save him! I was only away for a few minutes! He's dead and I couldn't do anything about it," I sobbed.

"Paul, did you really believe you could?" It was Dr. Foster's voice! I looked up. I was back in her office, sitting on the black leather sofa. I was drenched in sweat. I wiped my eyes, and looked at her. Suddenly, all the conversations we'd had on so many occasions about this "process," this "gift" of going back in time, the whole concept of hypnotherapy came sweeping over me like a tidal wave. And I felt a profound embarrassment, that when I needed to remember those things, they had all escaped me. Her face was soft, calm. "None of it mattered," I heard myself explain to Dr. Foster who needed no explanation! "I couldn't save him! I was so close! I was so damn close!!

"Paul, look at me," she said. I tried to wipe away the tears. "Tell me what you're feeling." She put her hand on mine.

"I was there! I knew what was going to happen! But I couldn't help feeling that I could have saved him if only I had stayed with him. There might have been SOMETHING I could have done? Why do I feel like his death was all my fault?" I gasped.

"Paul, listen to me. You've obviously been carrying a sense of deeply repressed guilt inside you for a lifetime. No wonder it pushed forward past all the warnings and rationalizations we paraded you through. It had to come out - play out, if you will - before your very eyes. Clearly, it wasn't your fault. What COULD you have done? You're father died of a sudden massive heart attack. It happened; it would have happened, whether you had been there or not. Take this gift and see it for what it is.... a piece of your past that you have been allowed to experience in a very personal, intimate way. It was *not* your fault. Treasure this, learn from it! Remember it. Listen to me: you're a man of faith, are you not?"

"Sure I am," I answered without pause.

"Well, have a little faith. Who's to know what this gift of insight into your father's death will mean to you in the future you've yet to see? Who knows what part this might play in the perspective you'll need in understanding what happened to your mother in the weeks and months following your father's sudden death? Paul, let's not be impatient to have all the answers just this minute, just now, just today. This is a journey, remember? And we have miles...and miles... still to go."

Chapter Twenty Three

Nearly two weeks had passed since my last appointment with Dr. Foster. It had been an emotionally draining experience but, upon reflection, it was oddly comforting, too. I found the mixed emotions difficult to interpret for myself...let alone explain to Connie. So without meaning to exclude her, I didn't try. I resolved to work at understanding these contradictions myself and to find some kind of emotional compass to help me along this journey.

I was home alone. Connie had gone to the grocery. I found myself sitting on the porch, not consciously trying to analyze what had happened during the sessions with Dr. Foster, but just letting my thoughts wander. I was still new to this process, and I couldn't stop my mind from trying to look ahead and prepare my psyche for what might be coming. Was any kind of healing already taking place? Certainly the nightmares had stopped. That, if nothing else, was *real* progress; and I was enormously grateful for it! But how did I feel about what was happening with these tantalizing flashbacks in time? Did I actually believe I was returning to a REALITY of half a century ago?

The clarity of "being there" was more real than any dream or fantasy I'd ever experienced in my life. Of that, I was completely sure. If all this was totally manufactured from within me, where did it come from? Was it need? Was it imagination? Was it some hoped-for wish fulfillment? Was it some unconscious memory somehow bubbling to the surface? Where was my rational mind when this emotional side of me was taking over with such unprecedented force?

Suddenly, my thoughts flashed back to the box! Was this seemingly random thought the answer to my mental questions? Maybe so. It was the arrival of the box that had precipitated this entire quandary, right? Was I making that connection for the very first time? Perhaps if I went there... more might be learned. Perhaps the kind of understanding I was looking for still awaited me within that box.

Without making a conscious decision to do so, I was suddenly on my way to the hall closet. Since the first day it arrived – with my cursory but overwhelming review of its contents – the box had been relegated to the back of that closet. Pushing aside the coats, past a hamper of mittens and scarves, I reached into the darkened corner and lifted it out.

I had come to view this box of letters, photos and yearbooks as some kind of sacred vessel that might contain some keys to my past. But it was almost *too* sacred. When I initially began the process of looking through its powerful contents, the experience had been clearly uncomfortable for me. It seemed to be filled with sadness, grief and lost opportunities. Now, I could see for the first time that I'd actually re-buried it in this closet – behind a buffer of heavy coats and protective winter clothing. That revelation – alone – was interesting. Maybe I WAS making progress with Dr. Foster, after all. I was encouraged enough to begin to look further and explore what other answers this box might hold.

In the library, I placed the box on the floor and sat down cross-legged before it again. I studied it as if staring into a campfire. Lifting the lid, that familiar musty aroma of old papers drifted up to greet me. Gently, as I'd done before, I lifted out one pack of letters, most of which I had read on my first visit to this "shrine" of my origins. There was another group of letters also tied with blue ribbon that all seemed to have later postmarks – mostly from 1947. These, I put aside. I wasn't ready for 1947 – in more ways than one.

Among the stack of my mother's high school yearbooks was a letter I had not noticed before. The humidity from some non-air conditioned summer long ago, I decided, had stuck it to the back of one of the books where it had managed to hide from me. A trace of the envelope's seal – long since torn open and folded back – had adhered to the back of one of the yearbook covers. But a gentle coax released it into my hands.

Immediately, I recognized the handwriting on the envelope as my mother's. The letter was addressed to my maternal grandmother. The postmark was Culver, Indiana. The date of the postmark caused a shiver to go down my spine. It was October 20, 1945 – the week immediately following my father's funeral.

As I gently pulled the pages out of the yellowed envelope, I realized I was intruding on an incredibly tender moment between a grieving daughter and her mother – a conversation of intensely felt need for comfort and familial love. It was a very long letter; multiple pages written on both sides of each sheet, I almost stopped and slid them back into their fragile sheath of privacy from the past. But at the same time, I realized the letter was here FOR me to read; that it was saved and sent TO me for a reason. It was now MY letter, mine to read, my job to be a part of whatever it had to say. And I felt prepared....

It began:

October 17, 1945

Dear Mother,

It's after 3:00 A.M. and I still can't sleep. I need to share some of my feelings with you. This is my first night alone here in the apartment. Even little Paul is still with Aggie and Emmy. They thought it best to keep him through the night – as people have been staying here with me rather late – and he'd need feeding during the night. They were right of course. I am exhausted. But I ache to hold him right now. I need him desperately – he's still so tiny, but so like his father in a hundred little ways. But it's best he's not here tonight. I still feel numb – and I can't seem to be able to concentrate on anything. I'm so lost, but writing to you seems to help. All I can think about is the memorial service for Paul. It plays like a record – over and over again in my mind.

It was a good service, wasn't it, Mother? Paul would have wanted things done the way we did them. The caravan of cars moving slowly through the campus. It was all such familiar ground to him. There was a mist rising over the lake. It completely obscured the far shore. That was odd, wasn't it? And there was such a chill in the autumn air. I couldn't seem to get warm. The only sound was the rumble of tires over the uneven brick roadway.

I remember looking up at the faces of the cadets lining the route, as the limousine approached Logansport Gate. I could see their eyes following the hearse. They are only boys, and most of them were fighting back tears. They were trying so hard to be men.

The minister's words still echo in my head, like the repeating toll of a distant bell. He gave me a copy of his remarks. I've read them over and over. Here is the most beautiful part, I think, of what he said, 'There was youthfulness about Paul, an eagerness for life at its youthful best. Although he was very much a grown man, it was such a strong characteristic – we shall always recall his youthful side as we remember Captain Bradshaw in our midst. It would be difficult to think of him as anything but young – in attitude and activity. Even in his chosen field of music, it was as though he wanted to express a melody of youth, of life at its most energetic best.'

Then, he said something that hadn't occurred to me, Mother. And it's really true. 'As we reflect upon his work among us, he will be eternally young. Now it will be impossible to picture him as an aged impresario leaning heavily over his keyboard with uncertainty or diminished skill. Help us, Lord, to gain the perspective to see this blessing – as the gift it is.'

I can't think of him as playing somber compositions, Mother. Not from his hands...or from his heart.

Mother, remember the cadet who spoke? He said he'd always remember Paul leading the "sings" in the First Class Ring? And his glee club, and coaching his *team on the playing fields? Will they, Mother? Do you think they will remember? They must, you know. He was so gifted. And I loved him so much.*

After the service, Rev. Sexton told me that the unspoken wish of Paul's life had indeed been fulfilled with the birth of our son. He said that Paul's determination to never grow old was granted in this way. How did he know Paul felt that way?

I'm so grateful, now, that we named our baby Paul. He'll have his father's name and in that way, at least, we will never be separated."

I paused. If she could only have known how separated I would feel from them...

The letter continued, "*Oh, Mother -- how is it possible that in the midst of our greatest happiness this tragedy could happen? How could God let it happen? I'll never understand! Paul was only 41!*

I still see the black hearse with the dark velvet curtain over the windows taking my Paul away from me. My world has turned upside down. All our hopes and dreams, our joy at the arrival of our baby, our lives together have ended.

What does the future hold for our baby and for me? Will there ever be another day when I look forward to what life has in store? Will there ever be a day when the sun will shine as brightly as it always did when I knew Paul was nearby? I keep asking myself those questions.

When we arrived at the cemetery, I heard Doc Baxter's voice. He asked me if I was all right. He called me 'Margaret.'

I put the letter down and looked out the window. "Margaret." How odd that name sounded. To my parents, he was almost family. Yet she had written in this letter that Doc Baxter called her 'Margaret.' Was he unconsciously saying this was a changed woman, someone he no longer knew as the playful and buoyant "Shippy?"

I recalled the stories I had heard from my Uncle Bill... about the three of them; Doc, Paul, and Shippy. They'd been friends for years...shared many good times together. I looked down at her words on the written page. It was as if she was somehow following my thoughts – or was I following hers?

She continued:

"I remember all the wonderful times we – the three of us – spent together. We would all sing after dinner in our apartment with Paul at the piano. One of the songs we always sang was 'After You've Gone.' What a cruel irony that is now! Here we were at my husband's graveside... people were saying prayers...and I was thinking of the lyrics to, 'After you've gone....' Oh, Mother – I'm honestly frightened. Sometimes I hurt so badly, I think I might lose my mind.

On the way back to the car, Doc asked me again if I was all right, and I said I was. But, of course, I wasn't all right! I wanted to hold little Paul so much just then. We drove straight over to Aggie's. He was perfectly fine, the little dear. I'm glad he's too young to know what's happened. I couldn't bear to tell him, but how could I tell him what I don't understand myself?

I've been past the little Culver cemetery countless times, but I never really noticed it. The finality of death it represents apparently never made much of an impression on me. Why should it? Death has never occupied my thoughts. Now I find my thoughts hopelessly locked there among the rows of granite and marble headstones in the cemetery.

Mother, as I walked into that wine colored tent, every step I took was harder than the one before. Doc gave me his arm, but I felt weak – it was like a terrible dream. How could it be that I was actually looking at my Paul's grave? As I stood there, I could almost feel it pulling me, drawing me into cold nothingness. After the cadets, all dressed in gray, removed him from the back of the hearse, something happened to me. I stopped hearing, seeing, almost breathing. I felt completely, utterly alone. I know what transpired – it all happened just as planned. But I wasn't there somehow.

The minister said the words we agreed he would say. But I tell you -- I heard no part of it. 'With the firm assurance of the resurrection of the body and life everlasting, we commit his body to the earth, from whence it came. And in the sure knowledge that Paul and his beloved wife, Margaret, will, one day, be together once again in Paradise.'

Mother, can you understand if I tell you that I look forward to that day? I feel torn and actually broken beyond repair. No matter how hard I try – I cannot see past this terrible and dark place right now? Mother, does that make me bad? Am I letting Paul down if I refuse to accept him leaving me?

Maybe someday my senses will return. Maybe someday the effects of shock and exhaustion will subside for me. But it will take time, Mother. Time and rest. And love from you and Dad. I so want you to be proud of me, and of little Paul. He's all I have now. I'll try. I promise I'll try. I think perhaps I can sleep now...

I love you,
M."

Instinctively, I turned over the page in my hand – wanting to find more of my mother's words. But these were the last. No more in this letter; no more in the box. I ran my fingertips over her handwriting as if to feel the touch of her skin, to comfort her and transmit my deep understanding and profoundly shared sense of loss.

How very sad this had all been for her. My mother's whole world – everything she had counted on – was gone. But it was more than that; I understood something else was going on. The life she was looking forward to with such joy had been torn from her at a critical, emotionally vulnerable time. Her body was still reeling (medically) from the throes of childbirth a mere eleven days earlier.

How could anyone emotionally cope with all that? The grief! The despair! The unreality of her loss! The...loneliness! Loneliness that would come and stay and infect every part of her soul, despite the arrival of a son...despite my arrival. And yet, I thought, none of us really live our lives alone. Despite my father's death, she was not alone; there had been many people around to help her, but the loss she felt must have been too profound for anyone to reach her.... help her. How else could you explain it? My father had defined the boundaries of her world, as she had defined his. Upon reflection, I could understand the loneliness, the same loneliness I had felt as a child and, to be honest, still felt...sometimes. Perhaps that was at least one thing we shared. How ironic, sharing loneliness....

I felt a sudden warm connection to her as I held those pages in my hand; then I heard Connie's car pull into the driveway. The moment passed. Quickly I put the letter back inside the box and returned it to the hall closet. I wanted to tell her about the letter, about the loneliness, but how could I possibly do that? How could I share such deep emotions, even if I could put all I was feeling - all that I sensed my mother had felt - into words, how could I make Connie understand? I couldn't, at least not yet.

"Well, what have you been up to?" Connie asked as she came in from the garage, her arms draped with plastic sacks full of groceries.

"Not much, just relaxing, you know, enjoying the day. Want some help with those groceries?"

"Sure! They're in the trunk."

I grabbed an armload of sacks and headed back to the kitchen. Apparently, I had never been very good at masking my feelings. Connie was looking at me in that slightly off-hand way that always let me know she could tell that I'd been doing more than just relaxing. "Paul, what's on your mind?" I could tell by the look on her face that she wasn't buying my attempt at relaxed indifference.

"Oh, just reading some letters I found in that box in the hall closet," I said casually, trying to avoid her eyes. I felt embarrassed, ashamed, and I didn't know why.

"I thought you'd gone through all that stuff?"

"Well, I did too, but I found some papers I hadn't noticed before."

"What were they about?"

"A letter my mother had written to my grandmother. I must have overlooked it."

"May I read it?"

Connie had never asked to see any of the things in the box before. Why now? No. I didn't want her to read it; I wanted to keep it to myself. It was too personal, too private...too close to the heart of what had been happening all these months.... but heard myself saying, "Sure, you can read it if you want to."

I retrieved the box from the closet and carefully lifted the letter out and gave it to Connie. She walked into the living room and sat on the sofa. Slowly she read each page, carefully placing each one face down on the coffee table to keep them in order. I felt as though I was exposing more of myself to Connie than I ever had before. Her eyes softened as she read on. She wiped away tears. It was not like Connie to be moved by things like this. She was pretty tough when it came to keeping her emotions under wraps. Nor did she have a very high tolerance level for emotionality in others - especially me - men, in her world, weren't supposed to show that depth of feeling.

"Oh, Paul!" She looked up at me, her voice choked with emotion, "I had no idea! It was almost as though I could feel what she was feeling. How terrible it must have been for her. I can't even imagine..." She carefully handed me the faded pages. "There may be more to all of this than I thought. What can I do to help?"

At that very moment, I felt a surge of inner strength, at least for the moment, that let me reply calmly, "Nothing, really. Just be patient with me a little while longer. I guess the deepest wounds take the longest time to heal." I took in a deep breath. "I'm afraid my mother's never did. I hope mine do." Connie looked at me and smiled with a glow of understanding I had not seen before.

Chapter Twenty Four

My appointment with Dr. Foster couldn't have come too quickly. I was anxious now to find the healing I knew this process could bring. I was anxious to be there for her...my mother. I had brought the letter with me for Dr. Foster to read. She, also, slowly read each page. Carefully, as if she knew, she gently handed them back to me. The letter didn't seem to have the same effect of her as it had on Connie. She had, I supposed, seen far worse. "Paul," Dr. Foster said, "I don't believe this is going to get easier for you. To be honest, I think we're approaching the most difficult part of all. It is very important for you to remember that this is about you, not her." Her comment sounded callous. "You can't help her anymore, but you can help YOU. That's what this is still about. Don't forget that!" She paused. "And, by the way, call me Joan. I think we've come far enough to justify that level of familiarity," she said with a smile, "Are you ready to begin?"

I looked at her for a long moment. "Yes...Joan...I think so."

I found myself walking up the steps of the Infirmary. The dogwoods on either side of the entrance were in full bloom.

The fragrance of spring was in the air. Just inside the double doors I saw Doc Baxter, balding, reading glasses drooping from the end of his nose. His white medical coat unbuttoned, stethoscope around his neck. He glanced up when he heard the sound of the door shut behind me. "Newkirk! Just the person I want to see! Have you got a few minutes? We need to talk," he said with a detached professionalism. We walked through the reception room; past the nurse who had been so perfunctorily indifferent the day my father had died. She still had that look of crisp formality about her. He motioned me past her as he held the door open. "Have a seat." Up to this point, I hadn't said a word. "How are you getting along, Newkirk," he said as he eased himself slowly, painfully, into the chair behind his desk. He looked like he needed rest, badly.

"Oh, I'm fine Doctor Baxter, just fine. What's up?" Doc Baxter put his glasses on the desk, rubbed his eyes with his thumb and forefinger, like a man who had had too much on his mind for much too long. Then, suddenly, I heard footsteps coming down the hall, coming nearer, echoing off the tile of the brightly polished corridor floor. I looked toward the door, then back at Doc Baxter. Bright afternoon sunlight streamed in the windows, glistening off the white aseptic walls and chrome examination table. It was almost too bright. Then came the knock at the outside door, the door that led straight into the corridor.

"Doc? You in there?" The door swung open. Neither of us could see the face for the sunlight, but Doc Baxter clearly recognized the voice.

"Yes, Frank, I'm here. Come in. Newkirk, this is Frank Wilson, the pharmacist from the drugstore in town. Frank, this is Paul Newkirk from the business office, relative of Shippy's."

"Doc, that's why I'm here, I'm worried about Shippy. Paul's been gone nearly six months now. You'd think she would be getting over it - what with the new baby and all..." His voice trailed off. "She was in the store just yesterday, and she looked awful. She's lost weight and there's hollowness around her eyes. Looks like she hasn't been sleeping much to me." Six months! This had to be sometime in April 1946!

Doc Baxter leaned back in his chair and sighed. "Yes, I know. I'm worried about her, too. I've seen some strange things happen to perfectly reasonable, normal, healthy women after giving birth to a child. I don't understand why that happens. There seems to be no rhyme or reason to it - medically. For some reason, many women seem to go through a period of depression after a child is born. I wish we knew why. But when you add in losing your husband less than two weeks after giving birth, well, I can't even imagine what that's like. We usually want a new mother to stay in the hospital for at least two weeks. Shippy was only there a week when Paul died. Then the trauma of the funeral. I can't imagine what a shock that must have been. I just wish we could understand." Doc Baxter looked at Frank, "When did you see her last?" Frank looked away, and then at me, hesitated. "It's OK, Frank. Newkirk's here essentially for the same reason." I looked at Doc in surprise, but then, I really wasn't surprised. Shocked, but not surprised.

"Well, Doc, she was in the store just yesterday asking me to refill that prescription you gave her. Doc, I couldn't do it! That last prescription you gave her for Milltown was supposed to last thirty days. That was just two weeks ago, and she's out! She's taking too much! And, well," Frank paused, "I think she's been drinking, too. You know what alcohol and Milltown can do. I'm worried Doc, I really am!"

Doc Baxter looked at Frank and saw the fear in his eyes. He'd seen that look before. "All right, I'll go see her this afternoon. It's time to have a look at the baby anyway. Maybe I can talk to her. Maybe she'll tell me what's going on inside. Newkirk, I'd like you to come along, if you don't mind. This is what I wanted to talk to you about. "

"I don't mind at all. Maybe I can be of some use, but I don't want to intrude...."

"Not at all, I wouldn't be asking you, if I didn't think it was proper. Maybe seeing you will help. I wish we knew more about all this, medically speaking. Paul and Shippy and I were so close. It's been very difficult on me, too. If only I had been here...maybe I could have done something the day.... the day Paul.... died."

Doc Baxter and I walked slowly from the Infirmary to his car, his black bag under his arm. "You know, Newkirk, I've been thinking back to all the good times we shared together. I remember one particular Saturday afternoon last summer when the three of us, Paul, Shippy, and I, made some studio recordings in the Music & Art Building. She really has a beautiful voice, an alto, but you could argue that she was really a contralto at heart," he added, absentmindedly. "What fun it was making records directly onto the wax discs and being able to listen to them the same day! We sang trios together. Paul played the piano and Shippy sang some solos while we listened.

"They were so natural together, as though they knew what the other was thinking. They were so happy; it made me feel good just to be with them. Her best number, I think, was a throaty rendition of 'After You've Gone.' Everything seemed so perfect for them. How could a man have two better friends? Then the news that a baby was on the way! In a way, it seems like yesterday, and yet, it seems like a hundred years ago, too. What a shame. What a tragic shame."

We drove up to the now familiar apartment building where Shippy and Paul had lived. It really wasn't much of an apartment building by city standards, just three stories. We walked up to the second floor, south side. He knocked gently at the door. I heard the deadbolt lock open and the saw the door slowly open. "Oh, Doc Baxter! Mr. Newkirk! I'm glad you're here." It was Agnes Cable. "Please come in. Miss Margaret is so blue today. Don't seem like anything can cheer her up, not even that precious child. Maybe you can help her some."

We walked into the apartment. I knew where everything was. The living room was the same. Same sofa. Same easy chairs. The little end table with the photograph of my Uncle Bill, and his new wife, my Aunt Maxine, taken just before the war. The living room seemed darker than usual, though. It had always been such a bright cheery place, full of life... but the blinds were pulled nearly down, keeping out most of the light. There was a cold emptiness about it that made me shiver. A hollowness.

Funny, I thought, a room is just a room, four walls, ceiling and floor. Everything was the same, but in a peculiar way nothing was the same. A room doesn't have a life of its own, but still... The sensation was the same as I'd experienced at the house on Perkins Street after Aunt Nell had passed away. Then I saw the baby grand in the corner. I gasped out loud. It was as though I could almost see my father sitting there, working on a new composition. But, no, he was not there.

Doc Baxter had felt it, too. "I know what you're thinking, Newkirk. I feel it, too. It's just our imaginations; the mind plays tricks on us sometimes. I remember how long Paul and Shippy saved to buy that piano. I remember the private lessons Paul had given cadets to make a few extra dollars to supplement his small instructor's income from the academy. How they scrimped and did without so many things." Doc Baxter looked at me intently, sincerely, "I remember the day they finally could afford to buy it, a shiny dark mahogany Steinway baby grand! It became the medium through which they expressed the creativity they shared. I thought it was a foolish purchase until I saw how it brought them both to life." Doc Baxter looked off to some faraway place. "Music was the center of their world. It was the means through which Paul and Shippy could release the music that filled them both." Now, there it stood, the piano, useless and untouched in the half-light of the melancholy living room.

"Aggie, let's get some light in here. Damn! Reminds me of a sick room at the Infirmary!" Doc said.

"Miss Margaret doesn't seem to like the sunshine like she used to. Told me the light hurts her eyes." Doc asked about the baby - asked about...me... "Oh, that little angel is doing fine, just fine. He's taking his nap just now. Best child I ever saw. He doesn't fuss or carry on at all. I'm just glad I can be here to help Miss Margaret. It doesn't seem right that a body should have to go through what she's been through. Happy as can be one minute, most sorrow anybody can endure the next."

Aggie walked out into the hallway. "Miss Margaret! Doc's here to see you! Mr. Newkirk, too! Shall I send them back?" Faintly, the reply came, "Yes, please ask them to come in." Doc Baxter gave Aggie a gentle pat on the arm and walked down the hall toward the bedroom. I followed. "Careful now, don't wake the baby," Aggie called quietly after us.

The bedroom door was closed. He knocked. "Come in." Slowly, almost reluctantly, he reached for the dull brass handle and slowly opened the door. The door squeaked as he pushed it aside. I saw her sitting in an armchair by the window in a dull half-light that seemed to fill the room with only shades of gray. No color. The thin curtains were nearly closed. Doc walked closer. I stood in the doorway, my heart in my throat. She looked small and frail. She didn't look up. Doc walked around the bed where he could see her in the light from the window. Her face was empty, blank. It was as though she was staring into some faraway place. He tried to be cheerful, upbeat. "Well, Shippy, how are you feeling? How's the baby?" She looked up at Doc. I saw what Frank Wilson had seen. I felt an instant tightness in the pit of his stomach. I wanted to reach out and hold her, but she seemed very far away. Her eyes were dark and she clearly had lost weight. She looked tired and weak.

"Oh, our little darling is doing fine. He looks just like his precious daddy. He's the only thing that keeps me going. Paul will be so proud of him."

Doc Baxter sat slowly on a nearby straight chair, listening intently to her words. He put his black bag on the floor. "I'd like to have a look at him when he wakes up. But how are you doing?"

"I miss Paul so much. We've never been apart this long in all the twelve years we've been married. Sometimes I cry until I can't cry any more. I want to sleep because I dream about him, but I dread waking up because he isn't here. Sometimes I feel so frightened and so lonely I think I'm losing my mind.

Sometimes I don't feel anything at all. I just stare and feel nothing."

Doc sat forward in the chair. Looked into her eyes. "Margaret, it's time to get on with your life. You have a son. A fine healthy child who needs you as much as you needed Paul...probably more." He looked intently at her, but it was as though she was looking right through him, drawn into some world he could not reach. "Margaret, can you hear me?"

"Of course, I can, Doc," she whispered.

"Have you thought about going home? I'm sure your folks would be happy to have you stay with them until, well, until things seem better. They have to be worried about you and the baby. I know they'd love to spoil that little boy. This is their first grandchild, you know. And you could be around old friends. I think that would do a world of good for both of you."

"Oh, Doc, I can't. I've got to be here when he comes back." She reached forward, held back the thin drapes, looked out through the small opening into some faraway place where no one could reach her.

"When who comes back, Margaret?" Doc asked. I took a deep breath. I knew what was coming...

Her face brightened. She turned toward Doc Baxter. For an instant, there was a twinkle in her eyes and a hint of her beautiful smile. "Why, Paul, or course! We've got to be here when he comes back to us! He's coming back, Doc, I know he is. We can't go. I know how disappointed he would be if he came home and we were off visiting Mother and Dad."

"You think Paul's coming back?"

"Oh, yes!" There were tears running slowly down her cheeks. "That's all little Paul and I live for."

Doc Baxter sank back heavily in the chair. It was worse than anyone had thought, than I had ever imagined. She was in total denial. She thought, somehow, Paul, my father, was actually coming back! The tightness in my stomach increased, like a clamp. She seemed so fragile, so vulnerable. My God, what could he say to her now? Doc Baxter looked at the floor, considering what he ought to do, what he ought to say. After a long pause, he looked toward the light coming through the narrow opening in the curtains. "Well, I think he'd understand if you went home for a little while. Aggie's here. She could, ah, tell him where you are."

There was a small cry. From down the hallway came Aggie's gentle voice. "I'll see to the baby, Miss Margaret. You just rest yourself."

Doc reached for his medical bag. "As long as I'm here, why don't I have a look at you, too?" He reached for his stethoscope, placed it just under her left collarbone. He listened. "Normal heartbeat, but slow, too slow," he barely whispered, looking up at me. He put his hand under her chin, gently lifted her head so he could look into her eyes. Her pupils slightly dilated. There was the faint odor of alcohol on her breath. "How often are you taking those pills?"

"Not very often, Doc. No more than I need."

"Margaret, you mustn't take more than one tablet three times a day. Morning, noon, and just before you go to bed. Frank tells me you were in for a refill just the other day. Those were supposed to last a month."

She looked away, avoiding his eyes. "That's what I try to do, Doc, but sometimes," she sobbed, "it just hurts so much. Please try to understand! I've got to be here when he comes back." Tears fell on her worn cotton blouse. Her voice trailed off.

Slowly, Doc sat back down. Gently, he took her hands in his. "Shippy, look at me." She lifted her head until her eyes met his. Doc swallowed hard. "Shippy, I want you to listen to me. Paul is gone. He's not coming back. I can only imagine how empty you must feel, but you've got to accept the fact that Paul is gone. He'd want you to get on with your life. You're young and you have a beautiful baby boy in the other room who needs a mother." I could see that she wasn't listening. "Shippy!"

This was not a scene I wanted to see. It was all I could do not to sink to the floor. The feeling of profound grief for her had so engulfed me I wanted to cry out! Run to her! Tell her! Embrace her! Do SOMETHING! Doc Baxter looked up at me again, I could see the frustration etched in the lines of his face. He could not reach her, either as a friend or as her doctor. "Here, you're a relative," he said to me. "Maybe she'll listen to you. I'm going to check on the baby."

My stomach tightened into a knot, I felt frozen to that spot, incapable of uttering a sound, let alone being able to think of anything comforting to say to her...my... mother. In that instant I could see the past, the present and the future before my eyes. Her past, this present, and my future. She was staring vacantly out the window, looking like a broken doll. Quietly, slowly, I moved to the straight chair across from her. I don't know where the words came from, but I could hear myself saying, "Shippy, no one can ever understand exactly how you feel. No one can ever be where you are right now." I paused. It was though someone else was speaking through me...a lost, frightened, little boy. "Loneliness.... is a terrible thing. But I'd like you to know that I, perhaps more than anyone else, understand the loneliness...the awful sense of loss. I've felt that same loneliness for a long, long time.

And I know it's real and totally overwhelming." She turned her head toward me. She reached out her hand. I watched it move toward mine. Very gently, she placed her hand on mine. I could feel the warmth of her touch flow through me. She seemed to have felt something, too. She looked at our hands and then lifted her eyes to meet mine.

"Why, Paul, have you lost someone you love, too?"

"Yes...a very long time ago...when I...was very young.... my...mother..."

"Oh, Paul, how awful!" she signed.

"If only I had been old enough to tell her how much I needed her, loved her, would have given anything to be there for her...perhaps I could have helped.... but...I...I couldn't. I was too little..." I leaned toward her. "I...wish...very much.... that I could tell her now. I...I'm sure your son...would tell you that right now.... if he could...how much he loves you."

She looked at me tenderly. Her eyes softened, as though, perhaps, for an instant, she knew. Then, her hand slid away from mine. "I don't know if I can stand it, Paul...." Her head turned back the window. I was losing her!

"Moth...Margaret, Shippy, the pain of this will pass! And one day soon, very soon, before you know it, you'll have the cherished memory of the loved and lost. That's more than I have! Do that for yourself for.... your son!"

"Thank you for trying to help, Paul." Her voice sounded distant...detached. "When I'm with my Paul again, I'll tell him how kind you've been to me."

I was losing her! There had to be something, some way, to distract her from her grief and disorientation from reality! There had to be something I could do to show her that there could be...a tomorrow to which she could look forward... something real she could hope for! Some reason to go on living! A way to give her a perspective on the future that could be! I could feel my heart racing. I looked around the room in desperation, in a vague attempt to find some inspiration, an idea, anything to keep her from slipping away from me into some dark distorted world of depression and helpless isolation where no one could ever reach her...before it was too late!

What? What could I do? I took a deep breath, looked at the floor, felt helpless. Then, at that moment, at that very instant, it came to me! I knew what I could do.... what I could do to, perhaps, give her a glimpse of a future with something in it to live for. Even in the dim gray light of her room I could see it!

"Shippy," I said softly, choosing my words as carefully as any I had ever spoken, "I want to give you a present for the baby." Before she could turn toward me, it was clasped tightly in my hand. Startled, she looked at me curiously. "I want to give you something very special..." I slowly opened my hand. "This...Culver ring." A thin shaft of light from the narrow opening in the window reflected off the highly polished gold finish and made it sparkle, even in the dimly lit room. For an instant the ring glowed as if radiating its own inner light.

I could remember the day in 1962 when I received it. I was only seventeen then. I remembered the excitement and pride I felt opening that velvet blue silk-lined presentation box from the L. G. Balfour Company on that long ago day. It was one of the happiest days of my life! I had worn the ring every day since, for over thirty-five years. It was one of my most prized possessions. As much as I loved that ring, had loved it for so long, had seen it as a connection to my own past...perhaps by giving it to my mother... "I, ah, had this ring made for the baby, for little Paul, for the day when he graduates from Culver. I felt sure you'd want him to go to school here someday. Look, I've even had his initials put on it and the year he'll graduate! It would mean a very great deal to me if you...would keep it... for him. And give it to him...when that day comes." My mother looked at the ring and then at me. There were tears in her eyes. I held the ring out to her. Carefully, she took it and held it in her hand. Tears rolled down her pale cheeks.

For a breath-holding moment she didn't speak, then, "I promise you that one day my son will have this ring," she said quietly, as a faint smile drifted across her face toward me like a gentle caress. That was the last thing she said. She clasped the ring with both hands and held them against her breast. Then, slowly, she turned toward the window once more. It was too late! She was gone. I had lost her...

"Newkirk!" It was Doc Baxter. "Come here a minute." I looked at my mother again. She was sitting very still, looking vacantly out the narrow opening in the dull curtains, just as she had done when we came into the room. I walked into the dark hallway. "Newkirk, come see this fine baby!"

The baby! The BABY!! Oh, God, how would this work? I walked into the little nursery room. Doc Baxter was smiling and looking at the infant being held in Aggie's safe protecting arms. She turned toward me. "Mr. Newkirk, would you like to hold him."

Aggie gently held the baby out to me. Instinctively I cradled the little head in the crook of my left arm and supported the little body with my right. Gradually, cautiously, I looked down at the tiny face...my face! Everything was silent, the world was silent, everything except that tiny face seemed to have drifted out of focus...behind a silken curtain. The moment was magical, almost a oneness of spirit. Almost. Oh, what you have before you.... little Paul.

Chapter Twenty Five

"Well, Paul, how do you feel?" It was Dr. Foster's...Joan's voice. I was back!

I let out a deep sigh. "Very sad, I think. I was there, with her...my mother...seeing the effect my father's death had on her. Joan, you wouldn't believe how much I've seen her change! She's not the same person anymore! It's like her world is gradually slowing down, coming to an end. And there's nothing I can do about it. Even the people in her world, Doctor Baxter and the others, don't seem to be able to do anything about it! It doesn't seem as if too many people are all that concerned about her! Joan, there's more to this...emotionally... than I bargained for. To see it happening...right before my eyes! To witness all this...and not be able to do anything about it, well, it's a very sad and depressing emotional trip, I guess I never really expected I'd have to take, at least not like this."

"But, Paul, it's an emotional trip you *need* to take!' Joan said slowly, but emphatically, "That's what all this is about. I know this isn't easy for you, but it *is* what you bargained for. We know that the early life experiences, even of very young children, profoundly affect their development in a wide variety of ways. Sometimes those experiences are very good. Sometimes they're not. And when they're not, they can affect the rest of your life.... you already know that the emotional wounds you suffered haven't healed, but you didn't know they were even there until we started this journey."

"I know you're right, but.... it's like a two-edged sword. I really want those old wounds to heal, for my sake, but I also want to help, for her sake...and now I know...I can't...and that's very, very sad." I could feel my eyes welling up with tears.

"Paul, I think you may be mistaken about how much other people were trying to help your mother. You said there were other letters, in the box. Between now and our next session - read them. I'm sure you'll find that a number of people back then were feeling the same way you are now."

Joan was right. The letters were bound together by more than another faded blue ribbon. They were bound together by the deep concern they expressed about my mother's grief and about.... me.

Not until I untied the ribbon did their true significance reveal itself to me. I shuffled through the first few letters in the stack and could tell from the postmarks that they were all written after my father's death. They seemed to be a collection of correspondence exchanged among and saved by various relatives and friends of my family. Somebody felt strongly enough about me to save these letters for some reason. At some point – and it must have been for the sake of recording this difficult, confusing time – someone compiled these letters in this particular stack. And that person lovingly tied them together with yet another, now-faded, blue ribbon.

It was eerie to pull one end of the ribbon and untie the little bow. It seemed like breaking some sacred seal. And yet, I knew instinctively this bow had been tied -- originally -- for me to do this very act someday. And that someday was here; it was now.

The first letter was from Agnes "Aggie" Cable to my grandfather. It was dated October 1, 1946. Aggie, of course, was employed for most of her life as a domestic of some kind. She was a proud and wonderful woman...who wore her dignity like a fine new dress. But at the same time, I could imagine Aggie was not in the habit of addressing my grandfather in the written word. This letter must have been difficult for her.

"Dear Mr. Winship:

I am glad to tell you that little Paul is doing just fine. Since he started walking, it's all I can do to keep up with him! He's been eating solid food since last week and he's a real delight to be around. Miss Margaret has even enrolled him in a Sunday school class!"

Included with the letter was a black and white photo of me in a stroller with my mother kneeling nearby, handing me a toy and smiling. In the background was a little stuffed toy rabbit. I recognized it – and remembered the colors; bright yellow with pink ears! Actually I still had it. It had been years since I had seen it, but I remembered the colors vividly and that it was stored somewhere, safely wrapped in plastic, in the basement. My mother looked happy enough in the photo, but Aggie expressed growing concern over her health in her letter.

"Mr. Winship, I'm worried. Miss Margaret tires so easily and, if it weren't for that little darling, I don't know what she'd do. I try to be there as much as I

can for her. But when she's feeling particularly blue, I just take little Paul home with me where he can play in our back yard while I work. He loves to be with my husband, Emerson."

Emmy! I remembered him! How was it possible for me to remember that far back? Kids don't remember much about their first few years of life, but suddenly I remembered Emmy and, according to the letter, I was a few days short of being only a year old! I specifically recalled the times when Aggie wanted me to take my nap I would run to Emmy, clamber up on his lap, and ask him to sing to me, "Sing, Emmy, Sing," so I wouldn't have to go to bed! Where had that memory come from? The vision was stunning! Then it occurred to me that perhaps I was taken on visits to Aggie and Emmy's more than once – perhaps a great many times -- as things deteriorated with my mother. Maybe I even went to see them after my mother was gone. If that was so, then Aggie and her family CHOSE to care for me – even after my mother's death. This was something that had never occurred to me before. I felt strangely warmed by the affection of this wonderful black family who had been so protective of me as a child.

Next, was a letter from my grandfather to my mother – written October 4, 1946. I recognized his handwriting from when I was a kid. My grandfather was required to sign my report card after each six-week grading period at school. His signature was indelibly imprinted in my memory - *W.S.Winship*. In this letter he seemed to be imploring his daughter to come home. But as was his nature, he did it indirectly.

"This is the best place for you to be right now," he wrote. *"We both miss you very much."* My heart went out to him. He

was only telling part of the truth. He knew, by this time, that my grandmother had been diagnosed with cancer. She would be gone by July of 1947 – less than a year from the date of the letter. I also knew that my mother had even less time left. For that reason, this request was all the more poignant to me.

Reading between his lines, I strongly suspected, he needed her as much as he felt she needed her parents. By October of 1946 he KNEW there was nothing he could do to save his wife...my grandmother. By the fall of 1946, she was too ill to travel. I wondered if my mother knew that, or if Granddad actually kept it from her - sensing the depth of her problems at Culver. The letter gave me no clue. Just the urgency and the undeclared need were obvious to me.

My grandfather, the man I knew as a child, was never the same after the loss of his wife and daughter within the span of five short months. This seemed like an entirely different man trying to reach out to his daughter. I refolded the letter tenderly and put it back in its yellowed envelope.

Next was a letter from Doc Baxter to my grandfather, written in November 1946. In it he expressed growing concern for my mother's health. He, too, felt that she should return home to Rushville to be with her family. One paragraph was particularly telling:

"Mr. Winship, I am extremely concerned about Margaret's ability to care for her child, your grandson. She is working for the academy on a full-time basis, which is demanding enough, but clearly – she still has not recovered from the loss of her husband. She is suffering from a serious depression and, in my medical *opinion; she needs a long rest away from this place and all the memories that surround her here."*

It was clear that my grandfather was looking for some way to give my mother the help she needed. There was a note from him to my Aunt Nell. He minced no words with his older sister. The note is dated November 24, 1946.

"Dear Nellie,

I need your help. Margaret's no better. Frankly, the doctor up there thinks she may be getting worse. You know that with Floss' illness, I can't bring her and the baby home now. Floss just isn't up to it. Would you and sis be willing to take care of her and the baby for a while? I'll take care of everything. I don't know where else to turn."

How terrible this must have been for my grandfather! How helpless he must have felt.

Aunt Nell's reply was dated just a few days later, written in pencil -- as if in haste.

"Dear Will,

Cora and I will be happy to help care for Margaret and the baby. We would either need to open Mamma and Papa's house on Perkins or we can go up there and take care of them, if one of the fellows from the store can drive us up there." (Neither of my aunts ever learned how to drive an automobile.) "Just let me know what you want us to do. We'll do anything we can to help."

And, of course, it is a colossal understatement to simply add – they did just that.

Their father, my great-grandfather, had died just two months earlier, in September of 1946. My great grandfather's once flourishing general contracting business had barely survived the Great Depression; then the war came along and suddenly he had nothing to do!

While my grandfather gamely held on to his farm implement business – and tried to keep things afloat for his parents, my unmarried great aunts, his sisters, made their own sacrifice. To help make ends meet, both went to work at the Indiana Soldiers and Sailors Children's Home in northern Rush County. They lived on-site and had closed my great grandfather's big old brick house on Perkins Street in the fall of 1946, where they had lived with "Mamma" and "Papa" since the 1930s.

It all must have been extremely difficult and embarrassing for two women whose strict and perhaps somewhat narrow Victorian upbringing had led them down such an unexpected path in life. They had just ASSUMED they'd grow up to marry a couple of wealthy young blades from Rush County and lead gracious lives – just as their mother had – in due comfort and high social regard. But for some reason, that never came to pass. To think that after making that adjustment, they'd consider entering another whole new lifestyle – caring for their ailing young niece and her infant son.... It amazes me still. But they did it. The proof was in my hands. The proof was my childhood!

I was beginning to get a strong sense for the DEGREE of concern everyone in the family had for my mother's mental and physical health. But nothing I read even hinted at any kind of negative reflection on her. Instead, it felt more like a warm blanket of love and support being directed toward us... toward me. This was a perspective that was completely new to me. A true revelation!

Another letter was to my mother from her brother, my Uncle Bill. He was just home from the war and living in a big, rambling, white frame farmhouse in the country. I remembered it from when I was very small. Perhaps he had a better sense of what was happening to my mother than anyone else in the family.

"Shippy: I know you believe that Culver is the best place for you and little Paul, but Maxine and I would love to have you stay with us so you can take some time off. You need a break, Sis. We've got a big house here in the country, we're close to Mom and Dad, and it would be a wonderful chance for all of us to be together again. Please let us come up and bring you home for a while. Won't you even consider it? Love, Billy"

Apparently no one's plea could assuage my mother's determination to stay her course and continue down a path that would ultimately lead to tragedy. But these letters were saved; it was now very clear to me, to PROVE how hard everyone had tried. In the post-war years when loss was so much a part of every American family's life, at a time when the Winships, themselves, were under tremendous strain with illness and economic hardship, their hearts were still extended to us. I was humbled by that fact, as I'd never been humbled before.

I carefully retied the ribbon around the stack of letters – I don't know why. I put them back in the box with a realization that reading through them was something I couldn't have faced before I started the sessions with Dr. Foster.

It was clear now that I could only have done this when I was "ready" to do it. Now, I knew I was ready, and I had Joan to thank for it. I also recalled that, after one of our early sessions together, I had asked her – point blank – when she thought I'd be "finished with this therapy, this process, this journey -- whatever it is." She had quietly told me I would know when that time had come.

I thought to myself -- that time must be getting near.

Chapter Twenty Six

I saw motion out of the corner of my eye. I glanced up from the box toward the open window, Connie was outside planting her autumn mums again, near the front door in what had become something of a yearly ritual at our house. The welcome sight of her working there surrounded by the golden yellows, warm rusts, and rich maroons reminded me of something. And it was not about flowers.

She had been planting mums on that hot day last September, a full year ago, when I first brought home "the box" from the office...the box that contained so many of the missing pieces of the puzzle of my life. A year later, it suddenly occurred to me, some of those pieces were finally starting to fall into place. A year had passed since my unique journey had begun.

"Time for the mums, already?" I asked halfheartedly - my mind really in another place.

"Hi Honey," she answered, still working. "Well, maybe it's a little early, but the nursery just got these in and they were so fresh and full of blooms, I thought I'd go ahead and buy them while the selection was good. Aren't they pretty? Might as well get 'em in the ground and off to a good start for the fall.

The advent of fall and welcoming clusters of mums at our front door spoke to me of the circle of life itself. A year ago, I think I had fussed a little at Connie, seeing her pull up the still-blooming geraniums that welcomed me home each evening like bright red flags. I always hated to see the summer geraniums go. This year, it didn't seem to bother me. Seasons come. But they must go, as well. It's a cycle. It's all life. Then and now.

It was mid-September again, but 1998. This year was different. The difference, the huge, life-altering difference, was that now - however it had been happening; however hypnotherapy worked - I was different. I understood so much more about the flow of events in my childhood that I had been avoiding for so long, but that still had carried me along so helplessly, like an abandoned raft swirling down a river at flood tide. Somehow, I had a new found sense of comfort about the tragic, early deaths of my parents, the difficult choices that confronted my remaining family. Even about the arrival of fall mums replacing my faithful geraniums so early in the year.

My next appointment with Joan came on a late summer afternoon toward the end of September. I looked forward to the visit for a number of reasons. There were still pieces of the puzzle yet to be put into place. There was still healing to be done. So, I drove the now-familiar route to her office in Indianapolis with mixed emotions. I thought of the letters I'd found in the box and how reading them had given me so much new insight into the difficult period of time after my father's death. For so many years, it had been a time no one wanted to discuss with me. It was so much easier; it seemed, to recall when my parents were together and happy in their lives at Culver. So much easier to envision my mother as the carefree high schooler and the fun-loving college co-ed.

But the dark days at the end of her life were forbidden territory – held back from me with love and the best of intentions, I knew. But now, at least, I had some clue to the nature of those times, the unhappy convergence of fate, illness, and economics and, yes, even medical and psychiatric ignorance.

Driving through the tall cornfields that bordered old State Road 52, the green walls rustled in the wind as the car sped along. I passed through the little towns and lowered speed zones without restraint. I was in a hurry to get there and discuss with Dr. Foster this strangely comforting insight – which had come from an old stack of letters in an old cardboard box.

When I arrived at her office and opened the door to her office, there – as it had been from the start – was the same aquarium with the same tropical fish. How close the parallel was of the world of the aquarium to the one I had visited so often through Dr. Foster – the past. How like a fish out of water I was in a world of unknown golden yesterdays – separated from reality by an artificial veil of glass. I heard the door open behind me. "Paul, welcome! It's good to see you again! I hope you're well."

"I'm not sure I'd go that far," I chuckled, "but I genuinely believe I'm making real progress, Joan, I really do. I'm hoping that, today, we might work a bit on processing some of what I think I've learned."

We entered her office at the end of the corridor; and, after exchanging a few more pleasantries, we took our usual places.

She in the red overstuffed chair, me on the black leather sofa.

"You know, I finally read the letters," I said, looking at the floor, avoiding her gaze. "And I learned there *were* people who really cared, people who were trying desperately to help. It was between the lines sometimes, but it was all there. Trying to help my mother...trying to help us, our little family unit. Somebody even bothered to keep the PROOF of that all together. Tied up in a blue ribbon! And, somehow, I think it was meant for *me*, strange as that may sound."

"All this was in the letters?" she asked softly.

"My grandfather, my mother's doctor, my nurse, my aunts, even her brother, my Uncle Bill...all their letters were full of love and concern. It was almost more than I could take in.... I found compassion and, I guess, a sense of desperation. It was before people really knew what to do. But you could almost feel the emotion, the love." I went on. "It was all there in the words they wrote all those years ago."

"Paul, that's an important point." she interrupted. "Have you ever stopped to think just how different things are today for a family faced with those tragedies... that set of circumstances?"

"I guess not."

"So much more is known about post partum depression, now. In that time, it was practically unheard of. People called it 'the baby blues,' and expected it to simply pass with a little time and good luck. And for most women, it did. But for a small percentage of unlucky women, then as now – for reasons we still don't fully understand even today – it doesn't go away. Instead, it gets worse. For some, it becomes toxic, lethal, and literally life-threatening. Clearly, your mother was among those unfortunate few. It's seldom referred to, even today. Your mother was undoubtedly in such a profound state of denial that it would now be called 'perceptual defense'. It's a mental process that protects us from the things that, at some level, we determine we can't handle or that we simply can't face."

I listened intently as Dr. Foster spoke to me – not only as a psychologist, a hypnotherapist – but also as a woman. And a friend. "We think it has to do with hormonal imbalances brought on by pregnancy. No one knows for sure. But there are wonderful new medications that seem to give relief...far more effective than anything available in your mother's time. And because we understand this process more than we used to, there are support groups and help is abundant now – available for women with serious post partum depression."

"Sometimes these physical problems are exacerbated by grief. We understand the grieving process and the stages everyone goes through that mark a healthy progression back to normalcy. None of that was fully dealt with back then."

"It still seems unfair," I countered, "she had to suffer this... so alone."

"That's just it, Paul," Dr. Foster answered. She leaned forward, "Don't you see? She wasn't alone. And more importantly, neither were YOU. Everyone tried to help. It's all in the letters; you saw it yourself. They did everything they knew HOW to do. But you have to accept something...." and her tone suddenly changed dramatically. "We all have to live in our own time. Your family made the best of the lives they were given. Paul, that was another time, another whole world."

Suddenly, all I could picture was that glowing aquarium out in the waiting room – the fish living out their short and fragile lives under that pink light. My therapeutic journeys into the world of my parents' time had brought me new understanding and enlightenment, but it was a foreign world...their world, not mine. I didn't belong there any more. I had been given the gift of making these journeys to know them, to understand the context of their lives, to discover what had been missing from my own life for so long.

Now, I understood. As a child – even as a motherless infant – I was not alone. Never really had been. But what was the price of KNOWING this? The price of NOT knowing clearly had been very high for a very long time. Was I never to go back there again and see those people and those times that impacted my life so dramatically? I felt an overwhelming surge of emotion as I thought about these journeys to the past coming to an end. They were my only link to my parents. To close that door forever would be like losing them all over again! I wasn't sure I was ready for that...and from afar, I heard my voice telling Dr. Foster so....

"Please, I'm not ready. Give me one more chance...."

A cold wind was blowing in my face. There were patches of ice on a sidewalk beneath my feet. Neatly shoveled snow was piled on either side of the walk. Snow? I looked around at the vintage cars lining the street. People in heavy overcoats were walking toward a large, white frame house up the street. Even from where I stood, I could hear the crunch of very cold snow under their feet. They seemed to slow as they climbed wide, stone steps fronting the impressive-looking home. I saw men removing their hats as they stepped inside the door. Intuitively, I walked toward the house. In the yard, I passed a snow-dusted sign. It read "Easterday Funeral Home."

So this was it. The town of Culver. Tuesday, March 11, 1947. This was a place I did *not* want to be. But at the same time, I knew this is where my "journey" had to take me.

Somewhere deep inside I understood this was a pre-ordained destination that could not be avoided. I slowly walked up the front steps that were covered by a dark blue canvas awning coated with ice and new fallen snow. At first, I felt invisible as I walked inside. Then, just as suddenly, it seemed that I was expected there.

"Mr. Newkirk, hello," came a soft voice from across the hall. It was a nicely dressed middle-aged man who apparently worked for the funeral home. "We've been expecting you. The hope was expressed that you might serve 'at the door' today, to greet callers and show them where they might put their coats and things. Would that be all right?"

"Of course," I heard myself say in response. I walked back to the wide front door with its heavy beveled glass and stood there – my mind reeling at the thought of finding myself in this terrible, sad place. The over-ripe smell of flowers seemed to permeate the house and it wrapped around me like a smothering blanket. I was extremely uncomfortable, yet I felt compelled to stay. Just a few feet away was the black felt board sign with white letters confirming what I already knew. "3:00 PM: Services for Margaret R. Bradshaw." *My mother was dead...*

This was the day of her funeral. Thirty-six years old! What a terrible loss, what a waste of life and love and talent and beauty. Her casket must have been lying in the very next room! I decided I couldn't – wouldn't – go through those large silent double doors that separated this room from the room in which she lay and see it. I didn't need to.

Yes, I knew this day would come – had to come – for my journey to be complete. But while this was the place for one journey to end, I also knew it was where another would begin. Clearly, that's why I was here. It was the only thing that made any sense, any connection, to me. While I struggled to cope with all this, another realization became apparent. Most of the people with whom I had made my journey were likely to walk through this heavy door just beside me. They would be the people, the instruments of love, allocated to my life. My grandfather, the good friends from Rushville, my aunt and uncle, and more than anyone else, my dear, selfless, and loving great aunts. It was as though I was here to greet them and welcome them all... to my life.

"Well, Newkirk, a sad, sad day," I heard as I pulled open the heavy front door to see walking up the front steps none other than Colonel and Mrs. Gregory. He removed his garrison cap and brushed the snow slowly from the visor. Mrs. Gregory held fast to his arm, her head down, weeping. "Such a tragedy. I don't think any of us realized how profoundly her life had changed. She put up a good front; but, damn it, we should have seen it! We should have seen it!" He clenched his teeth as he spit out the words, angry with himself.

"Sir, I don't think there was anything anyone could have done. It's difficult, I guess, to keep someone from...well, from dying of a broken heart."

"Oh, I know you're right, Newkirk," he said softly, "but I...we...all feel so helpless, so responsible for what's happened. We should have seen it coming." "But dear, what will become of the baby?" It was Mrs. Gregory. Her voice filled with emotion.

Colonel Gregory patted her arm gently, compassionately; "I believe arrangements have been made for two of Shippy's aunts to care for him, her father's sisters...down in Rushville, I think. He's so young that, thank God, he won't remember any of this."

"No, Colonel, I won't remember any of this, but perhaps I would have been better off through all the years if I could have understood some of what had gone before," I thought to myself.

"Neither of them has ever married. I believe that's right, isn't it Newkirk?" The colonel looked at me for some reassurance.

I hesitated. "Ah, yes sir, that's right I think."

Colonel Gregory looked at me intently, the same way he had the first time we met, that day in Sally Port. "You know, Newkirk, I don't think I've ever been associated with two more wonderful people. So talented. So in love with each other. So much.... well, with so much living yet to do. Sometimes I wonder what God is thinking when tragedies like this happen. I wonder what lesson He's trying to teach us, or if there's a lesson in it at all." Mrs. Gregory was weeping more.

"Well, sir, I suppose the only thing we can do is appreciate the fact that our lives have been enriched a little by knowing them...that, somehow, something that made them who they were together...survives, lives on...in others."

Colonel Gregory stared at me. "I hope your right. My God I do. Perhaps we'll see little Paul again. Perhaps...in a way... they will live on through him. Perhaps... Maybe his family will send him to school here one day. I hope so. He's part of this place, too...just as they are." He smiled warmly at me, and then gazed off into some unseen future. He reached out, patted me affectionately on the shoulder and escorted Mrs. Gregory through the double doors into the next room.

Other people, most of whom I didn't know, filtered quietly in from the cold. Some were in uniform, some in civilian attire, all expressionless, quiet. Then, entering alone, I saw a face I knew. It was Cadet Billingsly, the young man from Cincinnati whom I had met down by the lake, who sang in the

Glee Club, had played intramural football on my Dad's team, and who had been my first contact with this world. He looked a little older and he was wearing a suit and tie. He looked uncertain, scared. "Billingsly! How are you?" He looked at me, smiled faintly, came over.

"Coach, it's good to see you again, although I wish it wasn't under these circumstances."

"Neither do I." I groped for something to say. "So, what have you been up to lately?"

"West Point, just finishing up my third-class year." I could see the scar just over his eyebrow from that intramural football game...the day...my father died. It was hardly noticeable, but it was there nevertheless. He stared toward the double doors.

"Is this spring break for you?'

"No, sir. I wanted to be here for the funeral, just came in on the train. Even at the Point, the word about happenings at Culver gets around quickly. Lots of us will be coming back today..." He paused. "No two people meant more to me during my years at Culver than the Bradshaws. It's almost impossible to believe they're both gone. She was so beautiful, had such a wonderful voice. I think I had a rather serious crush on her." A faint smile crossed his face. He looked again toward the doors. Almost absentmindedly he said, "She's the standard by which I've been judging girls out East, not sure I'll find one like her, though." He looked back me. "She was very kind to me during my plebe year. I was so homesick, and she knew it. Captain Bradshaw invited some of us over to their apartment on weekends, and she would sit and talk with me, not about anything special, just talk. It really helped. I wish... I just don't understand it. It makes no sense to me at all."

"I don't think there is an explanation for things like this. It's just life...a tragic part of it, but just life," I said.

"It's good to see you, Coach." We shook hands as he slowly walked toward the double doors, hat in hand.

Other people arrived, a steady sorrowful stream. Several younger women came in who I assumed had been sorority sisters. Other, more familiar, Culver people arrived, Colonel Payson, Coach Oliver, even General Gignalliet. One by one they passed, nodded, I hung up their coats, they signed the register and then walked slowly by...a solemn procession...a parade, I thought, a final "pass in review" of all the people who had, in their own ways, given me the gift of insight into the world in which my parents had lived.

Another gust of cold wind. Doc Baxter had arrived. His face looked drawn, careworn. "Hello, Doc." He looked at me briefly somehow lost in his own thoughts.

"Hello, Newkirk," he said softly. It was almost as if he was carrying the responsibility for my mother's death on his own shoulders. He fumbled with the buttons of his overcoat.

"Let me hang that up for you, Doc."

"You know...I've lost my two dearest friends in the whole world...I can't believe it." It was as though he was thinking out loud, not really talking to me. "People think being a physician is such a damn noble calling.... but there are times when I just feel helpless...totally helpless. Their lives just slipped through my fingers, and there was nothing I could do about it." He looked at me. I could see the pain in his eyes.

"I know, Doc." He sighed heavily and walked toward the doors.

Then, slowly, the outer door opened again. It was Ruth Moran accompanied by her sister and brother, Esther and James! I would have known them anywhere! They looked so young! Ruth was one of the first people I had asked about my mother...we had shared martinis in her living room while she shared memories with me. Now, she was here, clutching her rosary. Her brother, James, supporting her. They stopped, hesitated; Esther leaned forward and spoke quietly to her sister. Ruth nodded. I could not hear. How incredible to see them here! How ironic to see them in this place, all alive, and my mother now gone...from both worlds...this world and the world to which I knew I would return. They had driven all the way from Rushville...a long journey in 1947. I did not speak. Ruth opened her handbag and pulled out a linen handkerchief and wiped her eyes. Slowly the three of them crossed the room and passed through the wide doorway.

Then I heard a slight noise behind me. I turned toward the door. I could see a gloved hand carefully pushing it open. Oh, my God! It was Aggie, my black nurse, and her husband, Emerson - Emmy! The couple who had cared for me, loved me, protected me, during those times when there seemed to be no one else... They looked tentative, almost frightened, as they walked silently through the door. Oh, Aggie! How much you have meant to me! I took a deep breath. I could feel the tears welling up in my eyes. This was still a segregated world, between black and white. I took another long deep breath. "Aggie, Emerson, I'm so glad you're here, may I take your coats?

"Oh, no, Mr. Newkirk, it wouldn't be right! We'll just sign the register and leave," Aggie said quietly, almost in a whisper. "Please just tell Miss Nell and Miss Cora that we love that baby, too. And if there's anything we can do..."

I could not help myself. The tears flowed as I reached out to Aggie. Once more, she held me...one final time. I could feel the warmth of her embrace, the love this black woman felt for that little white boy who, in a way, had once been hers, and I loved her. In a brief instant, I experienced that same warmth and safety I remembered from so long ago. I wept as we embraced; yet she was as strong, even in this moment of tragedy. She held me tight in her warm and loving arms as she had a half a century before. It was a timeless moment that neither the past nor the future could take from me. "Mr. Newkirk, Emerson and I shouldn't be here. Please." I let her go, as I knew I must let go of this time. But once more, I looked at her, at Emmy, those two wonderful loving people who had loved and cared for that lost little boy... Quietly they signed the guest register and left.

Sing, Emmy, sing! The words re-echoed in my mind.

I had always hated funerals, all my life, but none more than this one. I hated the fact that it had to happen at all. More people arrived. I greeted them as best I could, most of whom I didn't know. Quietly I asked most to sign the register. At least I seemed to be serving some useful purpose. I was thankful that I had no conscious memory of this time, this place...that I had been spared this experience, at least until I was ready to see it for what it was - an end - and a beginning. This was where her life had ended and my life, at least the part I could remember, began. That was the price I had paid for a lifetime of feelings of abandonment!

This was also the end of my journey to this time, I knew that. I hoped it would continue to be a time of understanding and, in a strange way, a re-birth for me into the world to which I belonged.

Perhaps life really was like a river, I thought, flowing on endlessly, filled with twists and turns, eddies, and tranquil pools, but always flowing on...perhaps as it is supposed to... from one generation to the next, a river of life...flowing on endlessly.

I felt a rush of cold air. The door opened again. In walked my Uncle Bill, a young man in the early prime of his life! Quiet, determined, dutiful, and sad. He held the door for my Aunt Maxine, so gentle, so lovely. It would be over a year before they would have their first child, my cousin Bill, Jr. She stopped, turned, behind her were my two Great Aunts, Cora and Nell, arm in arm. They, too, seemed sad, but grimly determined to make this ceremonial event as dignified as it could be. Aunt Nell was fussing with her little purse, making sure she had an extra handkerchief. Already in their sixties, silver-haired, wearing silk scarves, heavy cloth overcoats, and white gloves, they had come to say good-by to their only niece, the little girl they had spoiled on so many summer weekends so long ago. They stopped in the entryway. My uncle looked at me. I nodded. The funeral director approached. Uncle Bill spoke to him. They talked quietly. They seemed to be discussing something about the order of the cars for the procession that would take place later.

Suddenly the outside door opened again. I knew the face but couldn't place the name - there had been so many faces in so many pictures so long ago. All I could tell was that this was a high school friend now, from what I could hear, the wife of some successful Rushville businessman or lawyer. I had seen people like this before. Much too eager to gush over the "tragedy" with the Winships she had encountered in the vestibule. "Billy, this is just too, too awful of course. Everyone at home is.... just so upset about it. Why, just the other day, somebody said they'd not seen Shippy for months; but, when they last saw her she looked so, so bad. Like I say, we're all extremely upset! We just knew - something up here just wasn't right. Maybe if we'd been able to persuade her to come back home.... well, you know. So when we heard...."

I could see the pain this boorish woman was causing my Aunts. Aunt Nell's eyes were downcast and she almost seemed unsteady on her feet. Uncle Bill took her elbow and glared angrily at this woman and her mindless chatter. His icy stare made the point. This woman quickly excused herself to "get a seat" as she quickly moved to the viewing room. Uncle Bill's eyes angrily followed her through the doors to the next room.

I could hear him say, "You don't have to stay. If you're not up to this. No one in the world would say anything - they'd understand this was too much for you, right on the heels of losing Granddad." This was where I was supposed to be...I couldn't help but overhear. "Do you want to wait for Dad?"

Aunt Nell opened her little purse again and took out a dainty handkerchief, exchanging it for the pair of white gloves. Closing her purse with a resolute "snap," she looked at her nephew, "Billy, we don't want to make this any more painful for him than it already is. We're fine. We've loved Margaret since she was a baby - just as we've loved you. We're staying!"

"I understand. I just want the two of you to know that Maxine and I would be happy to..."

"Now, Billy," Aunt Nell interrupted, "We've talked about this with your father. You'll be starting your own family one of these days. Raising little Paul will be something for us to live for, now that Papa's gone. It's something we can do for Margaret. It's what she would have wanted. That's one of the reasons we wanted to be here...we want to promise her that we'll take care of her little boy."

Aunt Cora added, "Billy, we think this is what God wants us to do with the rest of our lives, Nell's and mine. Perhaps it's why neither of us ever married, so we could be here for

Margaret.... to take care of her son. We took care of Mama and Papa, now God wants us to take care of a little life, to help it unfold. We owe this to our niece...your sister."

"Billy," Aunt Nell added emphatically, "God saved us to do this one last job! Now let's go on in!"

Aunt Maxine reached out and took my uncle's hand. He looked at her tenderly, and then back at my aunts. "I believe He did," he said softly.

I saw the same resolute posture in Aunt Nell I would see a thousand times as I grew up, on Sundays as we walked into Main Street Christian Church, as the holiday table was set for family gatherings, as she gardened in the mornings in her broad-brimmed straw hat to avoid the heat of summer. She knew about life...and death, she knew about home and family and love. She would be fine. And she was.

It was nearly three o'clock; the time the service was scheduled to start. I stood alone in the room. Silence, except for the muffled sound of voices from beyond the double doors. Then, slowly, deliberately, the outer door opened once more. A tall, solemn, silent man entered. It was my grandfather... my mother's father had arrived! This was his sixty-fifth year and he was here to be with his only daughter one last time... to say farewell. At home, his wife was dying of cancer...would be gone in four short months. He knew that day was coming. How could any man endure this? His own father had died in the fall of 1946. His son-in-law, my father, had died just one year before. What emotional price was he paying for this magnitude of grief? He removed his hat. He did not see me. It did not matter. Before my eyes he was becoming the man I knew as a child; stoic, silent, keeping the grief inside, keeping it to himself. This day, the days that had come before, and the day he knew was coming would change his life forever. How could it not? What must he have been feeling, how crippling was the pain, as he stood there, jaw set, eyes glistening, looking straight ahead...looking at that doorway?

What I had been through, I thought, was nothing compared to the losses he endured. Why had I not seen that before? I felt a wave a compassion for this man, my grandfather, whom I would have liked to have known so much better. He had been there when I was a child, but what must he have seen when he looked at me? Was I a comforting reminder that, in some way, life goes on, or did I remind him of all he had lost? I never knew. He could never tell me. Carefully he removed his overcoat, placed it slowly over his arm, never taking his eyes off that doorway. What a horrible nightmare must this have been for him? In only a few short days his family would be gone, except for his one son, my uncle. Slowly he started for the doorway. Then organ music...the service was about to begin.

I had not been alone! They had been there for me, for her, for us, all those years ago! The courage of these people during this time of tragic, unexplainable loss was more than I could stand. I gasped for breath. I could not control the emotions that were surging through me. I had to get away from this place of sorrow and pain and courage of a magnitude I could not comprehend! I bolted through the outer doors of the funeral home into the falling snow...one foot in front of the other, step after step...away from that terrible scene that was the meeting of my previously unknown past, that present, and the future of my childhood memories.

Everything around me was cold. I could feel the icy wind blowing in from the lake, gripping me in a frozen vice. I could feel the numbness of my feet, through wet moisture-stained wingtips. I hurried down the ice-covered sidewalk, the snow swirled around me, I nearly ran from that place where past and present had finally come together, like the colliding of two different worlds.

Suddenly, unintentionally, the thought that I had not been alone at all engulfed me again. I stopped. I stood alone in the blinding show. A strange feeling of warmth swept over me, it was no longer snowing. I glanced down; the wet brown wingtips I had been wearing seemed to have become a warm dry pair of comfortable penny loafers. I knew this journey to the past was nearly over. I was gong back, I could feel it, but I had seen, heard, and felt the outpouring of love and support that had sustained me as a child. Still, how tragic it had all been.... for so many. At least I was not alone in that.

"No, you weren't alone." It was Joan's voice! I was sitting once again in her office. "You never have been, that's been the purpose of this journey...to help you see that." Joan looked at me, smiling warmly. I was back! This was the here and now!

This had been the most difficult journey to the past. In some strange unexplainable way it had been to a place I had never wanted to be, never imagined, even in the darkest nights of the loneliness of my childhood. I had been to a place I would never have consciously wanted to go, but now realized it was a place I needed to see. Everyone who had counted had been there, everyone who had mattered, everyone I had loved had come to that terrible place of sadness and grief, all beyond my conscious comprehension until that moment. The unremembered past and the painful recollections of my childhood had come together, connected, becoming one continuous river of my life.

As I sat there, I realized the connection had been made, the connection with my parents, understanding who they were, healing the wounds from childhood of feeling abandoned. Now, I could see that life IS like a continuous river of events, that life is just life...and all of us make the best of what we're given. The floodgates of emotion overcame me and burst forth like a torrent. It was as though fifty years of unrecognized grief spilled from me. The anguish I had kept inside so long poured forth. "Joan," I wept, "it all seems so clear to me now. I don't know how to say it! Somehow it finally makes sense. Oh, God, Joan, it's like...like being released from all the fear and anxiety that have been with me for so long!" The tears streamed down, as I looked at her, for the first time, unashamed.

"What was really waiting for you at that funeral home, Paul?"

"I saw more clearly than I ever thought I would, that I've never really been alone, that I was never abandoned. The whole process was my chance to make that missing connection with my parents. And it was more wonderful than I ever could have hoped. I feel like I know, now, who they were. And the hunger for their love I felt throughout my childhood was understandable...but love was never really lacking at all. Not when I saw how hard everyone worked to compensate for their absence. Not when I could see from the perspective of an adult's eyes what sacrifices were made for me. I *was* loved and I returned it the best I knew how."

"Is it all about exchanging love and things balancing out?"

"No, it's more than that. Much more. Tragedy and loss are part of life...for everybody. At mid-life, I'm finally at a place and time where I can see friends and even family members around me dealing with parental loss and other personal tragedies. What they're dealing with now, I experienced long,

long ago, I just didn't understand it...until now. Everybody pays their dues sometime. And I now have the advantage of perspective. Both good and bad. If we're wise, we all make the best of what we're given...one day at a time." I hesitated...said, "Joan, you told me I'd know when the time was right and... I believe it has come. This is my last visit with you, isn't it?"

"If that's where these journeys have taken you, Paul, then you're a fortunate man, indeed. And I would agree with you; your work here with me may be done at last. That's something only you will know. It's not for me to say."

"May I reserve the right to come back here? Maybe not to this office, perhaps not to this same 'process,' and not even necessarily to you. But I'd like to reserve a return ticket to this place in my value system...where for a brief, glorious, break-through moment I can be in touch with the 'big plan,' the universal truth, the Higher Power of Understanding? I might just need to come to that place again, someday. Now that I've been there, I might want to catch the view from, say, ten or twenty years or so...down the river. That is, if I'm lucky enough to be on the journey that long."

"That might be arranged. I don't really hold any of those so-called tickets, Paul. But my experience has been this; we 'buy' them with simple gratitude. Being thankful for the gifts we've been given is the price we pay for discovering more of them... I've seen it a thousand times."

I stood up. "Joan, I don't think I can express my thanks for all you've done for me. You've asked me many times how these journeys have made me feel. Well, right this minute I'm feeling a strange sadness that it's all coming to an end but, you know, I'm also feeling something else."

"What's that?"

"A new-found inner peace and, somehow, a new determination...and belief, I think, that the rest of this journey is waiting for me at home...waiting to be found, not unlike the arrival of that old cardboard box...waiting for me to get there,"

She extended her hand, "I'm very glad, Paul. Good-by."

Chapter Twenty Seven

I went straight home; back down the quiet green corridor of swaying Indiana corn. As the miles passed, the world seemed to be brighter, the colors more vivid, I felt more alive than I ever had before. Why did the corn seem greener...and why did that season of bounty and fruition seem so symbolic just then?

Of course! My eyes had been opened and I could see with a new light. Where there was void, I now had substance. Where there were questions, I now had answers. This world, my world, had become a different place since my final trip back in time. It was almost a euphoric sensation. My relationship to the world, my view of the here and now...had changed. My view of who I was had also changed. This was where I belonged! This present! This reality! The end of my journey was yet to be reached, but I knew it was just beyond the horizon. I couldn't wait to get home.

It was nearly dark when I pulled into the driveway. The lights were on, but Connie's car was not in the garage. I walked through the hallway to the kitchen. She had left a note on the counter, "Stock Club tonight at Sue Master's. Dinner is in the refrigerator. Home soon. Love, Connie."

This was the time. Immediately, I walked to the hall closet, opened the door and reached far back into the corner. It was a spot where even the light from the hallway barely reached, but I could feel it. The box. Carefully I lifted it past the coats and the hamper of gloves, scarves, and knit hats. I carried the box into the library and closed the door. This time, for the first time, I was not dealing with the layers it contained; I was finally going to reach the bottom of it and the end of my journey. Neatly folded in half, I saw a new sheet of yellow tablet paper. It read:

Dear Paul,

I think Grandma must have known that these letters, photos, and all the rest would mean so much to you someday. She must have been saving things for years! Some letters, yearbooks, and other things of your mother's must have been added later. Mom and I found them in an old steamer trunk in the attic. She asked me to send them to you.

I only wish I could have seen the letters that Grandma wrote to each of her children, they must have been wonderful.

I read everything and I learned so much - particularly about your mother and father. I loved the way your father, Paul, wrote to Grandma and all his endearments to her. Mom said they had a very special bond.

I was so moved reading all the letters, especially the ones written by your mother. So many of my memories of Grandma are tied to you, your father and mother.
I hope you enjoy it all.

Lots of Love -
Cousin Jean

What I was doing now, it seemed, was searching for those last few missing pieces of the puzzle of my life, past the yearbooks, past the annuals, past the photographs, to the time that connected me with them. I glanced up once more at the photograph of my mother as a little girl – it was exactly where Connie had placed it – on the little table next to the slipper chair. I felt sure now that it would stay there, always in its place.

Looking back to the box, I noticed a small envelope. The return address said "N. Winship, 519 North Perkins Street, Rushville, Indiana." It was addressed to "Mrs. Warren Bradshaw, 1105 St. Joe Street, Rapid City, South Dakota." The postmark said January 10, 1950. My Aunt Nell had written this letter to my father's parents when I was four years old. Carefully I opened the envelope. I recognized her handwriting from the daily letters I had received during those summers at Culver and years at IU. It read:

"Dear Mrs. Bradshaw,
The toy fire truck arrived in good condition in time for Christmas and Paul is having loads of fun with it."

That sounded so much like her, *"loads of fun,"* I could almost hear her voice as I read on. *"He loves the book you sent him, too - the illustrations are so colorful and pretty. Our darling had a wonderful Christmas - he got everything from a Jack-in-the-Box to an electric train."*

I remembered that Christmas and all the toys she mentioned! In my mind's eye I could still see the little bright red metal fire truck with its white ladder attached to a tiny handle that made it extend! I still had it! The electric train, now nearly fifty years old was also in the basement, safely tucked away in a cardboard box.

Aunt Nell's letter continued,

"Paul loves to play and has quite a large playroom and I believe he has one of everything...he loves music and likes to sing. He has the sweetest voice and a wonderful ear for music. Cora and I are glad you enjoyed the picture we sent of him. He is a happy, healthy, and a handsome child - and his Aunts worship him. Thanks again for remembering him at Christmas.

Sincerely, Nell Winship."

I hadn't thought of that playroom in years, but that's what it had been, a room dedicated to play, a quaint holdover from the Victorian Age - the time when my Aunts were still young.

Stuck behind the first letter was another written by Aunt Nell in June 1950. It also was to my father's parents.

"Dear Mrs. Bradshaw,

My sister and I want you both to know that we are doing the best we can to make a home for our darling. Strange as it may seem, we somehow have found joy in the process, even in the midst of this awful tragedy. Little Paul is keeping us young and has given us a sense of purpose and happiness that we would not have known otherwise. Still, we share your terrible sense of loss over the untimely death of your son and our only niece. It was through God's grace that we were here and able to take care of their little boy. Our brother, Margaret's father, is making sure that we want for nothing. Since the death of his wife a few years ago, he has come to live with the three of us in our home on Perkins Street. It is a large two-story brick house and we are doing our best to make it a suitable home for our darling. It seems like only yesterday that his blessed mother was spending long summer weekends with us here - when she was a tiny girl, no older than little Paul is now."

"None of us will ever fully recover or understand all that has happened. What we are doing now, as you will surely understand, is trying to make the best of it.

Sincerely, Nell Winship."

I could feel the final pieces of the puzzle falling into place. I was nearly at bottom of the box. Beneath a few more snapshots, I saw a little black leather coin purse. I had not noticed it before. I wondered if it might have belonged to my mother. Gently, I lifted it from the box. The leather was still soft to the touch. Slowly, I undid the little brass clasp that had held it tightly shut for over half a century. There were a few coins. A thin gold chain necklace. Trinkets. Tiny keepsakes. A child's ring with a small ruby setting. Ruby...my mother's middle name, the name she hated, but the name someone had loved. Then I saw her sorority pin, her Kappa Key. There was no doubt about it! This little purse had belonged to her! Carefully I laid each item on the desk. A club pin from high school. A pair of cuff links with a script "W" on each one. A baby ring with her initials "MW" clearly visible.

These were tangible reminders of events in her life that clearly were important to her. It was nearly empty. But, far down in the corner, I noticed a ring. I held the purse closer to the light. Perhaps it had belonged to my father; it looked too big for a woman's hand. I lifted it out and turned it over in my hand...toward the light. My God! It was my Culver ring!! The ring I had given her during my last visit with her! But that was during a session of hypnotherapy. There were my initials... and the year - 1962! How was it possible? My mind reeled as I tried to understand, but there could be no understanding of this – I don't even know what to call it – this last miraculous "discovery!" There was no logical way to explain it. And yet, there it was! This ring was her gift of love to me somehow sent across the veil of time! My mother had kept her promise..."I promise you that one day my son will have this ring."

The circle was finally complete. It was clear now that my journey to find her had begun, somehow, with her journey to find me...and now I *knew* my mother still lived on - in me. At long last, I could feel that love...like a warm breeze on a perfect summer afternoon...love that had transcended time and space...and life and death. More importantly, I discovered that I had found something else.... I had found myself. Carefully, I put the ring back on my finger...where it remains to this day.

Epilogue

It was Thanksgiving Day, November 2002. All three of our grown sons were home, Paul Jr., Will, and Jon, along with my cousin Margaret, named for my mother, and her family, Connie's mother and stepfather, and my late cousin Bill's two nearly grown daughters. Also there were the wives of our two oldest sons, Kristen and Eileen, our youngest son's girl friend, Brooke, and a brand new grandson. A small family, but still seventeen people in all. Dinner was over, and we were all full and satisfied with the bounty of our good fortune and shared love. But there was something else; there was the unspeakable beauty and the promise of the next generation of our family there before my eyes...from one generation to the next...a river of life. Relaxed and happy people slowly drifted back into the living room to enjoy the fireplace and each other's company.

I looked out the arched windows; snow was gently falling, transforming the surrounding woods into a timeless scene from Currier and Ives. I leaned back in my chair. I was filled with a warm glow of contentment and the sense of resolution, as I recalled the year spent on a dynamic journey. It had been a journey, an adventure, beyond understanding, in search of something I only thought was lost. But the most profound sensation of all was the gratitude I felt for all that I now understood I had been given.

As I watched and listened to the happy sounds of laughter and love, my eyes were drawn to the piano in the corner of the room that had belonged to my mother and father. Resting there, as it will always be on family holidays like this perfect Thanksgiving Day, was one last item from the box, my father's hand-written manuscript that one he had written for his unborn son, "Love Once Again." It was no longer a Lost Lullaby.

The End

About the Authors

Paul William Barada was born in South Bend, Indiana, in 1945 and grew up in Rushville, Indiana. He attended Indiana University and graduated with a B.S. degree in 1967. He is founder and president of a firm providing reference checking and background checking services to a wide variety of clients scattered all over America. His writing credits include national magazine articles and an opinion column syndicated in several newspapers throughout the Hoosier state. He and his wife, Connie, raised their three sons in Rushville and now enjoy keeping up with their seven grandchildren.

J. Michael McLaughlin also grew up in southern Indiana and was a fraternity pledge brother of Paul's at Indiana University. After graduation, he was a war correspondent in Vietnam, wrote advertising copy in Indianapolis, and co-authored eleven editions of a guide book to Charleston, South Carolina. Today, he lives just outside Charleston where he writes about history and preservation topics for a number of local and national publications. This is his second book co-authored with Paul.

Printed in the United States
107208LV00002B/52-78/A